Thieves

Chapter 1: Child

MELVILLE BRYANT WILL never tell you what happened to him. He's not afraid or embarrassed, he just doesn't remember.

So I'm here to tell you his story. The first part of it, anyway. You don't have to know who I am yet. I'll tell you who he is.

Melville was stolen from his natural born parents when he was less than a year old. His mother had him in a stroller. She was pushing the stroller around downtown Portland, Oregon, where she lived, and she stopped in front of a department store window to admire a display of spring blouses. While she was thus distracted, Melville's future father figure casually walked by and stealthily pulled Melville out of the stroller with a minimum of motion and no fuss at all from Melville and walked away with him.

As simple as that. By the time Melville's mother turned her attention back to the stroller, it was too late. Melville and his abductor had disappeared into the throng of people crowding the sidewalk. It was mid-December, you see, the height of the shopping season, what with Christmas coming up and Melville's mother wanting to get Melville something special for his first Christmas in the world. Instead, Melville experienced the first robbery, though certainly not the last, of his life.

We'll leave his mother now. Not because her life was and is insignificant. In fact, it becomes very significant indeed, and we will pick up her story later. For now, I want you to simply be aware that anyone can come back from a terrible experience. They may be changed, even damaged, but they can survive.

And what of the thief who stole Melville? His name is Rex Anderson and he did a terrible thing. Now I don't want you to get the idea that Rex is a pervert or serial killer or anything like that. He wasn't. He isn't. He just has a different idea of personal property than the average person. To him, there is no such thing as property. You don't own anything. He doesn't own anything. All objects (and people) are independent beings. Sometimes those independent beings spend a few years with some people, and then with other people, and then with others. It's a circulation thing, where energy flows from person to person in the form of the objects and people that the person has around them. It's all abstract and up in the sky until you see what it means in practice.

See, Rex had a wife. Stella. They had been married for a few years. They wanted children. Very much. But they couldn't have children. They tried for years, but Stella never got pregnant. She got depressed instead. She didn't do much of anything. Mostly she ate junk food and watched a lot of television. Which made her even more depressed. Rex tried to get her to do things, to go out with friends, or take trips with him. But she wasn't interested. She didn't want to take control of her life and do something with it if she didn't have children.

You can imagine the way this made Rex feel. He already thought it might be his fault that his wife couldn't get pregnant. Not that he had anything to base this on, it was just his way of seeing the world: If something was wrong in his marriage, then it was most likely his fault and he had to do something to fix it. No big deal. He was not about to whine and moan about it. It was simply the way the world worked.

So think about it. Here's a guy who feels like ownership is a fluid thing and at the same time he feels like he's wronged his wife. Put those two things together and it's not hard to predict what came next.

Rex was on top of the world, let me tell you. He had Melville in his arms and he walked briskly down the Portland sidewalks. He had this feeling that maybe Melville's mother was following him, but he didn't dare look back. Instead he tucked Melville into his coat and walked ahead, determined to stay as far from Melville's mother as possible. Melville looked up at him and smiled. Rex smiled back, like Melville was his own child, like he had come out of Stella's womb. Yes, it was that quick, the transformation in Rex's mind. Not five minutes before, Melville was nowhere in Rex's consciousness or immediate vicinity. But just five minutes later it was as though he had once been in a birthing room with Stella acting as her Lamaze coach, helping her usher Melville down the birth canal into the doctor's waiting arms.

I already mentioned that Rex had no violent aspect to his personality. That is not to say that he wasn't prone to mutability. He could change at a moment's notice. In the short time it took him to remove Melville from his stroller and walk the few blocks to the next MAX station, Rex had become, in his own mind, a father. Now he could hardly wait to show his son to his wife, who would, in due course—within a few seconds, in Rex's mind—become a mother to Melville.

He rode the train east. People on the train smiled at him. Rex knew they smiled at him not because of himself, but because he had Melville. This helped Rex justify in his own mind his hold on his new-found role as father. It made him feel good that simply by having Melville in his presence, people thought more highly of him. There was now no possibility of Rex ever voluntarily parting with Melville.

Rex was well aware of his position. He was fully cognizant of the fact that society did not like kidnappers. And that's what he was, in the eyes of society at large. It did not matter that Rex had a different code of ethics. Society did not respect such things when it came to thievery. Rex had stolen Melville from his mother. The mere fact that Rex was now Melville's father would not help him a bit with the police or a judge. Rex could only hope that the unfolding of events would never bring him before either.

The train took Melville and Rex along Interstate 84 to the east part of town. Rex watched the stations pass by. He did not get off the train until it was well past the airport. By that time, late afternoon, a cold wind chilled Rex and he became conscious of a strong urge to protect Melville. It was a strange feeling for Rex, but he reasoned that it must have something to do with his new role as father.

He wrapped Melville up even more tightly in his jacket. He knew that once he got home he and Stella would do what they needed to do to make his son comfortable. Rex was aware that infants required regular feeding, warm clothes, changes of diapers, and lots of sleep. He was fully prepared to provide his son with all these things and he knew that Stella, once she got over her depression, would pitch in. He boarded the bus that waited at the train station and settled in for a half hour ride that would take him close to his house.

Stella and Rex lived near the edge of town in a neighborhood of mostly poor people. Stella and Rex were poor. That wasn't their choice, it was merely the way life was. No one on the bus looked at him or at Melville. They all occupied their own worlds, staring blankly into space or reading a newspaper or paperback, or listening to music on their iPods. Rex had noticed a long time ago that people on trains were much friendlier than people on buses. Why this should be always puzzled Rex, but he did not give it a great deal of attention. As with so many things, Rex believed it to be one of those facts of life that no one understood or ever could understand.

About half way home an elderly woman got on the bus and sat in the seat across the aisle from Rex. She looked at Melville but did not smile. This put Rex on alert. Why wouldn't she smile at his son? When you looked at a baby that was what you were supposed to do. Everyone knew that. It was not something that had to be taught to you, either. It was the sort of knowledge that you were born with.

Rex drew Melville tighter to him. He wanted to protect his son from this strange woman.

"New baby?" said the woman.

"Yes," said Rex. "My wife gave birth a few months ago."

"That baby don't look happy to me. It's like he don't want to be with you."

"That's crazy," said Rex. "I'm his father. I take him places all the time."

The woman nodded, but it was clear she did not believe Rex. Rex had half a mind to get off the bus at the next stop, just so he wouldn't have to hear anything else this woman had to say.

"Men don't usually take children nowhere. My husband never took our kids no place."

"Things are different now," said Rex. "Men do things with their kids."

"Uh huh," said the woman. There was so much doubt in her voice that Rex wanted to tell her to shut up and mind her own business. But he knew that was one of those things people did not care for. You should never insult people or tell them to do things they would not ordinarily decide to do completely on their own.

Why was she interrogating Rex about his child, anyway? Didn't she have better things to do with her time?

"All I'm saying," said the woman, "is that whenever I see a man with a baby like that I think there's something wrong."

Rex's whole body tensed. He looked wildly down the aisle of the bus. If the woman tried to do anything like take Melville away from him he would run down the aisle as fast as he could and get off the bus with Melville.

"But," said the woman, "that's just my way, I guess. I'm old and I don't understand how you young people do things nowadays. It was so different back when I was having my babies."

"I'm sure lots of things were different back then," said Rex. He wanted it to sound friendly, but it came out slightly hostile.

Melville had decided to become restless. He kicked at Rex and began to mewl.

"The boy's hungry," said the woman. "You got a bottle for him?"

"Um, no," said Rex.

"You go out with your baby and you don't take his bottle with you?" The woman shook her head.

"It was an unexpected trip," said Rex.

Rex began to rock Melville, but it didn't calm him down one bit. His crying got louder.

"Give him to me," said the woman sharply. "You don't know how to soothe him. He needs some loving."

Rex almost did hand over Melville to this stranger. He almost gave up his child to a person he knew nothing about. This startled him and he stopped himself before he did something he could not undo.

"He's fine," said Rex.

The woman looked skeptical again. "You sure this baby is yours?"

"Of course he's my son," said Rex.

"What's his name?" Suspicious like, again. She was a busybody. Rex had no idea how to get her off the subject of his baby. He thought wildly of a name. He took too long. What father didn't know the name of his son?

They passed a street corner. Rex saw a green street sign flash by the window behind the nosy woman. Morris Avenue.

"His name is Morris," said Rex, as though the fact might get her to mind her own business.

"Oh, I knew a Morris once. A horrible person. He was the pastor of our church, but he was no kind of good person, no sir."

"That happens," said Rex.

"We got rid of him, once and for all. He was a liar and a thief. Can you imagine a pastor lying and stealing? But he did. Took money from the church, like it was his own." She shook her head and clucked her tongue.

"This is my stop," said Rex. He pulled the string over his head so a ding sounded through the bus. Someone else near the back of the bus got up and walked down the aisle toward the door in the middle of the bus.

By this time Melville was crying so loud that no one could miss the sound.

The bus came to a stop. Rex rose and slid by the woman.

"You take care of that child," she said. "I don't want to open the newspaper one day and find out he died because you didn't take care of him."

"Don't worry," said Rex.

"I do worry," said the woman. "I worry all the time. I worry about everything but mostly I worry about children. You got me? I'm going to watch you from now on."

Rex felt his head get warmer. He knew he was turning red, but he couldn't do anything about it. He just wanted to get his son off this bus and bring him home to Stella.

He had a short walk from the bus stop. He went by rows of trailers, lined up like tombstones to his left. Stella once told him that living in one of these trailer parks was the same as living with people who just wanted to die. This troubled Rex. It was even more troubling because Stella didn't seem upset by what she said. It was almost as though she thought there was nothing wrong with going to live someplace where people just wanted to die.

Oh, but all that was about to change. They had a baby now. A baby brings all kinds of joy to your life. Stella wouldn't want to die anymore, Rex was sure of it.

He looked down at Melville, with his face buried deep in the folds of Rex's coat. He was warm, so why was he crying? Rex made faces at him to try to get him to stop crying. It didn't work.

He went around a corner and saw his house in the distance. He would get home soon. Then Stella could take care of Morris. She would know what to do. He had been looking after him for over an hour. He needed a break.

The light of the day had drained out of the air. It was already dusk and he never liked that time of day. The darkness tried to snatch away who you were. In the light you could see everything and you could tell where you were in the world.

Not in the dark. Without light, your skin disappeared and it was just you in contact with the air. It was so awful sometimes, to be alone in the dark.

Only he wasn't alone. No. Not anymore. He had to keep telling himself that. He had a son now. A son who would revive his wife.

He came to the house they rented from a woman who lived at the trailer park. All the lights were out. That was odd. Stella hated the darkness just as much as he did. She always left the lights on.

He tried to open the door but it was locked. He banged on the door several times.

"Stella," he shouted. "Hey Stella, let me in."

Stella didn't come to the door. Rex shifted Morris onto one hand and fumbled in his pocket for the house keys. What was going on with Stella? It made no sense that she would not come to the door. He was having trouble with the keys in the darkness. It was hard to see which key was which and he couldn't find the right one for his door. He tried one key, then another. Three times he tried pushing a key into the lock but each wouldn't go. On the fourth attempt the key slid into place and he turned it and the door popped open.

"Hey Stella," he said to the empty living room. "What the fuck?"

No answer. Rex put Morris down on the couch. He was still crying. Wailing now, like he wanted to wake the universe from a deep sleep. Rex looked at him and felt a twinge of remorse. Maybe this wasn't such a good idea. Maybe he could take Morris back to downtown Portland.

He turned from the baby and went into the kitchen and turned on a light.

"Hey Stella," he said. "I didn't get any money. Picking pockets was not so good business today, but I got something better. Something that'll make us both happy. Stella?"

He went into the bathroom. Dark and empty. He went down the hall to the bedroom. Stella was stretched out on the bed.

"Stella," he whispered. "What you doing sleeping so early?"

He turned on the light. Stella's face was blank. Her eyes were wide and empty.

Rex stopped. He became aware of his own breath. So loud. It filled the room.

He bent down to look at Stella. She wasn't breathing.

A jar of pills lay open on the bedside table.

Morris cried and cried. His wails couldn't wake his wife.

Morris was half an orphan now.

And Rex was a single parent.

Chapter 2: Automobile

REX NEVER HAD much use for the law. It existed, in Rex's view, only to impede his ability to make a living. So it was not surprising that he did not call 911 when he found his wife dead on their bed.

He reasoned thus:

She's already dead. There's nothing the police or paramedics can do. Therefore, there is no reason to call them.

He also didn't call because he had Morris and would not be able to adequately explain a baby's presence in the house, especially since Rex and Stella had been childless until just a couple of hours ago. Rex could see the scenario unfold in his mind: Morris would be discovered and his connection to the woman whose child was stolen from the carriage would be made. Morris and Rex would be separated and Rex would most likely be in big trouble owing to the acute displeasure that law enforcement authorities generally displayed whenever the topic of kidnapping came up.

In for a penny, in for a dollar. Or something like that. He couldn't give Morris back now. And he couldn't just leave him somewhere. That would be completely unsafe and unfair to Morris.

Rex observed a moment of silence over Stella's still form. If she had only waited a few more hours, she would have been okay. But there was no time to dwell on that. Rex filed that fact in the back of his brain, to remind himself that it was never too early to try to fix a problem.

He reached under the mattress where he and Stella had stashed away some money for a rainy day. He pulled the wad out, counted it quickly, and stuffed it into his pocket. Then he retrieved Morris from the other room and went back outside. He remembered a couple down the street at the end of the block who had a child not too long ago.

They had a nice car and Rex could use a nice car right about now. He adjusted his son in his arms. Morris had cried himself out, for the most part, still mewling but not wailing terribly loud.

Rex walked down the block to the house with the new child. He saw the car parked in the road. Good. That would make it easier than if it was in the driveway. He looked at the house. Flickers came through the front window. They must be watching television. Also good. He saw the doors to the car were unlocked. Even better. He opened the back door and put Morris into the baby car seat that was already buckled into place. Morris seemed to like the seat. He grabbed at the straps.

"Good," said Rex quietly. "Keep yourself occupied for just a minute."

Rex went around to the driver's door and got in behind the wheel. He closed the door slowly so it wouldn't slam. He had learned to jump-start cars when he was just a kid. He would hot wire them and take them on joy rides. He never damaged a single car, and usually left them in a safe place where they could be easily retrieved by the owner.

Now he pulled out a tool from his pocket and used it to yank out the assembly by the steering wheel where the key went in. He reached inside and touched some wires together. The car started. He put it into drive and eased away from the curb.

The car was so quiet that he doubted the owners heard anything. When he was far enough away from the house that he thought it would be safe, he turned on the headlights and pressed on the accelerator to speed away.

The car had almost a full tank of gas. Rex saw this as a good sign, since he knew he had to get away and the less contact he had with anyone else the better it would be for him. He decided to drive south, away from the Northwest to a sunnier climate. He wanted to find some place little Morris could be warm. It was important for a baby to be warm. Rex was sure of it. He also knew it was important for a baby to eat. What did children his age eat? That woman on the bus said something about a bottle. That meant Rex needed to get a bottle and some formula.

He passed a drugstore and pulled into the parking lot. It was a risk, but Morris needed supplies. He needed to be taken care of in a proper fashion. Rex thought that if he was good to Morris now, then Morris would take care of Rex in his old age. Rex liked that idea. It fit in with his picture of the world. Everything was a deal, and if you held up your part of the deal, then the other person should do the same. It was only right, and without such bargains life would not be as good as it could be.

He found a parking spot near the front of the store and eased into it. He sat at the wheel and wondered if he should abandon this car and steal another one right away. Normally, if he was on the run like this, he would do so, but having Morris along complicated matters. He decided the next vehicle could wait, at least for a while. He got out of the car, left Morris on his own, and went into the store. A clerk asked him if he wanted some help. He looked away and mumbled "no."

He pulled a shopping cart from the front of the store and pushed it down the aisles of merchandise and found the section with all the baby stuff.

Immediately he was overwhelmed by the choices. First there were the baby bottles. So many designs. He picked one more or less at random after examining a few brands, and put it in the cart. But then an enormous variety of formulas confronted him. He had no idea how to choose, so he picked a few without delving into their relative merits and shortcomings.

He wondered if Morris was old enough for solid food. Just in case, he grabbed a couple of dozen jars of baby food from the shelf. Then he plucked some packages of diapers and went to the front to pay. While he waited in line he noticed a display of books. One of them was a paperback that told new parents how to care for their children.

Rex picked it up and examined some of the pages. It looked like it had good information, plus, it also had pictures: diagrams of procedures like changing diapers and techniques like how to hold a baby while feeding him. Rex tossed the book in with the other items.

He looked, he thought, completely normal, standing in line waiting to pay for his items, and yet, inside, he was consumed with despair. To pay for these things was hard. It was not his way to pay for anything if he could help it. If he did not have Morris with him he would have found a way to steal all of this stuff. But then, he told himself, if he did not have Morris, he would not need any of this stuff.

The thought sobered him immeasurably. He felt the blinding burden of caring for another human being, someone who could not fend for himself in any way. How did any person ever grow up, so completely dependent on the kindness of others, even parents who loved them? It seemed, at that moment, an impossibility.

And yet, people walked around every day who were once defenseless babies. It was a wonder, no doubt about it.

Let me pause here and say that though I understand Rex and am trying to present him as truthfully as I can, you should not therefore believe that I approve of his actions or his motives. It is much more complex than that. He should never have stolen Morris from his rightful mother, of course not. And yet, he clearly exhibited care and concern for the child and for others. He stole Morris to make his wife happy. It was not his fault that Stella was completely beyond help. How could he have known that?

You could argue that since Stella was gone, a truly selfless person would return Morris to his birth mother and take the consequences. Such is the course of action I would have counseled Rex to take. However, Rex did not know of me at that point in his life, and so that option was not open to him. Also, it is not likely that he would have followed my advice anyway. In case I have not made it clear: Rex did things in his own way.

Rex paid for the supplies and returned to his stolen car and got back on the road. He traveled for a couple of hours until he was far south of town. He stayed off the interstate and took some of the less traveled side roads instead. By this time Morris was asleep. Rex loved the sound of his son's sleep-breathing. It made him think of Stella, when she was happy and would sigh and tell Rex how much she loved him. That was such a long time ago.

Rex wondered when she would be discovered. It might take a while. They had no friends and no one ever came to visit. He thought maybe it was wrong of him to leave her there like that. But what choice did he have? He couldn't have stayed. Not with Morris.

It was after eight o'clock when he saw a motel that looked secluded enough for his purposes. He stopped there and took a room, which he paid for in cash. It broke his heart to hand over the bills, and he made a mental note to steal a credit card as soon as it was feasible for him to do so. He had left some credit cards at home, but they were so old now, having come into his possession several days ago, that they were useless. People reported stolen credit cards quickly. They usually had a useful life of only a few hours.

He brought Morris into the room and put him down on the bed. He needed changing. He also needed feeding, but Rex supposed the smelly diaper was a higher priority, so he tore open a package of diapers and opened the book he had bought at the drugstore and followed the instructions on changing his son's diapers.

It went pretty smoothly, all things considered. When he was finished, Rex noted that the diaper did not look quite as snug as the original one had, but he guessed that he would get better at it as he practiced more.

Food next. He opened the book to the section on feeding and absorbed the rudiments of bottle feeding quickly. He heated the formula in the room's microwave oven, even sterilized the bottle by dipping it in water he boiled in the microwave. Then he propped Morris in his arm and put the bottle next to his mouth. Right against his cheek, just like the book suggested. Morris recognized the sensation immediately and turned his head and began sucking on the bottle.

He looked up at Rex as he took in the formula milk. Rex locked eyes with Morris. So amazing that such a tiny thing could have such a big effect on his life. But then, thought Rex, how could it be otherwise? It couldn't.

Morris consumed the entire contents of the bottle. Then Rex burped him, as the book recommended, and then he put him down on the bed to sleep.

It was a wonder to Rex that Morris did sleep, but he did. Rex realized he himself was hungry, too, but more than that, he was tired. So tired he did not want to get up to go find himself something to eat. He laid down next to Morris and fell asleep.

He felt like he had been asleep for some hours when he was awakened by Morris's cries.

Why did Morris cry all the time? It was unnerving, his wailing. And Rex was sure it would wake up others in the motel, perhaps even bring out the manager. More complications that Rex did not want and had no time for.

Babies cried. He remembered that from the book. It was his task to discover why Morris cried and then try to find a way to help him to not cry.

Rex made more formula and offered it to Morris, who gladly ate it. Food. It was always about sustenance. Give someone support and they are happy. Not so mysterious, but it was still a surprise to Rex, as though Morris had taught him a secret of the universe.

They both returned to sleep until around 3:30 in the morning when Morris began crying again. Rex had some formula left over but Morris didn't want it. Rex held Morris in his arms and walked around the little motel room with him, rocking him back and forth, soothing him until his cries subsided. Morris returned to sleep, but Rex could not. He lay on the bed, Morris breathing beside him, but slumber eluded him. He thought it was just as well. They should be getting up and moving on anyway since they needed to keep distance between them and the authorities. But Morris was asleep. Rex did not want to disturb that tranquil and fortunate circumstance.

Rex lay on the bed and stared up at the ceiling. A dim light from the parking lot drifted in through the curtains. If Rex had been prone to such thoughts, he might have considered that this was a perfect moment, the solitude of the night combined with the proximity of his son. The two of them together and safe, for the moment.

But Rex was made of much more rational stuff. He didn't need the wonder of the joy of life to keep him going. All he required was the realization that his son depended on him to be strong.

So Rex got out of bed and roused his son from his slumber. He went out to the car and buckled Morris into his seat. Then he started up the car and headed down the highway again.

He knew the authorities would be looking for Morris and for the car Rex was driving, but it was unlikely they would be looking for these two things together, since he had left no evidence that would associate one with the other. Of the two thefts, Morris would be considered the more pressing since his disappearance involved a life. And a young life at that. Rex had noticed that the younger the person involved, the more likely it was that people would be upset about anything happening to that person.

Rex looked in the rear view mirror where he saw Morris reach for a small toy that had been hung from a bar over the seat. Rex watched Morris's spastic attempts to grasp the toy. He smiled. Here was his son's first attempt at theft. It warmed his heart to see Morris go for what he wanted, however trivial.

"That toy today," he said. "The world tomorrow."

Rex had read in the book that having a child was the most profound experience any human being could have. Rex believed it. Who would have thought that he would see so much meaning in the gesture of a child before today? But before today he was not a father himself.

Within a couple of hours Rex reached the coast highway, state route 101, and headed south. He had traveled this road before and liked to be near the ocean. He watched the sky lighten as he sped by beaches. The water, sand, and rocks caught the subtle milky light, which drew out and softened their features to a fuzzy non-focus. The water gave Rex an idea. He needed to baptize his son. Why not do it now?

He turned off at a state park, a small one that was little more than a beach fringed with grass and furnished with a couple of picnic tables. No other cars were in the parking lot. It was too early and it was too cold. That didn't matter to Rex.

He lifted Morris out of the car and cradled him to his chest. Such warmth in something so small. Morris stepped away from the car and entered a narrow path down a slight slope to the beach. Shadows clung to his feet as he walked. He wasn't sure of his footing, but he assumed it would be okay since this was a maintained path. He thought there wouldn't be too many rocks or roots anywhere and he was right. He made it down to the sand safely and walked to the water.

The waves came up the beach and lapped at his feet. He didn't step back. He welcomed the pull of the waves. He respected the ocean for its power, its need to steal him away from land and make him part of the sea again. Didn't everything come from the sea once? Rex was pretty sure it did. He thought he heard that once. Life started in the sea. That's why people should be baptized. It made the water part of them again.

The waves came in rhythmic pulses. They rose up to Rex's ankles. They made his feet feel as cold as ice.

He wondered if it was high tide or low. It wasn't possible to tell for sure in the dim light.

Rex waded in further until he was knee-deep. By now his legs were so cold he thought they might freeze off. Maybe they already had. He could barely feel his own feet.

Morris's eyes were wide open. They took in the sky and Rex's face. Rex saw stars reflected in his son's eyes. He bent down slightly and touched his index finger to the sea. He brought his finger up and placed it on his son's forehead and down his nose.

Rex knew from watching movies and television that people had the sign of the cross put on their forehead when they were baptized. He also knew that this was a sign of Christianity, of the death of the savior that Christians believed in. But Rex was not a Christian and so he did not make the cross on his son's forehead. Instead he ran a line of seawater from the spot between his eyes, over his nose, and into his mouth.

Rex felt Morris's mouth suck at his finger.

"That's the ocean," he whispered to Morris. "That's life, right there. I name you Morris in honor of the sea."

Morris said nothing.

Rex held him over the waves for several more seconds, then took him back to the car just as sunlight came peaking over the eastern horizon, painting the ocean with dabs of gold, stealing away the night, and tinting the sky and clouds an impossible shade of purple.

Chapter 3: Wallet

I OBSERVED REX and Morris at the beach but did not interfere with their activities. They followed a path unknown to me, despite my lofty position. I was charged with protecting Rex. However, that protection took many forms, and if harm befell him, that was not necessarily my concern. I will be completely honest here and tell you that I soon became much more interested in Morris. His situation, after all, came about through no fault of his own. I generally observe the widest latitude when it comes to thievery, bending over backward to understand and even condone the proclivity of so many to take what is not rightfully theirs, but I may have reached my limit with Rex's abduction of Morris.

I realized I was calling him by that made up name and I was beginning to resent Rex Anderson for putting me in such a position. Why did he not stick to objects and money? Picking a pocket I could rationalize convincingly but kidnapping? That was something altogether different and I had to face the fact that my charge was a less than exemplary human being.

Not that I was naïve. I knew he was not unique in this and I don't want to give the impression that he somehow needed to be singled out for his behavior. Many behave badly at some point. Some behave badly at many points, and as I have already indicated, the mere fact of thievery does not necessarily make one eternally evil. Let me illustrate by showing you something Rex did soon after baptizing his (stolen) son.

He continued to drive down the coast on Highway 101 through Oregon, past Gold Beach and Brookings into California. His plan was to continue all the way to San Francisco, then turn east and catch I-5 and continue south to Los Angeles. From there he would head east again toward Arizona where he and Morris would make a clean new start of their lives in Tucson.

All was going according to plan, but at a gas station south of Sacramento, Rex found himself ready to get back into the game. That is to say, he needed to steal again. It had been days since he picked a pocket and it was getting to him.

I don't expect you to feel sorry for him. Just understand that he was having a bout of anxiety and he knew the one thing that would relieve it. He went inside the mini mart attached to the gas station and gave the attendant a twenty-dollar bill and told her he wanted a fill up. As he did so, he noted the other people in line to get gas and pay the attendant. He picked out one likely victim, a man in a suit who had his wallet in his back pocket. The man asked for a fill up, which meant he would probably be back for change, just like Rex. Rex went back to his car and waved at Morris through the window. He liked having Morris along. People seemed to trust him more now that he had a child in tow. This was all to his advantage.

He put gas into his tank, being careful not to get the full twenty dollars, then waited until the other man had finished with his car and began walking back to the mini mart for change. Rex casually fell in behind him. The man went through the door. Rex followed and cut in front of him, as though he were angling toward the chip aisle. They collided. It was not a crippling collision. Hardly one at all. More like a bump. But it was enough.

Rex put out his hand and grabbed the man's elbow. "I'm so sorry," he said.

"Think nothing of it," said the man, who, at that moment, did not feel the momentary nudge of Rex's other hand as it dipped into the man's back pocket and retrieved his wallet. All in less than a split second.

Rex smoothly stepped away from the man and placed his now wallet-laden hand into his own jacket pocket. The man got his change from the attendant and went out the door back to his car.

Rex retrieved his own change and returned to Morris and his own (stolen) car. As he pulled out of the gas station, he saw the man, behind his steering wheel, pat down his own jacket and shirt, his face concerned, maybe even a little panicked.

Now. Rex had every right to gloat here. He might have slammed his hand on his steering wheel in a show of triumph. Or he might have put out his spread hand to Morris and asked for a high five. Or he might simply have smirked at the easy pickings the man had been. But Rex did none of these things. He whispered to the air, directing his remarks at the man in the car: "I'm sorry," he said.

You see what I am getting at, don't you? Rex was not a vindictive thief, or even one filled with animosity for his marks. He was, instead, filled with remorse and sympathy for those who ended up at the short end of the transaction. There are winners and losers in the world, after all, and it was not the mark's fault that he had encountered Rex, one of the consummate winners of the world.

Rex drove a safe distance from the gas station, glancing frequently in the rearview mirror, alert to the possibility that the man might put two and two together and come up with Rex as the agent of his loss. But the man's car did not approach him.

Rex took the wallet out of his pocket and tossed it down on the passenger seat. He riffled through it with one hand while driving with the other. Morris made baby sounds in the back seat.

"That's right," said Rex. "Today's payday for your dear old dad."

Rex had hit a rich vein of wealth, mining in the man's pocket. The wallet held eight hundred and thirty dollars.

"Woo wee," said Rex. "I'm *really* sorry now. But no matter. Fortune has smiled on us today."

Usually Rex liked to take no more than a hundred dollars from any particular victim. Such a sum, though not insignificant, usually meant the victim could recover with very little effect on his or her life. But this much money meant something to most people. Even to a guy in a suit.

"I'll make amends by not taking from anyone for the next couple of days. What do you think of that, Morris?"

Morris spit up on his chin and waved his hands in the air spasmodically and kicked his legs against the child protective seat.

"I'm glad you agree with me," said Rex. "You'll learn that it is never right to take more than you need. This money will get us to Tucson and get us set up for a while. After that, it will be time to look for more paydays. They will always be there. That's the thing you need to understand. That's what I want to teach you more than anything else: There will always be abundance."

Morris said nothing. His hands and arms did not move. He seemed to be interested in Rex's voice.

"You like me talking?" said Rex.

Morris, as you can imagine, did not understand the meaning of Rex's words, but he did understand the caring behind them. There was something in the timbre of Rex's voice. A mellowness in the phrasing.

"Maybe you're getting too old for that seat," said Rex. "Is that it? Do you want to sit up here with me? I'd get lonely in the back seat too, especially since this is where all the action is."

Rex pulled into the next rest stop and took Morris into the bathroom where he changed his diaper. He also dropped the wallet, with all its contents (except for the money), into the garbage can by the door. Then he bottle-fed Morris in the car and opened a jar of baby food and tried to spoon some of it into Morris's mouth. Morris didn't know what to do with it.

"Okay," said Rex. "Not ready for solid food yet. I get it. You about ready to continue our journey?"

Morris looked like he was about to fall asleep. Rex put him in the car seat and moved the car seat to the front of the car. He got back on the driver's side and was soon on the road again. Fields of cash crops drifted by on either side of the car. Morris seemed to like the hum of the road. He rocked slightly with the car and soon fell into a deep sleep. Rex remembered in the book how it said babies can sleep almost anywhere if they're tired enough. Rex thought back and had to agree. He had seen mothers in grocery stores with their babies, noise and bustle all around them, and the babies out like lights.

After a long day of driving, Rex came to a small town off the interstate. He was so tired he didn't even notice what town it was. The cars ahead of him on the highway snaked away like a train of brilliant stars leading to the future. An amusement park, with loops of roller coaster track arcing up like flowers, loomed next to him as he eased down the off ramp. A woman flew a sign at the end of the ramp: "Too old to work, too ugly to prostitute, too scared of jail to steal. Please help." Rex laughed. He stopped next to the woman and rolled down his window. She approached him. Rex pulled out 80 dollars from the wad of cash from the wallet and handed it to the woman.

"Great sign," said Rex.

The woman nodded, took the money and stepped back.

Rex continued through the intersection and turned toward a motel sign. He talked to Morris as he drove.

"The thing is, everyone should give to charity, Morris. It's not an option. Those of us who are more fortunate should give. Ten percent. It's one of the ways we can make a better world. And besides, those people who stand begging for money work hard. I wouldn't want to be out there in all kinds of weather depending on the kindness of strangers. No sir. Sure, what I do involves some more risk in that if I am ever caught I could be in serious trouble, but it all evens out in the end. That's what you have to understand. That's what I want to teach you."

As he drove into the motel parking lot, Rex looked around at all the cars. "What do you like?" he said to Morris. "Foreign model? They've got them here. How about domestic? Got that too." Rex looked across at a big SUV. "Oh no you don't," he said to Morris. "We aren't getting one of those. The owners, they love those vehicles. They'd kill us if they ever caught up with us. We'll just stick to something a little more our speed. Thing is, it's time we traded in. This one's getting to feel a little old, you know?"

Rex's habit, when he was in a car-stealing phase, was to keep a vehicle for no more than twenty-four hours. Any longer and it got to be too risky. Rex was nothing if not risk averse. He didn't even know why he had broken his rule this time, except that Morris made him sometimes forget to take care of business in the manner he knew was necessary.

They got into their room and Rex put Morris down for a nap. Then he fell into bed and slept for a couple of hours. Morris woke him up with his crying.

"Yeah," mumbled Rex, "time for food. I know." Except Morris's cries were different. It didn't sound like he was wanting food as much as he needed some attention. Even Rex, as inexperienced as he was, could tell the difference.

He put his hand to Morris's forehead. It felt very warm. That meant he had a fever. That was not good.

"Don't do this," said Rex. "You can't be sick. Not yet. It's too soon. I can't take you to a hospital until I have you longer. Get better, Morris. Don't ruin everything for us."

But Morris did not get better. His crying increased in intensity. He would not take any of the food Rex offered him, and Rex offered him a lot. Rex sat in the middle of the hotel room with Morris cradled in his arms and tried to figure out what to do. He couldn't let Morris die. That would be awful. But he couldn't take him to a doctor because that could get Rex put in jail.

Rex bit his nails and scratched at the back of his head. The motel manager would probably come around soon. All this crying was bound to get people upset. And when people got upset they did all kinds of things they shouldn't be doing. Rex had seen it a hundred times. It's why he tried to stay as anonymous as possible, so no one would get upset.

Rex thought about his predicament for a little longer. Probably about fifteen minutes all together. That might not seem like much, but it was forever to Rex, who did not know if Morris was going to flop over dead right then and there or if he was going to get better.

"Get better," he repeatedly said to Morris.

A knock came at the door.

"Everything okay in there?" A woman's voice.

"Um," said Rex loudly. "Yeah."

"Your baby's crying an awful lot," said the woman. "Is he sick?"

"A little," said Rex.

"Do you need some help?"

Rex put Morris down and went and opened the door about halfway. He didn't even think about it. Which was not like him at all. He usually played things ultra safe. Better for everyone involved. Only this time he didn't know what was better. The woman on the other side of the door was older, maybe sixty or so.

"I'm in the room next door," she said. "I couldn't help hearing your baby."

"Yeah," said Rex.

"Can I come in?"

Rex scratched his head. He opened the door all the way and the woman stepped in.

"Let's see about your little boy." She went right to Morris and picked him up and cradled him against her shoulder. "He's got a fever," she said.

"Yeah," said Rex.

"You need to take him to a doctor."

"We're on our way to Tucson," said Rex.

"Where's his mother?"

"She died."

The woman blinked. "Oh that's awful. Must have been not long ago?"

"Last week," said Rex.

The woman shook her head slightly, as though she was tut-tutting the world that such a thing might happen.

Don't look at me. I can't save people. I don't have that kind of power. Stella Anderson's death was *not* my doing, not in any sense whatsoever.

"Can you do something for him?" asked Rex.

"Heavens," said the woman. "I'm not a doctor."

"But you had children, right? I can tell by the way you're holding him."

"I had my children forty years ago. You get rusty about these things."

"No," said Rex. "I can tell. You know stuff. The book says a fever could be a lot of things."

"The book?"

"Here." Rex showed her the book he had bought at the drugstore.

"My God," she said. "Do you have any idea what you're doing with this baby?"

Rex didn't say anything.

"Are you in some kind of trouble?" said the woman.

"I need to get Morris to Tucson."

"Morris? That's his name? How old is he?"

Rex picked a number out of the air. "Five months," he said.

"Five months," said the woman. "It doesn't feel like his fever is real high. He is wheezing, though, which means he might have bronchitis."

"Bronchitis. That's bad, right?"

"Actually, not as bad as it sounds. All he needs is some baby aspirin and fluids. He should be fine."

"Baby aspirin," said Rex.

"You have some, don't you?" said the woman.

Rex shook his head.

"Lord," said the woman. "Go to the front desk and ask for some. I'll wait for you here."

Rex hesitated. He wasn't sure he should leave the woman alone with Morris. What did he know about her? Maybe she wanted to steal Morris for herself.

But he looked into her face and decided she had no such intentions. Rex could usually gauge the character of strangers, but he was never a hundred percent sure. However, he resolved that this time he would have to take a chance. For Morris's sake.

He left the room and went to the lobby where he asked clerk at the desk for some baby aspirin. The clerk gave him a bottle and asked if Rex would like him to call a doctor.

"I don't think that will be necessary," said Rex. "I have a nurse in the room looking after my son."

The clerk nodded. "If you need anything else at all, be sure to ask."

Rex went back to his room.

"You're back," said the woman. "I half thought you were going to run away."

"Why would I do that?" said Rex. "This is my son."

The woman nodded. "If you say so."

"Of course I say so." He handed the bottle to the woman who read the label and told Rex to go get some warm water for Morris.

"He needs to drink a lot of fluids," she said.

"Will he be better soon? We have to get going."

"Oh, you and your baby aren't going anywhere for a while," she said. "He's got to stay here and rest. Do you understand ?"

Rex blinked rapidly. "Rest," he said. "Okay."

They ground up the pills and put them in water and filled up a bottle and had Morris drink. He drank eagerly, like he was the thirstiest being on the planet. Rex's heart filled with joy as Morris grabbed the bottle with gusto.

"He's got his energy back," said Rex.

"He'll be fine," said the woman. "Just make sure he rests. Don't take him on the road. You don't want this to turn into pneumonia."

"Thank you," said Rex.

"You want me to stay here with him tonight?"

"We'll be fine now," said Rex.

"You sure?"

"Yeah."

"I think you're an okay person," said the woman, "but there's something about this that isn't right."

"I know," said Rex. "Lots of people tell me that. I'm still grieving over my Stella dying."

The woman nodded. "I'm right next door until the morning. Call me if you need me."

She left and Rex and Morris were alone again. The fever broke a few hours later.

"I think it was good she came over here," said Rex to Morris. "It makes me realize you need something. You need a good mother."

Morris looked at Rex with blank eyes. Rex held him above his head and touched his nose to Morris's nose.

"Oh yes," said Rex. "A mother. My little Morris needs a mother. I'm going to have to steal one for you first chance I get."

Chapter 4: Sling

Oh, how Rex wanted Stella to still be alive. He knew she would have loved Morris more than anything else in her life, just as Rex loved him and would, within reason, do anything for him. But Stella was gone. Rex had already faced that fact, though he had not had time to grieve for her. He also did not understand that he *needed* to grieve for her. To Rex, life events were simply that: things that happened. It was not up to him to lament their occurrences or to wail about the injustice of it all. Of course there was injustice. In Rex's view, that was a natural consequence of having justice. One gave rise to the other, and therefore if there was any justice in the world (and Rex truly believed there was) then there would have to be injustice as its counterpoint. This point of view was so ingrained in Rex that nothing short of a miracle would change his opinion on the matter. And Rex did not believe in miracles.

He did, however, realize that in order to obtain a mother for Morris, he would have to find himself a wife. Most men, given this dilemma, would naturally think of ways to attract and convince a woman to want to marry them. Rex didn't take that course of action. After he had put Morris down for the night, and before the sun came up, he went next door to the room where the woman had come from who had helped him.

Rex knocked several times. The woman opened the door just enough to see through. "What is it?" she said. "Is your son having trouble again?"

"Morris," said Rex. "His name is Morris."

"Is Morris still sick?"

"I think he's getting better," said Rex, "but I have a question for you."

"Yes."

"Would you marry me?"

"What?"

"My name is Rex Anderson. I liked how you took care of my son. I would like you to be his mother. Will you marry me?"

The woman closed the door without saying a word.

Rex knocked on the door.

"Go away," said the woman. The door muffled her voice, but her tone was unmistakable.

"I can provide for you," said Rex. "I have a profession and I'm good at it. Lots of money all the time."

"I'm going to call the manager if you don't leave me alone."

A couple passed by Rex in the hall. They glanced in his direction and he acknowledged them with a slight nod and a raise of his eyebrows. He waited until they were far down the hall and the man reached into his pocket for his room key. Then Rex put his mouth close to the small gap between the edge of the door and the door frame. "Won't you even think about it?" he said. "You're a lonely person. I saw the way you bonded with Morris. You would be a wonderful mother to him. He needs a mother now that his is dead."

He heard footsteps get close to the door, then the knob turned and the door swung open just a little bit. It shook as it stopped on the safety latch.

"Are you some kind of fucking psycho?" asked the woman.

Rex did not care for her choice of language. He saw no need, in the present situation, for profanity.

"Not at all," he said. "I'm just a father trying to care for his son."

"I can't tell if you're crazy or just simple."

"I'm a simple man, it's true. I don't need anything fancy. Neither does Morris. We both just need a woman in our lives."

She looked to her left, as though she could see through the wall to Rex's room next door. "You can't just leave babies alone like that."

"I know," said Morris. "I just took five minutes to ask you to marry me.

You don't have to say yes now. Give it some thought. We're going to be leaving in a couple of hours."

"You shouldn't do that to the child," said the woman. "He should stay in one place at least a day and rest."

"I see your point," said Rex, "but we can't stay in one place for long."

"Why not?"

"It's complicated. In any case, we like to rise with the sun. That should give you lots of time to think about what it would all mean." He touched the side of his forehead in a subtle salute. "You know where to find me." He stepped away from the door, just to show her how he wasn't desperate. He didn't need to be right up next to her. He could wait for her decision. Then he nodded and went back to his own room.

"That didn't go so good," he said to Morris, who had rolled over on the bed, but was still asleep.

Rex tried to get some sleep himself, but too many thoughts clamored for his attention. He had to find a good car in the parking lot to steal, and he had to do it quickly, while moving Morris and all his equipment into it. He also had to be better about taking care of Morris so his fever and his bronchitis wouldn't come back. And on top of all that, if the woman next door said yes to his proposal, there were wedding plans to attend to, not to mention licenses and such. So many considerations. It took him a long time to get back to sleep.

When he woke, Morris was crying beside him. He touched his forehead. Not warm. Yippee! He fed Morris and gave him more of the anti-fever medication. The sun was still not up. He looked at the clock. It was about four hours since he had talked to the woman. He made sure Morris was okay and went into the hall and knocked on the woman's door.

She did not answer. He knocked louder. "It's Rex," he said. Still no answer, and no sound of anything going on behind the door. Rex went to the lobby and asked the young man behind the desk if the woman in the room next to him was gone. "She's a friend of mine," said Rex.

"Your friend checked out an hour ago," said the young man with a tone in his voice that Rex did not quite get, but which sounded very much like sarcasm. Rex did not care for sarcasm. He thought it was unkind and, almost worse than that, useless, because it did not help anyone in any situation. It just made the sarcastic person feel better for a few seconds.

"You don't think she's my friend?" said Rex.

The young man spread his hands. "None of my business," he said.

Rex was prepared to continue the conversation, but he saw no point.

"She left you this," said the young man. He brought out a blanket from behind the counter. "For the baby, she said."

Rex took the blanket. It was small, just right for Morris. It was so soft, some kind of artificial fiber, he was sure. Certainly not wool or cotton. Morris would be very warm in this blanket. She *did* care about Morris. Rex had been right about the woman: She would have been a perfect mother to Morris.

"Thank you," said Rex.

The young man waved his hand in a dismissive gesture.

Rex felt touched and a little sad that the woman had given Morris this blanket. He also felt bad that the woman had left the motel without giving him her answer, though he had to admit that her absence was pretty much all the answer he required. He returned to his room and began to pack up Morris's things. Then he wrapped Morris in the blanket. Morris snuggled right down into the folds of the blanket. He appeared to adore the softness of it. Rex's eyes welled up with tears. There was no better feeling in the world than to see his son so content.

Rex found a beat up old car in the parking lot. It was so old and junky that he was sure the owner probably didn't even have insurance on it. Which meant it would be a safe theft because no police department was going to spend much time looking for it. And the owner might not even report it.

He got into it in about five seconds, got it started, and quickly got the car seat into the car and Morris installed in the car seat. He shot out of the parking lot with Morris staring straight ahead through the windshield. Rex got on the freeway and adjusted his speed so he was just under the limit. No point in attracting any attention from over-zealous highway cops.

He adjusted the heat and fan settings so warm air began circulating around his feet and especially around Morris. Traffic was already heavy on the freeway, which made Rex happy. There was safety in numbers.

As he drove he thought about the woman last night. Her blanket was a gift, he saw that. Also a consolation prize. She must have known that her refusal of Rex's proposal would be a disappointment to him, but just to show that she didn't bear him any ill will, she gave him a small gift to make him feel better. The only thing was, it *didn't* make Rex feel better at all. It made him feel ten times worse and he only now realized it. Last night there was the possibility of Morris having a mother. Now that possibility was gone.

Given that the woman did not want to be with Rex or Morris, how much of a gift was the blanket? It was more of an obligation, wasn't it? A way for her to make herself feel better.

Yes, Rex was sure of it. The blanket was not meant for him or Morris. It was meant only for the woman.

Oh, but wait. She didn't have the blanket anymore. Ownership of it had transferred to Morris.

Rex mulled this over. He did not like gifts. They obligated you to someone. Much better to take what you wanted; then you didn't owe anyone anything. He looked over at Morris, wrapped in the blanket. It occurred to Rex that far from being a freely given gift, the blanket was something he had wrested from the woman. Yes. Rex had used his cunning and thieving smarts to extract this blanket from the woman's grasp. Oh, this was better, so much more to his liking, because, in effect, Rex had stolen the blanket from the woman. Yes, yes. He had used his charms to make her give him the blanket, which is the best kind of con because she didn't even realize she was being conned.

I will pause here and allow you to consider the peculiarity of Rex's reality. In his world everything is about possession. To take something is of the highest moral value because it allows you to possess that thing. Possession also confers a responsibility. In Rex's view, possessing anything requires you to care for that thing. To understand Rex fully, you will need to understand that for him theft is no moral failing but the ultimate moral good. I don't expect you to agree with him, necessarily, but I do ask that you attempt to comprehend his point of view. It may make the subsequent pages of this narrative easier to follow.

Rex pulled off the freeway at a small town to change and feed Morris. Then he drove a short distance to a department store parking lot. He had decided that carrying Morris under his jacket would not do for much longer. It was too awkward. A sling would work much better. He left Morris in the car and entered the store. He located a sling in the baby supplies aisle and found it was packed into such a small container that it was a trivial exercise to steal it from the store. He merely opened the package, took the sling out, tucked it into his pocket, and walked out of the store with a completely convincing air of casualness. No one could suspect him of anything.

Two women stood near the car as he approached it. Morris surveyed the scene quickly, alert for the presence of authorities, but almost instantly saw there was no danger of that. These were just two local women. They looked vaguely in his direction, then hardened their stare as it became apparent he was heading directly towards them.

"Is this your son?" said one of the women.

Rex turned the possibilities over in his mind. Were they concerned citizens worried about a child left in the car? Were they busybodies not prone to minding their own business? Were they childless women who wanted to steal his baby? All of these were definitely alternative scenario's with a higher than zero percent probability. Did he need to engage the women? No, he did not.

He walked past them without acknowledging them and got into the driver's seat without saying a word. He heard the women outside, raising their voices.

"You shouldn't leave your kid in the car like that."

"We're going to call the police."

No, you aren't, thought Rex. That would be too much trouble. He put the car into reverse and eased out of the parking space. No need to rev his engine or do anything that might be misconstrued as anger. Keep calm. Stay on the agenda. He put the car into drive and turned slowly. The women had stepped back to let him pass. One had her hand on her hips. The other just shook her head at him. He examined them carefully in the rear view mirror. They didn't look like they were about to pursue this any longer. It was a story to tell their husbands over dinner tonight.

He got back on the freeway and realized to be on the safe side he would have to get another car.

"Do-gooders," said Rex to Morris. "They're everywhere, you know? You want to try to avoid them as much as possible. But we won't have to deal with that sort of thing again. I got us a sling so I can carry you around with me. I won't have to leave you in the car anymore. Isn't that great, Morris?"

Morris made some gurgling noises. Rex put his hand on Morris's forehead. Still not warm.

Rex drove for a long stretch while Morris mostly slept. At a busy rest stop not far from Tucson, Rex traded his car for one with Arizona plates where the single occupant had gone into the men's room. The poor sap had left his keys in the car. Rex transferred Morris and all their supplies into the new car in less than twenty seconds. Before another twenty had passed he was back on the freeway and guessed he was at least five miles away before the man came out of the men's room and realized his car was gone. Rex headed off the freeway to a side road bypass that would take him away from heavily patrolled areas.

"What do you say?" he said to Morris. "Should we try to find a place to stay, or just continue into the city?"

Morris gurgled and clapped his hands together. It was a spasmodic gesture but Rex took it as a sign. "Okay," he said, "let's keep going. We'll get in after dark, but we don't care, right?"

Three hours later they saw the lights of Tucson spread out on the desert valley floor as they came around the Catalina mountains. The clouds above the city reflected a yellow glow back to the earth.

"Oh," said Rex, "that is beautiful."

As he drove along the highway, he turned off his headlights to get the full effect of the sky. Stars illuminated his way along the road.

"I think we made the right decision," said Rex. "This is going to be our town."

Rex turned his headlights back on and drove into the city and parked the car a couple of blocks off a main arterial road. He put Morris into the sling he had stolen from the department store, hooked the sling around his neck, and packed up all of Morris's gear into a bag. Then he walked to the arterial road and down a few blocks until he found a bus stop. He sat on the bench. Purple pipes bent into the shape of a saguaro stood tall beside the bench at both ends. No one else waited at the stop. Rex rocked Morris very slightly, an unconscious motion, mostly, one that soothed both Rex and Morris.

The bus puffed to a stop beside him. Rex got on and slid a couple of dollar bills into the machine next to the driver, who nodded at him.

"Nice night," said Rex, completely forgetting about being anonymous. But he didn't have to be anymore. This was his home now. He could be friendly to people. No one was going to know about his past life in Portland.

"Little chilly," said the driver, smiling.

"Yeah," said Rex, automatically adjusting his definition of what cold was, now that he lived in the desert.

The bus carried only three other passengers. Rex took a seat next to a window and watched the lights of buildings float by.

When he had gone far enough away from the car, he pressed the strip above the seat to signal he wanted to get out at the next stop. The bus pulled over and let him out. Rex walked a block to a small motel. He got a room and took Morris into it.

It had a small cot, perfect for his son. He put him down and surveyed the rest of the room. A microwave in one corner. A sink and small fridge in the other. A bed for him, and a table and chair next to the door. Nothing fancy, but it would do for now.

"Welcome home," he said to Morris. "Welcome to paradise."

Chapter 5: Resistance

REX AND MORRIS fell into a daily routine in no time. Rex spent mornings feeding and bathing Morris, then playing for a couple of hours, developing his motor and cognitive skills. Morris liked the toys Rex stole for him, and began to understand some words, or so it seemed to Rex. He also took to scampering around on all fours with great gusto, reveling in his ability to propel himself from place to place. The motel room was not as spacious as Rex would have liked, but that would not last long. He planned to move them into better digs as soon as he could.

About mid-morning Rex would put Morris into the sling and they would walk down to the bus stop where they boarded the bus that took them downtown. Rex could easily have stolen a car for the purpose, but stealing cars in the place where you live is never a good idea. Much too easy for the authorities to find you. Besides, Rex liked riding the bus. It gave him a chance to get to know the citizens of his new town.

Rex got off the bus near the main library building and then adopted a casual gait as he made his way down busy sidewalks. He looked for people in expensive suits, mostly businessmen, and made it seem like he accidentally stepped in front of them. The suits, who were often on cell phones, hesitated, sometimes stopped, then tried to dodge around Rex quickly. Rex stepped to the side again, as though trying to get around the person as well, but, again, he "accidentally" ended up right in their way. A brief and slight contact then occurred, plenty of time for Rex to reach for the suit's wallet and liberate it for himself. Then he smiled at the suit, shrugged, mumbled a quick "sorry" and was on his way to the nearest trashcan. As he walked he took whatever cash was in the wallet, then discarded the wallet in the can. Most days Rex could repeat this operation several times for a profit of a few hundred dollars. Sometimes he took in close to a thousand dollars. It was hard work, but it was a good living and he did not complain. He noticed that people were not as easy to fool here as they were in Portland. He had to pick his marks carefully, looking for those distracted by business dealings or personal issues. He didn't have to talk to them to know this. He could tell just by looking at their eyes.

Once he completed the day's pickings, Rex took a late lunch at one of the downtown eateries. As always when he was out with Morris, lots of people, mostly women, would look his way and notice Morris and say something nice about him: how Morris looked or how lucky Rex was that Morris seemed to like to sleep in the sling.

Morris always answered them in the affirmative: He *was* lucky. Very lucky.

One afternoon Rex was enjoying a combination plate at a Mexican restaurant in the downtown core. Morris sat beside him in a high chair the restaurant had provided. A thin woman with leathery skin approached Rex from across the restaurant.

Rex looked up, wary that she might be a detective who had been watching his monetary procurement activities. But he saw immediately that she was not. She was simply interested in Morris, who was busy hitting the table of the high chair repeatedly with a spoon.

"I hope my son isn't disturbing you," said Rex to the woman.

"Not at all," she said. "I have noticed you here before and wanted to tell you how wonderful it is that you care so deeply for your son."

It seemed like a somewhat peculiar thing to be saying to a stranger, but Rex took it in the spirit in which it was intended.

"We have fun out and about," he said. "My son likes the fresh air."

"Not many men spend so much time with their children. It's usually the mothers."

Rex nodded. "So true, but my wife, Morris's mother, died. It's just him and me now."

"Oh, how awful," said the woman. Rex thought he detected the hint of genuine empathy in her voice and expression.

"Won't you sit with us for a minute?" asked Rex.

The woman hesitated only for an instant, then took a seat across the table from Rex. She put out her hand. "My name's Louisa," she said. "Louisa Hernandez."

Rex touched her hand. It was warm and soft. "Rex Anderson."

"My husband never much spent time with our kids," said Louisa.

"That's too bad," said Rex. "Too bad for your kids and for him. I love spending time with Morris. It's the most rewarding part of my life."

Louisa looked like she thought she might have made a mistake sitting with Rex and Morris. Rex was sure she was about to get up and leave. Morris regarded her with curiosity, as though she was the most fascinating thing in the world. Rex noticed this and determined that he would not let her go.

"What does your husband do?" said Rex.

"He's a mine engineer, always off somewhere digging up ore or sinking a shaft." She shrugged.

"You seem lonely," said Rex.

She blushed. "Oh, I don't know why I wanted to talk to you," she said, then put her hand over her mouth.

"Husbands can be a nuisance," said Rex. "I've heard it from the mothers at the day care."

"Oh," said Louisa. "You use a day care?"

"On occasion. When I have an important job to do."

"What do you do?" said Louisa.

"I steal things," said Rex. "Mostly I pick pockets. It's a petty crime and quick. I've never been caught yet."

It was a calculated thing to say. Rex, being a consummate judge of human character, had decided Louisa was looking for something new in her life, something dangerous. To be spending some time with a career thief might be just the thing she was looking for. If not, he could shrug it off as a joke, and they could part ways.

Louisa blinked twice but said nothing for a few seconds. Rex took a sip from his water and placed the glass back on the table without a sound. Then he tilted his head very slightly and looked at Louisa squarely in her eyes.

"You're kidding," she said.

"No," said Rex, "I'm not. Just this morning I stole wallets from three men."

"Show me," said Louisa.

"I don't have them anymore," said Rex. "I take what I want from them, then throw them away."

"I don't believe you," said Louisa.

"That's not quite true," said Rex. "You *do* believe me, you just don't *want* to believe me. You're hoping that I'm just spinning a tale to entertain you."

Louisa looked at Rex, then Morris, then back to Rex again. She had to be at least in her fifties, but she suddenly looked no older than a school girl. Her eyes were bright and her face was flushed.

"Go steal a wallet now," said Louisa. "Show me."

"Now is not a good time," said Rex. "It's after lunch. Much better during the lunch hour. People are out of their offices and they are distracted. Lots of times they have their wallets in an easy place to get to because they're getting ready to pay for lunch."

"Oh," said Louisa. She sounded disappointed.

"We could spend the afternoon together," said Rex. "Then I could demonstrate my profession during the evening rush home, when people are distracted again and out on the streets. It's not generally as lucrative a time as lunch hour, but it'll do to show you."

Louisa made a deliberate move toward Morris, tickling him under the chin. She was thinking about whether she should accept Rex's invitation and she needed time to consider the ramifications.

"I have appointments," she said.

"Break them," said Rex.

"I have a husband."

"He doesn't care about you."

Louisa paused. Rex was right about her husband. "I have grown children," she said.

"So you feel like you need to be responsible and a good citizen."

Louisa laughed. "Yes."

"Where do you live?" said Rex.

"In the foothills."

"A beautiful big house, right?"

She nodded.

"But it's empty and you're lonely."

She sighed and stood up. "This is crazy. Good luck with your son and your career."

She turned and went back across the restaurant to her own table, where she picked up her jacket from the seat of her chair and began to put it on. Rex, stymied for the moment, could not quite decide if she was worth pursuing or if he should simply let her go.

Louisa pulled some bills out of her purse, left them on the table, then went out the front door without looking in Rex's direction.

Most men would have taken this as a definitive no, but Rex noted that Morris did not take his eyes off Louisa the whole time she walked from the table to the door. And even when she was outside, Morris still did not look away from the door.

"She's something, isn't she?" said Rex. "I think she would make a wonderful mother. She's adventurous, but not reckless. She has some sense of responsibility and she likes you, Morris. I think she already loves you if you want to know the truth. Maybe she even likes me a little."

Rex paid for his meal, pulled Morris up out of the high chair and installed him in his sling, then went out into the afternoon, alert for signs of Louisa. He had the idea, or maybe the wish, that she was not so much brushing him off as hoping he would pursue her.

He turned and began walking toward the steel and glass buildings at the downtown core, where he had made some money earlier in the day. There were still a few suits out, most of them, no doubt, going back to their offices after lunch.

He picked out a likely mark from half a block away and began walking toward him. He adjusted his approach and managed to bump into a woman just as the mark went by. The woman he contacted turned and glared at him and Rex put up his hands. "Sorry," he said. "So sorry." He took a step back just as the mark went by. The mark, pushed off his balance slightly, slowed his pace just long enough for Rex to drop his hand and pull the wallet out of the mark's jacket pocket. He placed the wallet in Morris's sling in one fluid motion. Anyone watching would have seen Rex unconsciously checking that Morris was secure and safe. The woman was now long gone. The mark picked up his pace and continued as though nothing had happened. He would not realize he was wronged for quite some time, maybe not until he got home tonight.

Rex looked up the sidewalk and continued his slow pace as though nothing strange had happened. He saw Louisa in the distance, standing next to the curb, about to bend down to the car parked there. She saw Rex and stood up, shading her eyes from the sun.

She did not move until Rex was right in front of her.

"Hello," she said.

Rex pulled the wallet out of Morris's sling and handed it to Louisa. "Merry Christmas," he said.

"It's already the new year," she said.

"Merry late Christmas," said Rex.

She looked at the wallet. It lay on Rex's open palm like an offering. They stood like that for several seconds, neither of them moving. Rex felt the blood pulse in his head.

Finally she took the wallet and opened it. She found the man's driver's license and pulled it out of its little plastic window and held it up to compare the picture to Rex.

"You just stole this?" she said.

Rex nodded. "For you. To show you I wasn't lying. I don't generally lie. Unless it is absolutely necessary. Certainly not to the woman I hope will be a mother to my son."

Louisa ignored the last sentence. "You don't seem too conflicted about making a living by stealing from people."

"Everyone steals," he said. "We stole this country from the Indians. Companies steal from their customers by giving them less value for their money. Children steal time and youth from their parents. Your husband steals minerals from the Earth. We steal honey from bees. Without theft, we would have no civilization."

"You're a philosopher thief, then," said Louisa.

"I am a pragmatist," said Rex. "As are most people. As are you, I think."

"I can't associate with you," she said.

"But you waited for me."

At Louisa's house Rex went up into the attic where Louisa had told him there was an old crib. He brought it down in pieces and they assembled it in the living room and put Morris into it.

"He looks at home in it," said Louisa.

"I should get him one," said Rex.

"You don't have a crib for him?"

"No. I'm still getting settled. I don't know if we're going to be here long. After a few months of picking pockets it's best to move on to another city before you get discovered. Even the most dim marks will get to notice you if you show up downtown day after day."

"But surely you don't do your, um, work every day."

"Very good," said Rex. "You have good instincts for thievery."

She blushed again. Rex found this completely charming and laughed.

"What?" she said.

"You like being with a thief."

"About that," said Louisa. "I'm not exactly sure why I brought you here, but you should know that I'm not about to have sex with you."

"Of course not," said Rex.

"I just wanted to get that out of the way."

"I understand completely," he said.

"For one thing I'm way too old for that."

"Oh, hardly," said Rex.

"For another, you are just so completely wrong. You're a criminal for God's sake."

"You have me there. But, you see, I'm not looking for a relationship either. I just want to be married."

She laughed.

Rex grinned. "That does sound funny, doesn't it?"

"Only because you're right. Being married is not a relationship. Being married is death to any relationship."

Rex thought of Stella and a deep melancholy rose up in him. Louisa saw the change in his face.

"What's wrong?" she said.

Rex thought about brushing it off or telling her a lie but decided the truth would be more likely to get him what he wanted.

"My wife Stella," he said. "She was very depressed for a long time. She killed herself."

"Oh no."

"I didn't see it coming."

"Was it postpartum depression?" said Louisa. "I never had it, but it can be terrible for women. Just the worst."

Rex veered smoothly into lying, the combination of truth and untruth had a kind of pure storytelling power that appealed to him. "Yes, that was it exactly. When she died everything changed. Morris became the one and only focus of my life. I do everything for him."

"Yes," she said. "I can see that."

"And my work gives me the opportunity to spend as much time with him as possible."

"Another way in which thievery contributes to the well being of society."

"Yes," said Rex. "I hadn't thought of that, but you're right."

"You know," said Louisa, "none of this can go beyond today."

"I see," said Rex.

"Just so you know. This is something I'm doing as a lark, but only for this one day. Something completely out of my character."

"Everyone needs to do that sometimes," said Rex.

They left Morris in the crib to sleep and went into the kitchen where Louisa made coffee and set out a plate of cookies which Rex dug into with gusto.

"This is very good," he said.

She nodded. "My husband is cheating on me," she said.

"Sure," said Rex. "I knew that. I could see it all over your face as soon as I met you."

Her eyes were moist. Tears threatened to spill out over her bottom eyelashes. Rex watched them tremble, just on the precipice. He saw a box of tissue on the counter and went over and plucked a few sheets and handed them to her. She took them and dabbed at her eyes. "Thank you," she said.

"Think nothing of it," said Rex. "Are you going to divorce him?"

"I couldn't," she said.

"Why not?"

"I would end up with nothing. He has very smart lawyers. He told me years ago that he had things figured so that he would keep everything."

"That's crazy," said Rex. "I tell you what. You seem to like Morris, am I wrong?"

Louisa smiled. "No," she said, "you're not wrong."

"Why don't you take him for a few days? See if you like him enough to want to take care of him."

Louisa shook her head. "You are the most peculiar man," she said.

"The thing is, Morris needs a woman in his life. He needs some kind of mother figure and he doesn't have that."

She looked away and sighed. "I was happiest when the children were babies. When they grow up, you know, they become more and more of a pain in the ass."

Rex nodded. "With their own lives and everything."

"Yes. Their own lives. It was quite devastating when they didn't need me anymore."

"There you are. Morris needs you."

"What'll I tell my husband?"

"When's he coming back?"

"In a couple of days."

"Worry about that when the time comes. For now, just accept that Morris and I need you. It's for your own good."

"I'm afraid I'll love him too much to let him go."

"That's not a bad thing at all," said Rex. "Steal him for yourself. Steal his love. Otherwise someone else will get it."

She shook her head. "Who are you?"

"I'm just a guy," said Rex.

"I don't think so," said Louisa. "You're more like a force of nature."

Chapter 6: Saguaro

EVEN THOUGH REX wasn't sure if he wanted to stay in Tucson for much longer, he did know he wanted to be in Louisa's general vicinity at least for the next few months, so he and Morris moved out of the hotel room and took a more spacious, cleaner, and brighter apartment in the north of town, not too far from Louisa's house. He bought a car, used but sound, which he drove to Phoenix every day, two hours north, where he practiced his profession, then returned home. While he was gone he left Morris in Louisa's care.

Louisa and Morris got on very well. She bought him toys and read stories to him, put him down for a nap and later played finger games with him and sang to him. She took him to a doctor to make sure he was healthy and strong. All in all, she was exactly the mother to Morris that Rex had hoped for.

When Louisa's husband, Hector, returned home, she told him Morris was the child of a friend who couldn't afford day care so she was looking after him for a few weeks. Her husband, though initially irritated with having a baby around the house, soon let his irritation go. After all, he wasn't home that much anyway, what with his work and his girlfriend to attend to, so Louisa generally had the house all to herself when Morris was there. Around late afternoon Rex usually came back to pick up Morris. He would stay for a half hour or so in Louisa's house, have a cup of coffee, and enjoy some conversation with Louisa.

"I noticed all the saguaros today," said Rex. Morris sat beside him, chewing on a plastic pretzel from a collection of plastic food that Louisa had bought for him a few days ago. Morris was especially partial to the hot dog and the stack of pancakes.

"What about them?" said Louisa.

"I noticed that some of your neighbors have them in their yards, but you don't."

Louisa shrugged. "Our lot just didn't happen to have any. We wanted one, but it cost so much to buy that Hector said we should forgot it."

"Why didn't you go out and get one? They're everywhere."

"It's not that easy. They're a protected species. You can't just steal one. Plus it's a big deal to transplant one of them. They weigh a ton. It takes special equipment." She shrugged. "Why are you so interested in saguaros all of a sudden?"

"Your yard looks so bare without one. I wanted to get you one to thank you for looking after Morris."

"That's sweet, Rex, but you don't have to do anything like that. I like having Morris here."

"I know," said Rex, "but I want to do something. I could give you money."

Louisa laughed. "I don't need money," she said. "Hector gives me all the money I want. I'll say that for him, at least. He's not cheap."

Rex thought that couldn't be, if he didn't spring for the cost of transplanting a saguaro, but he didn't argue with Louisa. She seemed so happy sitting here with him and Morris.

"Was Morris good today?" asked Rex.

Louisa nodded. "He called me mama."

"He did?"

Louisa, her face radiant and flush, smiled and nodded.

"That's wonderful," said Rex. "I hope you don't mind. I mean, I hope you *feel* like his mother even if you aren't."

Louisa sighed. "I love having him in the house, I do. It makes my days feel worthwhile."

Rex felt happy for her. He looked to the cactus garden out back. An assortment of cholla, barrel cacti, and prickly pear, all low, as though wary of rising too far above the ground, baked in the sun. The landscape fairly screamed for a multi-armed saguaro to stand tall over them all.

"I've never been in your backyard," said Rex.

"Oh," said Louisa. "You want to come look at it now?"

Rex picked up Morris, who put his little arms around Rex's neck, and they walked out to the back yard. An adobe wall demarcated the area from the neighboring properties. A worn path meandered through the thorny cacti and underbrush. The sun burned a hole in the sky. Morris turned away from it, closing his eyes against the glare. A small tree with green bark occupied one corner of the yard.

Rex pointed at the tree. "What's that?" he said.

"It's a palo verde," said Louisa. "It's adapted to the desert by taking in sunlight through it's skin."

Rex raised his eyebrows and absorbed that little tidbit of information. "So its bark is like a giant leaf?"

"Kind of," said Louisa. "Desert plants are not like other plants in the world. Sometimes I think they're almost from another planet. Kind of like you."

"Oh yeah," said Rex. "I see it. In the desert you have to figure out how to steal water from the rest of the plants, and there isn't much of it so you have to be good at it."

Louisa hesitated. "That isn't *exactly* what I meant, but okay."

"Sure," said Rex. "It makes sense. Money is scarce so I learned how to steal it. Just like water in the desert. These desert plants are my brothers."

They walked down the path and around several barrel cacti. "Careful of the thorns," said Louisa.

Rex kept Morris away from the fish hook thorns and the sharp needle thorns and the nasty clump of yellowish thorns that sat atop a plump green globe like a cluster of glass shards. The fierceness of all the sharp needles did not repel Rex. In fact, he admired their power, the way they staked out their ground. He could learn from them, figure out ways to keep himself safe while he was on the job. To be prickly could save him from a nasty run-in with a mark. Or the authorities.

"One thing desert plants teach you is to be careful," said Louisa.

"Yes," said Rex. "I'm always careful, you know, but you're right. You have to be aware around all this bristle. It makes you think about your own skin."

"You like it here," said Louisa. "With all my plants."

Rex laughed. "How can you tell?"

"Most people I show my cactus don't want to be around them for long. They compliment me on the plants and then they want to get back in the house. Not you."

"They are amazing plants," said Rex. "We have nothing like this in the Northwest."

"I'll put one in a pot for you," she said. "So you can have one at your place."

"That would be nice," said Rex, "but I don't think I should do that. These deserve to be outside in the sun."

That night, after he fed and bathed Morris and played games with him on the floor of their apartment, Rex put him in his crib and then went down the hall and knocked on the door of Dan Randall, owner and operator of Randall's Landscaping, which consisted of one pickup truck, currently parked in the apartment building lot, loaded with rakes, hoes, shovels, and a lawn mower. Dan and Rex had met briefly when Rex moved in and Dan had helped carry a few pieces of furniture for the new apartment.

"Yeah?" said Dan when he opened the door.

"Dan," said Rex, "what would it take to get a saguaro into someone's backyard?"

Dan regarded him with suspicion, but Rex put on his best benign look, the one that always convinced people he was the most upstanding and moral citizen they could ever meet, and Dan's expression softened. He invited Rex inside. Rex sat on his couch.

"Your son at that lady's place?" he asked Rex.

"No," said Rex. "I got him asleep right now."

Dan nodded. "You want a saguaro here? Are you crazy?"

"No, not for me. For Louisa. As a thank you. She wants one for her cactus garden."

"You know it's illegal to harvest them?"

Rex nodded. "That doesn't bother me."

Dan laughed and shook his head. "Maybe not, amigo, but it bothers me. I'm not going to go to jail for a stupid cactus."

"I'm not asking you to," said Rex. "I figure maybe you know someone who can help me."

"Oh, that's what you figure? You think I'm connected with the criminal underworld or something?"

"The practitioners of most every profession know people on the edge, the ones who don't follow the rules."

Dan laughed, then rubbed his chin. "Yeah, I think I know someone who can help you. It isn't cheap."

"I have some money," said Rex. "And I know how to get more."

"I'll bet you do," said Dan.

"Just give me a name," said Rex, "and I won't bother you about this ever again."

Dan was not necessarily in agreement with the authorities on the subject of saguaros. He supposed saguaros should more or less be in the wild, but he didn't see any harm in taking a few here and there to put into people's backyards if they wanted one. After all, many other kinds of cacti were allowed to be traded on the open market. But saguaros were special because they didn't grow in very many places: too many frosty nights killed them, and they were potent symbols of the state and of the desert. Also, it wasn't his business what Rex did. The man was asking him for help based on his professional knowledge. That was kind of flattering in a perverse way. No one ever asked Dan for his expertise.

"You sure about this?" said Dan.

"Completely," said Rex.

Dan gave him the name and number of a saguaro rustler. Rex carefully wrote it down and Dan got a couple beers out of the fridge. He and Rex talked about kids and cactus for a few minutes while they finished their beers.

Let's leave them there for the moment while I tell you a little about what Rex was about to get himself into. First of all, you should realize that even though Rex had all the makings of an outlaw, his activities were very low tech. He used next to no equipment when he relieved marks of their money. His day-to-day profession was a model of efficiency in more ways than one. Not only did it require nothing more elaborate than his fingers, it generally left next to no trace or trail with which to track him down.

Saguaro rustling was an altogether different species of activity. It needed heavy equipment. Also more than one person. It required the cover of darkness and at least one expert in cacti to make sure the saguaro survived the ordeal of transplantation. The whole operation needed a detailed and foolproof plan to succeed. And if Rex was caught, the consequences would be much more severe than if some city cop saw him lift a wallet from someone's back pocket. Taking a saguaro was a serious offense in the state of Arizona People have gone to jail for months just for taking a saguaro out of a National Park. If Rex was caught, the consequences could seriously disrupt his life and cause no end of complications for Morris.

Why was he so interested in pursuing the procurement of the saguaro? Partly it was that he did not know all the ramifications. Partly it was that he had an over-inflated idea of his own abilities, and partly it was that he was in love with Louisa and wanted to get her something special.

For my part, I had a bad feeling about the whole business. I admit to having some affection for Rex. He had a spunk I admired and he truly did care for his son. Even though Morris was not his son, his behavior toward him almost made me believe they were related. That is not easy to do, let me tell you. I hope that in this narrative I have highlighted Rex's good qualities at least to the point that you share some of my affection for him. Despite his chosen profession, Rex was not an evil man. He was bad, in a way, but not truly evil. Do you see the difference? Perhaps not. Maybe it doesn't matter. Truth to tell, I wanted to swoop down on the scene between Rex and Dan and tell them to stop. Stop it right now. But, alas, I don't have that power. I can observe and sympathize. I can even cheer good fortune and lament bad, but I cannot intervene. Such frustration is an endless source of dismay to me, I can assure you. But none of us chooses our power. We are given what providence deems necessary.

I watched the two of them consume their beers. I shifted my attention to Morris, still asleep in his crib. I tried to imagine what his life would be like without Rex. Such thoughts should have told me something. But I did not see the change coming.

Rex put his empty bottle down on the coffee table in Dan's apartment, stood up and thanked Dan for the information, then returned to his own apartment and immediately called the number Dan had given him.

The voice on the other end was hesitant. Rex explained what he wanted, but the voice did not warm to Rex at all. Rex wished he was able to talk to the voice in person, but Dan had told him the man didn't like to meet his clients. Safer that way.

"You're not very smart," said the voice.

"What do you mean?" said Rex, who felt the opportunity slipping from him.

"You call up a stranger and propose a crime. Not very smart."

"I got your name from a friend. He said you could help."

"I got no friends," said the voice and hung up.

Rex sat next to Morris with the phone in his hand.

"That went well," he said. Morris, who had awoken, looked up at him and said "Mama" several times.

"Papa," said Morris. "Try to say Papa. Or Dada." He laughed. "I'm not your mother, you know?"

Morris gurgled at him and put out his hand and made a fist, then unclenched it.

"I guess I'll just have to do this on my own," said Rex.

Oh, how I died inside when he said that. It wasn't so much the idea of breaking the law, which, on balance, I can easily forgive under the right circumstances. It was more that I knew how ill-equipped he was for the task. I wanted to knock on his head and say "what are you thinking, dimwit?" But as I have already told you, I don't have that power. Instead I watched the next week unfold like a bad movie. Rex drove out into the state park east of town and walked the paths looking for a good sized saguaro cactus. He picked out a fairly tall one, maybe twenty feet, that had not yet grown any arms. Saguaro don't get arms until they are about fifty years old. So the one he found was still young and he thought he could take it by himself.

Oh no oh no oh no.

Rex went to the library and found a book on the theory and practice of transplanting large cactus. He was pleasantly surprised to learn that saguaro roots do not go down very deep. Instead, they remain shallow and spread wide. He though he could handle that.

Oh my oh my oh my.

He took Morris to Louisa's house and asked her if he could leave him overnight.

"Overnight?" said Louisa?

"Yes," said Rex. "There's a big marathon in Phoenix with lots of spectators. I want to be there bright and early tomorrow morning for some easy pickings, so I'd like to spend the night. Would that work for you?"

Louisa had her suspicions, but she took Morris from Rex's arms and hugged him to her shoulder. "If you want to," she said, "I'd be happy to keep Morris overnight."

"Hector won't mind?"

"He's with his girlfriend," said Louisa flatly.

"Oh," said Rex. "I'm sorry." He was not the least bit sorry. The more Louisa's husband stayed away, the more chance there was that Louisa would see how attractive a prospect Rex was and the more likely she would be to want to marry him.

Such are the delusions of people who live outside of polite society.

Rex did not go to Phoenix that day. Instead he stole a pickup. One with a long bed to accommodate the saguaro he wanted. He waited until dark and drove out to the desert and backed the pickup next to the saguaro. He jumped out of the cab and began to dig around a large perimeter of the cactus. This kind of manual labor did not come naturally to Rex. Before long sweat ran profusely down his face and back and in the cold night air the sweat chilled him to the bone. His back ached and his hand blistered within a few minutes. But he kept working. He wanted that cactus for himself. With every meager shovelful of hard dry dirt, he grew more convinced that the saguaro was his. His expenditure of energy and time made it his. That was the law of theft that he had come to formulate for himself over the years: the more you work for something, the more you are entitled to it.

That meant that people who sat around in cubicles punching on computer keyboards did not deserve the wealth they had. Typing on a keyboard was not work. It was play. On the other hand, someone who contrives to remove a wallet from a stranger's pocket without being caught, now *that* was *work*. And holy work, at that, because it spread the wealth around to those who deserved it: the poor and disenfranchised.

So, too, this excavating around the saguaro was hard work. Rex deserved whatever benefit came from that hard work. I did not agree with his assessment of the situation. After all, the saguaro did a lot of work to be in that place: decades of converting sunlight to food. Didn't that count for something? Of course it did. But Rex did not see this. Would he ever? I didn't know. I had hoped that Rex would grow up and understand how being a mature person meant you didn't always get what you wanted. But such considerations were far off. For Rex, nothing mattered but this cactus.

After a few hours he had dug a pretty good trench around the saguaro and had begun to dig under the root mass, with a view to loosening it enough to push the cactus over onto the truck bed.

I think it was about this moment that I despaired the most. The poor cactus would not survive the machinations of this misguided man. He had no idea the damage he was doing.

He dug out hard dry dirt and pushed it away with his hands, which were now bloody from cuts and burst blisters.

He heard the howls of coyotes in the hills behind him. They yelped in unison and in harmony, then broke into their own individual yips. Javelinas scuffled around him, then ran off. The desert bristled with activity. Owls flew above. He heard their hoots.

I will say that Rex's last hours on the planet were blessed with the abundance of life. I think that gave him some solace.

But I'm getting ahead of myself. When he sensed the saguaro was ready to tip over, Rex put down his shovel and stood away from it. His breath came hard and sweat fell from his forehead and into his eyes. This saguaro, without a doubt, was the most daunting object he had ever tried to steal. It made him proud to even attempt such a feat.

He spread foam and blankets over the pickup's bed, the better to cushion the saguaro during its ride to Louisa's house. Then he went around to the other side of the saguaro, put a blanket around it to protect himself from the thorns, and pushed. The saguaro moved slightly, then stopped.

Rex pushed some more, but the cactus was stubborn. It would not budge.

Rex thought perhaps his angle was wrong. He stood up on the pickup bed and wrapped a rope around the cactus and held both ends. He pulled on the rope. The saguaro shifted toward him, a little, but not enough to dislodge it from its home.

Rex took a deep breath, set his teeth firmly, dug his heels into the foam under his feet, and exerted a supreme effort of strength, the last he had in him.

A saguaro, even a relatively young specimen like the one Rex had lassoed, is a heavy object. It is mostly dense plant tissue wrapped around wooden rods, saturated with water. Think of the weight of a hundred gallons of water. Then think of pulling that weight down on yourself.

Rex thought he could scamper out of the way as the saguaro tipped over and fell onto the pickup's bed. Instead, his feet slipped out from under him just as the cactus crashed down, rolled towards his chest, and pinned his back to the edge of the truck bed. Further, it bent his head back and broke his neck.

A ghastly scene, indeed. Rex had no chance to escape. Also, you should note that Rex did not struggle. The saguaro did its job quickly and efficiently. The last thing Rex stole was the thing that killed him. If he had any last thoughts, they most likely would have been thoughts of Morris. He loved the child. Despite his faults, Rex had been capable of love.

Chapter 7: Heart

Louisa's night with Morris was not touched by Rex's demise. I would like to offer you some kind of cosmic connection between the two, such that, for example, when Rex died, Louisa and/or Morris felt a fracture in their universe. But this was not the case. At the moment the saguaro crushed Rex to death, Louisa had Morris in her arms. He had just woken and had begun to cry crankily. Louisa, roused from her own sleep, had noted the time: a little past two o'clock, and had taken Morris up from the crib and held him to her shoulder and patted his bottom rhythmically to soothe him while the formula she had put on the stove came to the proper temperature.

While Morris settled down and his crankiness began to dissipate, the front door of Louisa's house opened and in walked her husband, Hector. Louisa had not expected him. She knew he had planned to spend the night at his girl friend's place. Not that he told her that. He was officially supposed to be at a job site to the north. Too far to come back so he had to stay overnight. Such fictions had become a part of their lives. Louisa and Hector both knew he was lying but they both pretended he was not.

Hector had expected to find the house dark and quiet. He was surprised, and pleased, to find that his wife was still awake. He did not believe she was waiting up for him, but he did wonder if she was hoping he would come back early. A short time before, his girlfriend had told him she was not interested in seeing him anymore. Then she asked him to leave her house. Hector did so, with reluctance. He wondered what his life would be without her. He could try to go back to Louisa, but that seemed like a step in the wrong direction. The plan had been to transition away from Louisa and eventually leave her completely. That is what he had been telling this other woman for months, but she did not believe him.

"Hey," he said to Louisa. "You still have the little one?"

"Yes," said Louisa. "His father had business in Phoenix."

"Business?"

"He had some appointments early in the morning."

Hector put his jacket in the closet by the front door and came into the kitchen. Louisa looked happy and content. So at home with Morris in her arms.

"You should get paid for looking after his kid," said Hector.

Louis shrugged. "Being around the baby like this is payment enough."

"You always liked having babies," he said.

"Aren't you the smart one," said Louisa. "Knowing what I always liked."

Hector hesitated, unsure what to say next. He opted for silence. Morris gurgled and kicked his legs.

"And what about your business?" said Louisa.

"The, uh, job finished earlier than expected. I came home."

Louisa saw loss in his face. Some shame as well. Not enough, but some. She felt a small sympathy for him, but did not let it grow too large. He deserved her scorn, after all, not any kind of compassion, not for stepping out on her all these years.

"I see," she said. "And you won't have to go back to that job again?"

"No," he said.

"Not tomorrow?"

"No. Or the next day or the next. The job is finished."

She liked the sound of that. She extended her arms, offering Morris to Hector, who was unsure of himself at first, not ready to hold the child.

"Just take him," said Louisa. "I need to get his formula."

Hector finally accepted Morris and held him by the armpits. Morris's eyes went wide and unseeing, then focused on Hector's face.

"Oh for God's sake," said Louisa, "hold him like you should hold a baby."

"I was never good at this, Louisa, you know that."

She took Morris and told Hector to make a cradle with his arms. He did so and she eased Morris into the cradle. Hector's face softened considerably.

"Keep your hand under his head," she said.

Hector nodded. He moved his other hand and put his finger under Morris's chin. Morris smiled and gurgled at him. He made a sound. "I think he just called me Papa," said Hector.

"Impossible," said Louisa at the stove. "That was just a burp." She poured formula into a bottle and came back to Hector, who suddenly did not want to give Morris back. Louisa saw his reluctance. She gave the bottle to Hector who took it with more than a little enthusiasm and held it close to Morris's mouth. Morris turned his head and made a face. It looked like he was about to cry.

"What happened?" said Hector.

"You're a clumsy idiot is what happened," said Louisa. "Be gentle with him." She showed her husband how he should touch the bottle to Morris's cheek and how Morris then turned to it to accept the formula.

Hector, initially so clumsy, relaxed and found a small measure of contentment sitting with the child of another man and woman. How could such a small person bring him so much comfort so quickly?

"This father," said Hector. "He's a good man?"

"He cares for his son very much," said Louisa.

"How can that be if he gives him to you every day?"

"Don't be so old fashioned," said Louisa. "I'm like a day care."

"I don't like day care," said Hector. "Children should be with their mothers."

"The mother died."

"Yes," said Hector. "You told me she killed herself. That is very sad. Who would kill themselves if they had a baby such as this in their lives?"

Louisa wanted to hate her husband. She had every right to. He spent time with some other woman, then when it became inconvenient for the other woman and she tossed Hector out, Louisa suddenly became convenient and Hector came back to her. Such disrespect. And yet, she found it difficult to truly hate him.

"He'll be here all day tomorrow. Rex isn't coming back until the afternoon."

"Yes?" said Hector.

"Do you have to get up early?"

"I have to go to work," said Hector.

"I thought maybe, since they weren't expecting you, you might stay a little later. We could have breakfast together."

Hector stared at Morris's face, unable to look up at his wife's. He had wronged her, he knew that and he was sorry, but he also felt that being sorry wasn't enough. He had to pay in some way, but she wasn't asking him to pay. Why?

"Maybe a long breakfast with you and the baby would be good," said Hector. "I think that would be nice."

It's the baby, thought Louisa. The baby makes him want to stay.

THE NEXT MORNING a jogger who ran the trails at the Saguaro National Forest found Rex's stolen pickup across her path. She stopped to examine the scene. The saguaro was broken where it fell against the tailgate of the truck, and broken again where it touched the roof of the cab. The top of the cactus dropped over onto the hood of the truck like a fallen balloon. She looked around, not sure what to make of this. She had heard of saguaro rustlers, but had never encountered one. Certainly not a rustling in progress.

She walked around to the other side and saw Rex's arm stretched out on the edge of the truck bed. She gasped and bent down for a better look. She saw the side of Rex's torso and a small pool of blood that looked like it had dripped from his nose or mouth.

She pulled out her cell phone from her fanny pack and called the police, who arrived soon after. They looked for a wallet on Rex's person, but found none. They tracked the pickup truck to a man who lived in an apartment building across town from Rex's. They knocked on the man's door at six in the morning. The man, still sleepy, answered the door in his T-shirt and underwear.

"Yes," he said to the officer when asked if he owned the truck Rex had stolen. "That's my truck. What about it?"

They told him it was involved in a robbery and a death. The man, who did not even know his truck had been stolen until that moment, wondered if he needed to call a lawyer.

But the officer assured him that he was not in any trouble. It appeared some drifter had used his truck to try to steal a cactus.

"A cactus?" said the man. "Who would try to steal a cactus?"

"You'd be surprised," said the officer, who thanked the man for his time, but didn't tell him how he was going to get his truck back.

The police department tried to find out more about Rex, but with no identifying information on him, and no way to tell where he lived or where he was from, the police had nothing to go on. They pulled prints from the interior of the cab, but found no match. Rex had been careful to never get arrested, so his prints were not in any database anywhere.

They closed the file within days. The city disposed of his body.

I watched with more than a little interest. I anticipated Rex's visit to me with relish. I couldn't wait to lambaste him for his stupidity. Picking pockets I could understand. I didn't necessarily approve, but I could understand the Robin Hood mentality and the need to live on the edge of society. There are many who march to the beat of a different drummer and they should not all be abhorred. But stealing a saguaro? There is no excuse for such incompetence. Rex had a child, however ill-gotten, and he had responsibilities. If only I was able to intervene and make Rex see just how truly ridiculous his endeavor was.

But I could not.

All I could do was watch and worry. If I had nails they would have been chewed to the quick and beyond.

LOUISA HAD WONDERED, in the middle of the night, if she should have invited Hector to her bed. They had brokered an arrangement, ever since the other woman had become part of their lives, that Hector would sleep in his room and Louisa would sleep in hers. This had worked for both of them, and Louisa didn't want to see the arrangement end too quickly. Hector needed to feel some loss for his transgressions. There should be at least a little punishment, shouldn't there?

And so she did not give in to her urge. She had to admit, even though she would never say so to him, that she missed sleeping next to him. He had a nice warmth about him, did her husband. She felt so secure and safe when he was in bed with her, and it had been so long. Well, it would happen again. She would forgive him. Had already forgiven him. If he needed some silly fling for a few months, there wasn't much she could do about it. Now that it was over, things could maybe go back to the way they had been. Not right away, but eventually.

In the morning she rose and went to Morris's crib and picked him up. Then she went to Hector's room and knocked on the door.

"Yes?" said Hector from inside.

"I'll take breakfast in my room," she said, then returned to her bed and put Morris down next to her and played finger games with him. After a few minutes Hector appeared at her door.

"What would you like?" he asked.

"Some eggs, scrambled, would be nice. And maybe a serving of beans."

"I haven't made breakfast in years," he said.

"Then it's time you started again," she said.

He took a breath and looked up at the ceiling momentarily, then down at his wife and Morris.

"I won't know where things are."

"You'll figure it out."

"Oh?"

"Oh?" she said, mimicking him precisely.

He laughed. "You haven't done that in a long time."

"Go," said Louisa.

He disappeared from the door and momentarily she heard the crash of pans coming from downstairs.

"He's going to make a mess of it," she said to Morris, who stared at her blankly. "But we don't care, do we? No, we don't."

She took Morris to the downstairs bathroom where she had a small basin in which to bathe him. She did so now, while Hector struggled with breakfast. After she dried Morris off and put him into some fresh diapers and clothes, she took him into the kitchen.

"I thought I was going to bring you breakfast in bed," said Hector.

"I got tired of waiting."

"Hmmm," said Hector. "I don't blame you."

She noted the broken egg shells on the floor and the toast smoking in the toaster. "You might want to look into that burning smell," she said mildly.

"Oh, dammit," he said, then reached across the counter and nudged the knob so the toast popped up, charcoal black and leaking white clouds.

"I'll put in another couple of slices," he said.

"Marvelous idea," she said with a kind of dreamy faraway look in her eyes. He was completely useless at this. It was nice to see him try and fail so utterly.

He took two more slices of bread, slid the browning dial down a couple of notches, and plunged the knob down. He tossed the black slices into the garbage. Then he returned to the bowl with the eggs in them, noted the presence of small pieces of shell, and fished them out with his fingers, which took some work as they tended to slide out from under him. Meanwhile the pan began to smoke. He saw it before Louisa pointed it out and pulled the pan off the burner to cool down a little. He whisked the eggs with a fork. This, at least, he could do. He enjoyed the sensation of the eggs curling their liquid strands around the tines of the fork. They had weight and were also yielding. A charming combination. He returned the pan to the burner and poured the eggs in. They began to coagulate immediately. Hector rummaged around in the drawer for a wooden spoon and used it to push the eggs around the pan. All the while he was aware of Louisa looking at him.

"You're having me do this for a reason, aren't you?" he said.

"Reason?"

"You're trying to get me to see something."

"Maybe," she said.

"I'm sorry for what I did to you."

"You didn't do anything to me," said Louisa.

"I mean—"

"I know what you mean."

This wasn't going to be a conversation. Was it too early to say anything to her? Should he just let her direct things for a while? He was unsure how to proceed.

"Did you ever wonder," said Louisa, "how we are all thieves in this world?"

Thieves? What was she saying?

"I'm not sure I know what you mean," said Hector.

"That woman, she tried to steal you from me."

Ah, thought Hector. Here it comes. "Yes," he said. "I suppose you're right."

"This child here, he stole something from you last night."

"He's a baby. How can he steal anything?"

"He stole your heart. You were keeping it all to yourself. You didn't want me to see it, but he took it from you."

The eggs had completely lost their liquid aspect. They had solidified in the pan, dried out, and were beginning to brown. Hector didn't know if they were supposed to do that, or if he needed to stop their cooking process. He didn't want to ask Louisa. He pushed them around the pan some more and saw they were beginning to stick to the bottom. The toast popped. The sound of them springing up startled him. He jumped.

"You felt it," said Louisa. "A pure love. One that you could talk about to me. To anyone."

Hector could not imagine what to say to Louisa. He wanted to disappear. Wanted to be nothing for the next few moments. He concentrated on breakfast. He opened the cabinet door above the counter and pulled out two plates. He put a slice of toast on each one, all the while the air around him felt like it was made of cotton. And Louisa's eyes. Her gaze drilled holes into him. He wanted to scratch the back of his head, his shoulder blades.

He scraped eggs onto the plates, then had no more excuses to stay turned from her. He lifted the plates off the counter and faced her.

"Breakfast," he said, aware of how inadequate the word was.

"You steal from the earth," she said. "Did you ever think of that? You take ore out of the ground and crush it and roast it and form it into—stuff. That's theft, isn't it? To steal from the mother?"

Hector put the plates down on the table. Morris squirmed in Louisa's arms. Louisa took a morsel of egg from her plate and put it in Morris's mouth. He waved his arms and reached for more of the egg. Louisa took another bit and placed it on his lip. The softness of his skin was a wonder to her. How can anything feel like this? How can flesh be so ghostly?

"I don't steal," said Hector. "I transform. It all goes back into the ground eventually. In a million years no one will know what I mined here."

"Maybe not," said Louisa. "But right now, right here, I know. Everyone knows."

She ran her hand over the top of Morris's head. She pushed back his hair and felt his skull against her palm.

Hector was not the least bit hungry, but he took a bite of toast and a bite of his eggs. He chewed carefully, the food an invasion in his mouth.

"You're going to clean this kitchen up," said Louisa. "When you're done it will be spotless. You know that, right?"

"I know," said Hector.

"And you forgot the beans."

"Ah," said Hector. "The beans."

Chapter 8: Time

NEW ARRIVALS TO my realm often display symptoms of panic, unease, fear, distress, or dismay. Sometimes all those and more. I usually have to spend a lot of time consoling their sensibilities before I get around to explaining their situation. That didn't happen with Rex. I don't know if it's because he was used to life out of the mainstream, or if he had some intuition I was not aware of. In any case, he came out of the mist with a decidedly self-assured stride. I stood in his path.

"I didn't think heaven was going to be like this," he said.

"Don't be ridiculous," I said. "This isn't heaven. It's just a way station."

"Ah," he said, and smiled at me crookedly, like he thought the whole thing was a big joke. Which, in a way, I suppose it was. "So you're my guardian angel or something? Where's your wings?"

I don't mind telling you I was not amused by his nonchalance. He just died, for goodness sake. He could have had some sense of gravitas about his circumstances.

"There are no angels here," I said. "That's a delusion you all seem to foster for some reason or other that escapes me. I'm the avatar of thieves. I've been watching you."

"You get bored up here?" he said. "Is that it? You have to spy on sorry saps like me?"

You see what I'm saying? No sense of propriety whatever.

"Everyone has their destiny," I said.

"Yeah?" he said. "Why'd you let me die?"

His tone irritated me. That was not good for either of us.

"You mistake the nature of the universe," I said. "I did nothing to effect your death. That was all you."

"I don't believe it," he said flatly. "I knew what I was doing. It was a freak accident that got me. You had to be behind it."

"No," I said.

His face darkened. "You took years away from me. You stole my life out from under me."

I had half a mind to just let him go down the corridor to the soup line. That would have made my life (and his) a lot easier, but I was conscious of my duty to the spirit of thievery.

"Let me make myself clear," I told him. "I have no powers beyond observation. I am charged with observing thieves. True thieves, those who make it not only a hobby or casual pastime but who have undertaken it as a sacred way of life. In observing such as yourself, I come to a greater understanding of how the universe operates."

"But now Morris doesn't have a father."

"That's not my fault."

"I don't believe you," said Rex. "I think you brought me up here to tap my energy."

His interest in abduction narratives had escaped my attention. He did not believe me and I also saw that nothing I could ever say would convince him otherwise.

"Perhaps you would like to see your room?" I said.

"Show me Morris," he said.

I took him to a viewing room. I didn't need one, but we had several set up for newcomers. They often want to look at the world they left, but that usually lasted for only a few days. Sometimes a few hours. When you can't interact, the whole novelty of the thing wears off quickly. I wasn't sure that was going to happen with Rex.

He followed me through the door. The wall in front of us bore a wide view of Morris's mother. His real mother.

"Who's that?" said Rex.

"Don't you recognize her? Her name is Judy Bryant. You only saw her for an instant, but she gave you the most precious thing in your life."

He stepped closer to the screen. It looked like a flat panel television because that is the kind of technology Rex would be familiar with. In previous centuries newcomers looked into mist, mirrors, pools of water, and deep caves. But they always saw the same thing: the world they had vacated.

"Now I remember," said Rex. "She left Morris in that baby carriage. She was practically begging to have him taken away."

I have heard many justifications for thievery, from many thieves. I have grown accustomed to their bouts of perverse logic. I have even admired some of it at certain times. I cannot therefore say why this comment by Rex made me so angry, but it did. I felt the fires of rage rise in me. I turned on Rex and grabbed him by his hair and pulled his head back. I discerned a crookedness to his form, no doubt the result of his stupid accident. Ridiculous simpleton. For him to think that he could steal a saguaro. Such arrogance. Such idiotic foolishness.

"Hey," he said. "Be careful. I'm still sore from the accident."

I bent down to his ear and hissed into it. "This woman before you gave birth to the boy you so presumptuously call your son. Give her the respect she deserves. She suffers every day, not knowing where he is."

"Okay, okay," he said. He tried to twist away from me, but I held fast to his hair and pulled so hard that I threatened to tear it from his scalp. He rose on the tips of his toes. I angled his head so his eyes looked directly at the screen, which displayed Judy Bryant at her kitchen table sipping a cup of tea. She looked tired. In grief. So weary from concern and the long grind of months of panic and despair. Her eyes were swollen. She had obviously gone without sleep for a long time. I felt for her. I wanted to do something to ease her pain. I released my hold on Rex just a bit.

"She steals from her company," I said. "She's embezzled tens of thousands of dollars. A simple accountant's trick, sending fractions of pennies to her account electronically. Over the years it builds up."

"*Really*," said Rex, suddenly interested.

"Yes," I said flatly. "*Really*."

"So it wasn't so bad that I took her kid. I mean, it's not like she's all pure and everything."

I don't know why I told Rex those facts about Judy Bryant's life and activities. I suppose I felt some kind of guilt for the brief pain I inflicted on him. I suppose, also, that I didn't care for Judy Bryant's brand of thievery. It was entirely self-serving and did nothing to further the betterment of society. Not that Rex was a model citizen, by any means, but most of his thieving was for others. He stole Morris for his wife, he stole money to support Morris, and he even had someone else in mind when he attempted to take the saguaro from its rightful place in the desert. But Judy? She thought it an entitlement, the money she took from her employer. She thought she was underpaid and so, by her own ingenuity, arranged to be overpaid.

Now, you may say that her thievery helped create a better life for her child, but that was not in her heart. Or, at least not completely. She wanted to be rich for the sake of being rich. That was not a proper and just deployment of the urge to thievery. No. It was a perversion of that spirit. At least in my view. But I was charged with overseeing her. It was not for me to judge.

I released Rex's hair. He relaxed, smug in his perceived triumph against me. Did he think I would have his locks in my fist for eternity? Perhaps so. Newcomers always have strange ideas about what goes on in my realm. And who can blame them? No one tells them what the afterlife is like. No one can possibly know.

"If you mean by that comment," I said to Rex, "that she deserved to have her child taken from her, you have a lot to learn about justice."

"I was just saying that she's a thief herself. She should understand why I took her little guy. He shouldn't have grown up in that environment anyway." He rubbed the top of his head, trying to ease away the pain. I wanted to slap his hand away. I wanted the sting to remain for him. But I did not do so.

Rex had me turned inside out. I admired him, yet he was not admirable.

"Rex," I said. "I hate to say it. But I think I agree with you."

"Well, sure," he said. "She's got no sense of right and wrong."

He gazed at Judy Bryant's face. She took a sip from her cup.

"I wanted you to see," I said.

"Okay," said Rex. "I've seen." He rubbed the top of his head again. "I would have thought that heaven wouldn't have pain," he said. "It still smarts where you grabbed me."

"I told you this isn't heaven."

"Right," said Rex. "Now can I see what's up with Morris?"

I handed Rex a remote control, technology he was familiar with. He took it from my hand. "I can switch channels?" he asked. "How many are there?"

"An infinite number," I said.

"And still nothing good on, right?" He smiled his crooked little smile at me.

"Indeed," I said dryly.

He punched a few buttons on the remote. I didn't have to explain how the nested choices worked, even though it was different from the sort of television remote he would have been used to. In a few seconds an image of the interior of the Hernandez household popped up. A charming domestic scene: Morris in a high chair, Hector and Louisa on either side of him playing peek-a-boo, breakfast dishes scattered around the table. I immediately felt a wave of melancholy wash over Rex. He could not contain it all and some of it leaked out and crawled over to me and wrapped itself around my chest. I fought the urge to welcome it. Rex had no right to these feelings of sadness or grief. The child was not his. He had stolen him. I could not allow myself to sympathize with Rex. Not in this way. Not with him taking the lead and orchestrating the emotions.

I smacked his head. Hard.

He did not flinch. Indeed, he did not look away from the screen for an instant. His sadness lifted, a little. I spread and stretched my fingers so that my palm spread out flat. I repeatedly applied my hand to the back of Rex's head with sharp smacks until the last remnant of sadness left my body. It all went back to him. Or just crawled away to its own lair for all I knew. I didn't care. I simply wanted to be released from it.

"I guess you need to do that?" he said. On the screen Morris had his hand on Hector's cheek. Hector looked like he was in bliss.

"I have my reasons for what I do," I said, hoping Rex would not detect the lie in my voice.

"You hit everyone who comes here?"

"No," I said, "just the special ones."

He smiled again. "Here's the funny thing," he said. "I don't want to hit you back. Why is that? Any time before, I would have decked you good for what you just did to me. I'd smack you around and mess you up."

"You forget," I said to him. "I have watched you all your life. I know you are not a fighter."

He considered this. "Okay," he said. "But I would have wanted to. Now I don't. Why?"

"I have other people to attend to," I said. "Take your time in here."

"I'm not going to leave here until Morris grows up," said Rex. "I want to savor all his moments."

"Good," I said, patting him on the back, gently. He flinched this time, then relaxed.

"Say hi to God for me," he said.

I laughed and adjusted the temporal pacing to its highest setting. Then I left Rex to his "son."

I did have others to attend to, that wasn't a lie. But I had no intention of actually spending any time with them. Instead I retreated to my own kind. I found a cluster of avatars at the end of the hall, just a few steps from infinity, the bustle of them edging toward a grassy expanse that extended far beyond anything my eye could make sense of. All of us avatars, the powerless ones who are cursed to watch humanity's dramas unfold, we often congregate together for comfort and edification. My comrades saw me approach, nodded in my direction, and made room for me to join the group.

"You look tired," said one of them.

"I had to hit a newcomer," I said.

They all nodded sagely. "It happens," said another. Several murmured their assent.

"Just recently I beat one of them up so bad that I believe she was permanently scarred," said another.

"That isn't right," I said.

She shrugged. "It's not my fault," she said. "She challenged me to a fight. Wanted to know what my power was and if she could defeat me. She put up quite a fight, but I won in the end. Of course."

This did not make me feel better. Of course we could defeat them all. That wasn't the point. We should not *want* to defeat them in the first place.

"I think," said another, "you might benefit by time off from your duties."

"Such things are not allowed," I said.

"Many things are not allowed. That does not mean we can't do them."

"I don't know," I said.

The last speaker appealed to the rest of the group. "Ladies and gentlemen," he said, "who is correct here? Me or our saddened friend?"

They all embraced his position. I tried to argue with them, but they would have none of it. In the end, I took my leave, and gladly. I wandered the grounds of our enclosure. Everyone deliberately left me alone, I could see it. But I could not see exactly why. Was this some kind of test? Was my cruelty to Rex a sign of something? If so, what?

I had turned off my viewing attributes, but now found I no longer wanted to. If my colleagues could not support me, then so be it. I would find my own way to peace.

I cast my attention to Rex's view screen. It shimmered into focus in my mind and I saw Morris already six years old, in school and taking objects from his school mates. They were inconsequential things: pieces of trash found on the schoolyard, a length of multi-colored string, a cell phone case, a yo-yo, and so on. The detritus of boyhood which Morris had contrived to keep for his own.

Then the screen of his life sped up: more theft, more serious as the years went by. Hector and Louisa, having taken the roles of his parents by default, tried to set him on the right path, but as he grew older he began stealing from them. He took money from purses and wallets. Jewelry lifted from Louisa's jewelry box and hocked at pawn shops for cash. At first he used the money for candy and chocolate. Later for cigarettes and gambling.

Louisa and Hector tried to steer him on the right path, but their efforts came to nothing. Hector tried to beat him into reforming while Louisa tried to love and accept him into reforming. Nothing worked.

Morris, before he was fourteen, had graduated to breaking into other people's houses and removing anything of value. I knew, watching all this, that Rex's heart was breaking. How could the son, the son he tried so hard to show the proper way to live, take to this kind of life? To steal simply for the sake of stealing, and to invade people's homes as he did, these were the doings of a bad person. A wicked person.

Such were my thoughts as well. Did Morris ever have a chance? He was born of a thief and taken by a thief. His course may have been set by fate itself. In my position I should perhaps have known if such a thing was possible, but I know less than one might think. I am simply a cog in the vast intermeshing gear works of the universe. My horizon is limited.

Morris got caught during a house theft and ended up in a reformatory. There he learned how to be a better thief and how not to get caught again. Upon his release he returned to his former life. He still lived in the house of Louisa and Hector, but he came and went at all hours and did not even talk to them when he was there. He slept until the afternoon, came down the stairs for something to eat, then went out.

One night, when he returned, the house was locked and his key did not work. He thought to break into the house, but stopped himself before he began the operation. What was the point? He did not need Hector and Louisa anymore. He did not need this house anymore. He threw a rock through the upstairs window, the one in Hector and Louisa's bedroom. The glass sprinkled itself like ice on the floor under the sill. Hector groaned. Louisa rose and put on her slippers and went to the window. Morris looked up at her. She still felt something for him, but it was so dim that she could not call it love anymore. She wished him the best, but she did not believe he would ever achieve his best. She only wanted him gone now. Morris turned from her and walked away.

I slowed down the unwinding story and returned to the room where I had left Rex.

"My son's a punk," said Rex to me when I walked in.

"I thought it would be more merciful to show you quickly," I said.

He turned to me. His eyes were wide and so sad. "I never wanted that for him," he said. "Never."

Chapter 9: Money

THE NIGHT MORT Harney threw the rock through the window, his name was still Morris Hernandez, but he was already toying with ways of changing it. He didn't want to have anything to do with his parents, most especially their name, which clung to him like old sweat he wanted to scrape off his skin. He had invented a few aliases already, ones he used when he planned and executed robberies with other career criminals. He had been Morris for a while. He liked that. And once he called himself Mel. He thought he could go with that one for a while, a good one syllable name, non-threatening, which was beneficial when he wanted to bring someone into his trust. It was a little soft, however, which worked against it. It also felt vaguely like something from his past. Or from a past he did not want to confront, as though he had another life that wanted to intrude itself on his current life.

Such squishy spiritual considerations irked him. He prided himself on being a completely rational and level-headed person, as any career thief had to be, and yet sometimes, at the most unexpected moments, he would have this feeling of bigger things than himself. This was death to anyone in his line of work. You had to stay in the present and keep your entire being alert to the nuances of reality or you were dead. He had been to the reform school twice and if he learned nothing else there he could count the experience useful simply because he picked up this one survival skill. He learned it well. He managed to push away any kind of spiritual woo-woo that ever came near him.

The night we pick up his story was a typically hot August night in Tucson. He stepped away from his mother's house and walked down the driveway. The house felt like a dying monster behind him, one he had killed and put out of his life.

He turned north. The Catalina Mountains loomed dark and large on the horizon, but they did nothing for him. He had some vague idea that they should, that they held a grandeur which might enrich his life, but he was beyond enrichment. Such entanglements would only get him lost in unnecessary doings. There was only one thing that truly mattered in life, and that was money. To properly mark his life as a free man, Morris spent the next few hours before dawn broke wandering the city. He had no purpose, indeed, he had no conception of why he might want to wander the city, could not conceive that it was a rite of passage, a transition time to cleanse himself of his former life for good.

When he got tired of walking he hopped on the next bus to go by and pulled a hat out of his pocket and put it on. It was big enough to cover his ears and obscure his face. He rode on the bus until the sun rose. He got off at a corner with a convenience store. He waited on the corner until the store was empty of customers, then went inside and demanded the money from the cash register. The clerk, who was not the owner, readily complied when he saw the tip of a handgun peek out from behind Morris's jacket flap. Morris did not have a gun. Just the barrel of one. It was useless as a weapon, but extremely persuasive to anyone with even half an imagination. Morris was very careful not to look up, where he knew surveillance cameras would capture his face for purposes of identification.

The clerk put down the bills from the register on the counter, then began scooping up change.

"No," said Morris. "I just want the paper."

The clerk stopped and dropped his hands to his sides and nodded.

"You've been good," said Morris. He wanted to hand him one of the twenties, as thanks, and even started to make a motion to do so, then mentally kicked himself for almost being soft. He grabbed up the bills stuffed them into his pocket and was out of the store in another three seconds.

He walked rapidly from the store in a direction away from the mountains. A bus came by and he got on it. By this time the clerk would have called the police and they would be on their way. But they wouldn't find Morris. He was good at this. He knew how to fool them all. He leaned close to the window and watched the sidewalk roll by him. People were out on foot, even in this heat. All of them had money. All of them. Even the shabbiest looking person with rags on, he had money. Little kids had money. Not a lot, maybe, but some. And some kids had a lot more than a little. Rich parents made sure they had money. People in business suits, they had a lot of money. Everyone had money and everyone wanted money. It was the most basic law of the universe, even of survival. Morris had absorbed that lesson, and he had figured out how to get money. All the money he wanted, whenever he wanted it.

The bus stopped. An old woman got on and sat down in the seat next to him. She carried bags of groceries and let them all fall to the floor, obviously tasked by her burdens. Morris wondered vaguely if she might die of overheating walking around in the sun like that. She was old. He knew old people could die pretty easily. He had long since decided he wasn't getting old. He didn't want to live like that, with death hanging around like a friend you couldn't stand anymore.

"Oh, it's hot!" said the woman. She had a cheerful voice, which startled Morris. How could someone with such a miserable life, carrying groceries on a bus, for fuck's sake, sound so cheerful? He didn't say anything to her. He turned his body a little more away from her and pressed his forehead to the window. The glass felt warm, even with the bus's AC going full blast.

"Not that I'm complaining, you understand," said the woman. "I don't mind it hot. Better hot than cold, if you ask me. But some days it can get to you, you know?"

She tapped his shoulder. "You okay in there?" she said. "You sad about something?"

"No," said Morris.

"You seem sad. What's going on? Why don't you tell me? It'll make you feel better."

"What's it to you?" asked Morris.

"Oh, nothing, I suppose," she said. "It's just that I feel things, you know. From other people. It's a kind of a gift I have. Even though sometimes it feels like a curse."

"Yeah," said Morris, "you sound cursed, all right."

"What do you mean?"

"You don't even have a car. At your age. Must feel like you've had a loser life."

The woman laughed. "I guess it might seem like that to you," she said, "but I don't feel like a loser. Not a bit. I'm going home to make a nice meal for my daughter. She's coming to visit tonight."

Morris wanted to crawl through the window to the outside, just to get away from this woman who suddenly wanted to tell him about her life. Why? Why would she think Morris would care?

"I don't see her much anymore," said the woman, "so when she does come I want it to be special. I make her favorite thing: a kind of shrimp stir fry with vegetables and this special hot sauce she likes. It's nothing I ever make or eat, but she likes it so I'm happy to make it for her. What do you like to eat?"

"Eggs," said Morris, surprised that he even answered her.

"Mmmmm," said the woman. "Yeah. Scrambled or fried?"

"With bacon," said Morris.

"Yeah!" said the woman. "Bacon. Who doesn't like bacon?"

"My mother," said Morris.

"Your mother doesn't like bacon?"

"Says it's too fat or something. It's got chemicals that are supposed to give you cancer." He shrugged. The woman looked at him with deep soft eyes and a raised eyebrow. It made him feel like a baby, but he wasn't upset by that. If she wanted to think he was a baby, what business was that of his?

"Your mother's probably right, but even so it's hard to give up bacon."

"Maybe," said Morris. "She's not my real mother anyway."

"Oh?"

"She's just someone who looked after me when I was a baby. Then my father ran away and she raised me."

"That's quite a story," said the woman.

Morris shrugged. "It's nothing special. He was a shit. Couldn't handle looking after me, I guess, so he split."

"Oh, that's sad."

Morris shrugged. "It's no big deal."

"But the woman who raised you, she was good to you?"

"I guess," said Morris. "She and her husband fight all the time."

"Oh."

"About me. I disappoint them because—"

"Because why?"

"Never mind," said Morris, suddenly aware that he needed to be more on guard. He couldn't be telling his life story to a stranger.

She put her hand on his arm. Morris flinched to have some old lady like this touching him. But she didn't let go. He tried to shrug her away again, but she wouldn't release him. Didn't want to for some weird old lady reason he couldn't begin to understand.

"What about your mother?" she asked.

"She killed herself."

"Oh no," said the woman. She closed her eyes, like she was praying the world's shortest prayer.

"Right after I was born."

"That's the saddest thing I've ever heard."

"Yeah," said Morris. "At least that's what my adopted parents tell me. I actually don't know if any of it is true or not. People are such liars, you know? They say they'll take care of you but you ever do one small thing to upset them and they're gone."

"I'm sure it can seem that way," said the woman, who now pulled her hand away from Morris's arm, "but everyone is just trying to do the best they can, you know? You'll learn that when you grow up a little more. For now, don't cut them off completely."

She pulled away from him, like she didn't want to have any contact with a loser anymore. Except she just got finished saying things that made him think she never thought anyone was a loser.

"They hate me," said Morris.

"Oh no."

"I don't blame them. I suck. I steal stuff."

"That's not the end of the world," said the woman. "You'll grow up and stop that nonsense."

Morris shook his head. "No," he said. "I don't think so."

She looked past him to the window. "Would you press the strip?" she said. "This is my stop."

Morris reached up behind him and touched the signal strip. It chimed once and the bus began to slow down. The woman stood up before it came to a stop. She grabbed the handles of her bags and lifted them off the floor.

"Hey," said Morris. "What's your name?"

"Never you mind about that," she said. "We'll never see each other again. Just remember what I told you. Don't break connections completely. You need people in your life who love you."

She walked down the aisle to the exit. The air around him grew colder and it wasn't just the refrigeration. He felt lost. This irritated him. How could he feel anything for someone he hadn't even known five minutes before? And how could he tell his secret to her like he did? Stupid, stupid.

He watched her step down from the bus, slowly, gingerly, like she might fall any minute. She began walking along the sidewalk as the bus pulled past her. Morris watched her as his window approached. He knocked on the window to get her attention and waved his hand like a metronome against the glass. The woman did not glance up. She just kept waddling along like putting one foot in front of the other was the most important thing in the world, and maybe to her it was. What did Morris know about being old? Maybe it was a big deal just to get up and see the sun every morning. When you get old enough, it must seem like nothing is for sure. Maybe it's like the woman said, the only thing that matters after a while isn't money but people in your life.

Except, thought Morris, except this: without money no one wants to have anything to do with you. If you're poor, you're alone. That old lady was poor and she was alone. She said so herself, that her daughter only came to visit sometimes. Didn't that say it all? He bet if she had lots of money her daughter would still be living with her and soaking up all the stuff that she could get with that money. Morris was sure of it. Money always bought love. And lack of money always killed love.

Not that he cared about love. Sometimes he liked to be with girls, do things with them, but that wasn't love. Not what people meant when they talked about love. And the girls, they didn't mind being with him, until they found out about what he did, how he stole things. It was a lot easier for him to go downtown and buy that kind of thing anyway. Not that he did that a lot, but it just proved his point about money. With money you can have anything. Without it you have nothing.

When Morris was a safe distance from the scene of his latest crime, he got off the bus and boarded another going north toward Louisa and Hector's house. He hoped neither of them was home. There were just a couple of things he needed.

When he got to the house, both their cars were gone. That made him feel better. He could get in and out quickly. He went around the back of the house where Louisa kept her cactus garden. Prickly nasty place, that was. He never liked it, not from the time he was a kid and no time after that, either. It always seemed like all those thorns were just waiting to stab him, and who wanted that? Who needed to feel like if you took the wrong step you were going to get pricked?

He walked between the cactus to the bottom of a set of wooden steps and went up them to the door into an apartment over the garage. This had been his room for a few years, whenever he got out of reform school and he and Louisa and Hector had a short honeymoon when they all fooled each other that Morris had gotten better and become a more productive and docile member of society.

Those were pretty good times, he remembered. They were sweet on him and he appreciated their attention, but it usually didn't take long for him to feel the pull of thievery. Sometimes it seemed like there were forces, maybe guardian spirits watching over him and pushing him into the life. He never liked thinking about that too much because then it felt like he was some kind of puppet and someone else was pulling the strings, so he usually pushed those thoughts away. He got good at that, pushing things away. It helped him survive.

He tried the door. Locked. He put his key into the doorknob. It didn't unlock it, which was pretty much what he had expected. He took a card from his back pocket and slid it between the door and the frame and worked it down to the door latch and wiggled it around a little until he heard it slide across and the door swing open. He walked to his room.

The bed was still there in the same place. His little TV in one corner, a few books in another. On the shelf he saw what he wanted: a picture of his father and his mother. From when they were young, only a couple of years older than him now. In the picture they stood in front of a waterfall, which Louisa had told him was up north somewhere in Oregon because that's where his real father had come from. He took the picture, tore it out of its frame, and slid it into his pocket right next to where he had put the money from the robbery.

His hand froze.

The money. It wasn't there. His pocket was empty. Jesus. He tried his other pockets. They were all empty.

He snapped his head up. That old woman on the bus. She had put her hands on his arm.

He laughed at himself. He had been sitting with a career criminal, just like himself, and didn't even know he was getting a lesson in how to be a professional.

He wanted to be mad at her, but he couldn't work up the energy.

"Well done," he whispered to the air. "Well done, you miserable old fake."

Chapter 10: Solitude

MORRIS HAD SOME money stashed under his mattress. He retrieved it and put it in his pocket. Then he left Louisa and Hector's house and decided he would be Mort Harney.

He went downtown to the train station. He had always wanted to travel by train and this seemed as good a time as any. There were some good things happening in Oregon, he had heard. The economy was tanking up there and that meant a lot of land was available for cheap.

At the train station he considered how he might steal himself a ticket north but decided that would be too much trouble. Instead he used the money from his room, and bought himself a ticket to Portland.

I observed all this with a certain detached amusement. After all, Mort was going back to his birthplace. This could hardly be a coincidence. And I should know, being one of the observers of the universe.

While he's at the station, on his way to the boarding platform, I'll tell you what Rex was up to. After Rex had watched Mort's life unfold into a panorama that he greatly disapproved of, he spent most of his time looking at other screens and other people. He found lots of lives he liked a lot better. Periodically he would come to me and ask why Mort hadn't followed some of those other paths, the ones where the person became rich and well-thought of and provided for large families and generally prospered and made their parents happy. The part about making parents happy was the crucial point for him. To Rex that was the whole point of children. They didn't have a life of their own, they existed to serve their parents, even if those parents were surrogates. It was why he stole Mort in the first place, to try to cheer up his wife.

"You know," I told him, "I'll bet you never pleased your own parents in your life. Not once."

That stopped him. I knew that his mother and father, when they found out that Rex was a career thief, broke all ties with him. Even when Rex tried to explain to them that he was a Robin Hood kind of thief who was only interested in a more equitable spreading around of the wealth of the country, they would not accept him as he was. They told him he was wicked. Evil, even. They disowned him when he was just about the same age as Mort was now, boarding a train to Portland.

"When I was a baby I bet I did," said Rex.

"Okay," I said. "I'll grant you that. But scarcely a moment after that."

"They didn't understand," said Rex. "I had a higher calling."

"Maybe Mort has a higher calling, too," I said.

Rex made fists with his hands, then relaxed them. He had a lot of excess energy, I could see that, and he needed to do something with it.

"Why don't you go to one of the fighting rooms?" I asked. "Get yourself knocked around a little. You'd like it."

"Fighting rooms?" he said.

"You don't know about them?"

"How am I supposed to know about them?"

He had been here for years now, and he knew next to nothing about where he was. Granted, the years seemed like days, but still. I had never known a dead person like Rex. He seemed completely oblivious to the scramble around him. Most people when they get here spend some time at the screens. It's a natural curiosity. But eventually they leave them and start exploring. The fighting rooms are only one place. There are also places to eat a lot, the feeding rooms. And you can do art in other rooms. Have a lot of sex, of any variety you want, in other rooms, and so on. Most people indulge themselves in at least a few of the rooms for a short time before they leave again. Some people try them all. But not Rex. At least, not yet.

"Look," I said to Rex, "you need to let go of your past life. Your former life. You've seen what happened to your stolen son. Now let it go and just enjoy yourself."

"Enjoy myself?"

"Yes."

"By getting beaten up?"

I grabbed him by his shoulders, spun him around, and sent him in the direction of the fighting room. He took a step and then looked down at his feet. "Is this hell?" he asked. "Am I in the underworld?"

"There's no such thing. You all made that concept up. Now go."

He went. I watched him recede into the distance. I have to admit, I felt more than a little envious of him. He was about to get the tar beaten out of him. I hadn't had that experience in I didn't know how long. The best thing was that it wouldn't do him any permanent harm. He was already dead.

I turned my attention to Mort. His train pulled out of the station and slowly gained speed heading west towards Los Angeles, where he would have a several hour layover before heading north to Oregon.

Mort had no luggage. He found a quiet corner on one of the cars and sat in the seat next to the window. He had an overwhelming feeling of déjà vu as he stared through the glass at the landscape, dry scrubland extending for mile after mile, but could not think when he had been here before. He had never been here before, he was sure of it. Now that he thought about it, he had rarely left Tucson. A couple of times to go south to Mexico for a few days. Once to the Grand Canyon. That was all. Never this far west. Even so, he had the overwhelming sensation that this was *not* new to him. He didn't like the feeling. He stood up and decided to walk the length of the train, to see what was up with his fellow passengers. The space between the cars wobbled and bucked. He was momentarily thrown off-kilter and knocked his shoulder against a fire extinguisher in the corner.

How can I explain what happened next? I can't. As I told Rex and as I tell you now, I can only observe. It is an ability, even an extraordinary one, but it is not power, except in the most pathetic sense.

Mort's mind tumbled down a memory hole, like a rabbit going into its lair. That is the best way I can describe it to you. Something about the way his shoulder blade touched the fire extinguisher heightened his already sharply attuned sense of the past living inside him. I do recall that his mother, who we will come back to at some point in this narrative, rest assured, once tripped and collided with a fire extinguisher. That must be it. And yet, it doesn't seem enough. In any case, as I said, something happened inside Mort. He had a vision of a piece of land. It was flat and expansive, covered with yellow grass and sprouting white windmills, with blades turning with stately grace in the air, swooping around and around.

He grabbed a handhold on the wall to steady himself. The vision of the land was so strong that he had to pause for a moment and take it in. He sensed immediately that it was not anywhere in Arizona. The mountains in the distance were all wrong, and he knew of no large fields of grain in the state where he grew up. No, this had to be a vision from somewhere else. He considered that his decision to go to Oregon was not completely rational and had some mystical component to it. He decided to find the place he saw.

He steadied himself and continued into the next car. It was a revelation, suddenly, to be amongst people again. Most of the seats were filled. He studied some of the passengers. Why did people always look so sad when they traveled? It was like they were not with their souls. Mort didn't even know what a soul was, but he could tell that these people were nothing but paper. No real substance underneath them. He could poke his finger through them and they would crumble into dust.

He wanted to steal from them.

This startled him. They were ordinary people. Why did he suddenly want to take their possessions? He didn't even want possessions. Traveling as he did now, having nothing but the clothes he wore, was the best way to be. He had already decided that. And he had enough money for now, even with the loss of cash from that old woman on the bus, so crafty with her poor-elderly-woman routine. He would have to watch out for that sort of thing in the future. Don't be too sympathetic to old people. That was the lesson there. They became old for a reason: They were smart and knew how to survive.

But these people on the train? He had only contempt for them. And why? Because they travelled by train? He was travelling by train.

He kept walking down the aisle toward the end of the car. He was usually so sure of himself and now he didn't know if he wanted to put one foot in front of the other or retreat to the other car. Was this how other people went about their lives? People like Louisa and Hector, always questioning their own motives and the purpose of life. There was no purpose to life. Mort believed that. It was all about survival.

"Hey, Morris," came a voice slightly behind him.

Mort stopped. "Yeah, you," said the voice.

He turned around. A young man, more or less his own age, grinned at him.

"You don't remember me," he said.

Mort searched his memory, now fragmented and spread across his brain like shards of glass. He sorted through the shards quickly. He found nothing that would tell him who this guy was.

"I'm Jake," he said. "Jake Smythe."

"I'm sorry," said Mort. "My name's not Morris."

"What? Of course it is. I used to take care of your mom's yard."

Mort had some memory of a kid with a rake and a set of garden shears. A watering can. This was that kid?

"Her cactus," said Mort.

Jake laughed. "Yeah. Her cactus. She loved all her cactus. Never made sense to me. There's cactus all over the state but she wanted some of her own in her back yard."

"She liked the thorns, I think," said Mort. "They suited her."

Jake nodded. "Hey, why don't you sit here with me? I'm traveling alone. You, too?"

"Um," said Mort. "Yeah." Jake slid over to the window seat. Mort sat down next to him.

"I'm going north," said Jake. "To Seattle. Got some friends up there that do landscaping. Tell me they'll take me in as a partner. Sounds like a pretty good deal so I'm going to check it out. You?"

"First of all, my name's not Morris anymore. It's Mort."

"You change it?"

"Yeah. I need a new start."

"I hear you there," said Jake. "Where you headed?"

"Not sure, exactly. Some place different."

"You got a job lined up?"

Some of Jake's characteristics were coming back to Mort. He liked to ask a lot of questions. Always interested in what was going on with people. Louisa said she appreciated that. It was one of the reasons she kept hiring him to do the yard work, even when there wasn't all that much to do. Now Mort wasn't sure how much he wanted to tell Jake.

"I have some prospects," said Mort.

"That's great," said Jake. "You over that rough spot in your life? You know, when you were into petty crimes and stuff? I heard you got sent to reform school for a while. Your mom was pretty torn up about that."

That was the thing about Jake. He was always nosing around in people's business.

"They weren't petty crimes," said Mort.

"Oh, yeah. I didn't mean anything by saying that."

"Just so you know," said Mort. "They were pretty serious things."

"Right." He looked at Jake, then let his gaze slide down and away to the floor, like he was embarrassed.

"I was messed up there for a while, but now I'm on the right road," he said.

Mort found some comfort in sitting with Jake. He was a link to the life he was leaving behind and it felt right to have that link for the moment. He wondered how much money Jake had on him. He should steal Jake's money. But not yet. They still had some hours on the train. Maybe just before they got to LA.

"It's nice to have a friend to talk to," said Jake.

"Yeah," said Mort.

"But you don't *really* think so," he said.

Mort looked at him.

"That's okay," said Jake. "You like to be alone. I get it. I like to be alone too, nothing wrong with that. But sometimes it's better to have a friend. Like in Seattle. I wouldn't go up there if I didn't have friends. It would be too scary."

Mort felt his head get warm. "Yeah," he said. "Scary."

"You don't have to think about it," said Jake. "I don't want to make you uneasy."

"No," said Mort. "It's not that. We're different, is all. We don't see the world the same way."

"Okay," said Jake. "How do you see the world?"

"I have this feeling," he said. "It's not anything I can explain, exactly, but there's someone watching over me."

"Oh yeah," said Jake. "Like a guardian angel. I think your mom believed in them."

Mort hadn't known that. But it didn't surprise him. She believed in a lot of woo-woo stuff.

"No," he said to Jake. "Not angels. Angels are dead. I'm talking about something different."

"Okay," said Jake. He raised his eyebrows, as if asking Mort to continue.

Mort took a breath and let it out slowly. "I always sound like a crazy freak when I talk about this."

"Don't worry about it. We're on a train. Train life is different than real life."

Such a peculiar person, thought Mort. Where did someone like this come from?

"Okay," said Mort. "Let me see if I can explain it right. When I was a kid, I thought there was a camera in the sky and it was watching me all the time."

"Whoa," said Jake, grinning, "that could get *way* embarrassing."

"Not like that," said Mort. "More like someone paying attention to my spirit. Looking after me, but not caring about me. It's not even a person. More like a force."

"You lost me," said Jake. "Is there something watching over you or isn't there?"

"Yeah, there *is*, but it's complicated because they—or it or whatever it is—doesn't see the *whole* me, just a small part of me."

"What part?"

"The part that's good."

"We're all good, don't you think?"

Mort shook his head. "No way. Some people are good. You're good, I think. But a lot more people aren't."

"That can't be," said Jake. "Why are we born if we aren't good?"

"Being born or not born has nothing to do with it. It's mostly all about the way we get along in the world. It's about what we do to other people."

"But what does that have to do with these beings or whatever watching over you?"

"Those beings steal stuff from us," said Mort. "If you're not careful, they take away everything you think you know. You think you're in the world and safe and everything, but you're not. You never will be. Because you have all these—people—crawling around above your head. They make you doubt everything you do. Got it?"

"I'm trying, Mort," said Jake. "But I have to say, I don't really get it."

"Never mind. I shouldn't have told you anyway."

"No, I'm glad you did. I think it made you feel better."

Mort didn't want to admit it, so he didn't, not out loud, but Jake was right. He did feel better. How was that even possible?

Night fell. The lights in the train car came on automatically.

"We'll be getting into LA in a couple of hours," said Mort. "We'll have some time to kill. Anything you want to do?"

Mort shrugged. "Are the Dodgers playing?"

"Hey," said Jake. "Maybe they are. We should find out."

"Yeah," said Mort.

He settled back into his seat and stared up at the ceiling. The funny thing was, he didn't like that he wasn't alone anymore, even though, like Jake said, it was good to have a friend.

The train squealed and screeched into Union Station and they were glad to get off the train. Mort noticed that Jake had no luggage either. They looked at each other.

"Two vagabonds, huh?" said Jake.

"Let's get a car," said Mort. "Drive north. That train was no fun at all."

Jake considered the proposition. "Where we going to get a car?"

"Don't worry about it," said Mort. "I know how to take care of that little problem."

Chapter 11: Memory

REX RETURNED FROM the fighting room while I was engaged by a particularly interesting case involving a young child. I won't go into the details since dying children cause much vexation among many people. I understand the trauma completely. Children seem so innocent and death should not touch them. Isn't that the way the sentiment runs? However, that view of the universe assumes that death is some kind of punishment. It's not. It's a byproduct of the laws of the universe. For that matter, life itself is something of a byproduct. Don't blame me. I didn't set up the rules. As I have indicated previously in this narrative, no one set up the rules, at least not deliberately. Rules, or the laws of nature as they have come to be known, are completely arbitrary. If this is news to you, I am sorry to have to be the one to tell you.

In any case, it had been some time since I had last seen Rex and he was almost completely unrecognizable. His face bore bruised skin and caked blood. His eyes were puffed up so bad I couldn't see his eyeballs at all. He walked with a limp, and his clothes were torn and bloody.

"Hey," he said with a gurgle in his voice. He stopped, as though he had stepped in something he would have preferred to avoid, looked as if he was considering a deep question of personal morality, and spit out a pink gob onto the ground. Then he resumed walking toward me.

"Looks like you've been busy," I said.

"That was the best advice," he said, "sending me to the fight room."

"Glad you liked it," I said. Or that was what I intended to say. Before I could get the words out, he was upon me, throttling my head with his fists. His bloody fists. I had thought him weakened by his experience, but that was far from the case. He held my head in one hand and pounded on my nose, cheek, mouth, and forehead with the other. I was so surprised that for a moment I did not fight back. Then he let me go and stepped back and put up his fists in a defensive stance.

"Sorry to jump on you by surprise like that," he said. "But you're this immortal being. Or something. Figured I needed a little advantage to begin. You got two seconds before I come at you again."

Now, please understand that I have nothing against fighting. I also approve of inflicting pain when the situation demands. But I was not prepared to engage Rex in battle. For one thing, I had fought many in the past. The bloom of novelty associated with combat had long since withered. For another, I had plans for Rex. He had already overstayed his welcome and was overdue in the soup room.

However, his surprise throttling of my face got my blood going. I raised my own fists and stepped closer to him. We circled each other for a time, each looking for an opening.

"Do you remember activities like this from when you were young?" I asked.

"Sure," he said in reply. My face began healing itself. I saw dismay register on his features. Did he actually think he could beat me in fist to fist combat?

"Did they usually end well or badly for you?" I said.

"Badly," said Rex. "We usually ended up wrestling on the ground and I was always the smaller one so I was the only one with my face in the dirt."

"We can stop this right now," I said. "There's no need for more humiliation."

He set his teeth and glared at me. "You sent me to the fighting room."

"I did."

"I loved it in there. I fought dozens of people. Men, women, children. We kicked and scratched each other. We drew pint after pint of blood. I kicked guys in the balls. I got kicked in the balls a million times. I broke bones, mine and others. It was the best. Just the best."

"Okay," I said. "Do you want to continue?"

He advanced on me, moving like lightning. His determination impressed me greatly, but not enough to give him a break. I stepped to one side as he tried to connect with my jaw and brought my fists down on the side of his neck. Hard. I heard his spine snap and he went down like a stone. He ended up sprawled at my feet, his head bent at an odd angle. He looked up at me. And he was smiling. Such a simple soul. He made me smile back, which felt pleasant, coming as it did while my facial features swirled and coalesced into some semblance of normality.

I will leave him there, all twisted and bent for the moment, while I tell you about Judy Bryant.

After her child was taken from her, she entered an extended period of depression. She lived in an apartment in the northwest section of Portland, with a view of the Fremont Bridge out her window and Mount St. Helens beyond that, its white round shape, curiously suggesting a mound of snow more than a mountain. In the weeks following the disappearance of Melville Bryant, she spent most of her time sitting in her living room chair looking at the mountain and feeling so sorry for herself. Most of her friends abandoned her. Another hard fact of life, or the laws of nature, if you prefer. People have little tolerance for the misery of others. They want you to get back to being cheerful as soon as possible, and if that isn't possible, then they usually look elsewhere for friendship.

You can't blame them for that. It's a survival strategy. The more time you spend around depressed people, the more likely you are to be depressed, and therefore the less able you are to fend for yourself in an indifferent universe.

Judy wanted to move away from Portland, but the lethargy of depression prevented her from taking the necessary steps in that direction. She waited for a call from the police. It never came. She hired a private detective to try to find her son, but the detective got nowhere fast. Rex had left no trail.

It took close to a year for her to decide that there was little possibility of her ever getting her son back. With that realization, she might have fallen even deeper into depression. It is not inconceivable. Surely you have known people who could not come out of their illness. There is no shame in this. Some people might have killed themselves under Judy Bryant's circumstances. I have witnessed such things myself. It is a kind of solution to a problem.

But Judy Bryant was not such a person as that. She reasoned that the enormous emptiness she felt in her heart, though it would never quite heal completely, could eventually be muffled. She turned to drink.

Oh, yes. The numbing she found there was more powerful than anything she could have imagined on her own. She would begin to drink in the late morning and continue throughout the day. She watched television while she drank. The mountain and the bridge outside her window were still there, symbols of something beyond herself that she could get to, but they remained that: only symbols. Nothing that held any interest for her at all.

She had a job. Some trifling cubicle drudgery involving accounting calculations, executed for a large retail chain, but she missed so many days that she was terminated. She had some money saved, money she had embezzled from her company, which she used mostly to buy alcohol. She let her bills lapse until she could not ignore things like the power and gas lines turned off.

I observed her situation with some alarm. Hers was not the worst life I have ever seen, but that didn't matter. I saw where she was headed. She did not care for herself. Eviction proceedings began against her as she had not paid the rent on her apartment in quite a while. Her parents had died some time ago. She had no family. Melville was going to be her family. She had made him with the help of a fertility clinic. She wanted a family, though she didn't want a man. Now that Melville was gone, she took it as a sign that the universe did not want her to achieve her desires. Such misunderstanding of how the universe operates lead to much misery in people's lives. If she had believed that things could change, then she might have done things differently. She might have seen a path to salvation from her pain.

But she did not.

One chilly spring morning the landlord, accompanied by a police officer, appeared at her door with a document telling her she needed to leave the apartment.

She spent that night at a homeless shelter for women, on a cot in the middle of a room, surrounded by dozens of other women, some with children. She decided she could tolerate the cot and the noise and the smell, and even the prohibition on alcohol, but not the children. They broke her heart every time she saw one. Especially the very young ones.

The next morning she left the shelter and never returned. She spent the summer begging on the streets. She learned to fly a sign and stood on a street corner where an off-ramp from I-84 deposited travelers onto city streets. Her sign was usually some variation of the following: ANYTHING HELPS. GOD BLESS YOU. Armed with this shield, she was able to keep herself alive. All of her time was taken up with survival, which suited her fine. That way she didn't have to think about her loss. Not only her son, but her life. The life she had but couldn't manage any longer. All she had to think about was getting food for the day.

She even found friends. People, mostly women, down on their luck like she was. They made a kind of community near the bridge she once saw from her apartment window. They called it Faith Village, a small settlement of tents that the city tolerated because the inhabitants were mostly well-behaved and female.

As the years went by, Judy came to see this as her rightful place in the world. The winters could be hard, but there was a freedom in being out of the mainstream of society. Each morning the women would scatter into the streets, flying signs or sitting on sidewalks asking for change. Eventually Judy had amassed enough money to leave Faith Village and begin a life like her previous life.

Here is the strange thing: She chose not to. She preferred life in the village with her sisters. And so she stayed there for almost 20 years. Faith Village became a self-sustaining community with it's own garden, and even began a Saturday Market where the residents sold craft items that they made. The city left them alone, reasoning that they were taking care of themselves and not bothering anyone. In fact, Faith Village became a model for sustainable city living for poor people. The basic setup was copied in other cities around the country.

Judy was aware of this, but it hardly mattered to her. She was happy that she had found some stability and prosperity in her life. She occasionally thought about Melville, but not too often, and when she did, it was more of a nostalgic little twinge rather than a painful ruin.

The fact was, she could hardly even remember what he looked like. She had no pictures, and her memories of him were wrapped up in the life she had then, which she could hardly remember at all. Faith Village had taken all that away from her.

Which she appreciated. Even welcomed.

I understood Judy Bryant's attitude. It was one I shared.

REX GROANED.

"Sorry about that," I said. "You awakened the fighting spirit in me."

"Glad to hear it," he said.

"Does your neck hurt?"

"A little. But that's okay."

That was the standard answer from those who had been in the fighting rooms. All that punishment awakens the life force in them. They love the pain and punishment so much. Such a curious thing, but unremarkable to me now that I have seen it so often. To connect with the world, even in violent ways, seems to make so many of you so damn happy.

"It'll take a few minutes for your neck to heal," I said.

"I feel it," he said. "I'm already missing the pain."

"Yes," I said. "In the meantime, we have to talk about something."

"Talk? I'd rather fight."

"Please pay attention. Do you understand that you can't stay here forever?"

"What?"

"This place is not a permanent residence for you. It is more of a way station. A resting up. A transition place. A—"

He interrupted me. "Okay, Mister Thesaurus," he said. "I get it."

I stopped to compose myself. I never liked this moment. The loss was intolerable and I didn't like being made to feel so human. I was not human. "The thing is," I said, "you have to return."

"To Earth?"

"Yes."

He tried to lift his head, managed to raise it a couple of inches, but his neck was still broken. He groaned, then let it plop back to the ground. "Oh man, that feels good," he said.

"Savor it," I told him. "You won't have the sensation much longer."

"No," he said "I suppose not. I never much cared for pain in my previous life."

"Of course not."

"But here. It's so different. It's like food. I could take it in forever."

"Speaking of food," I said, "there's the soup room. Have you seen it?"

"No."

"Everyone who goes back needs to pass through there and have a bowl. It sustains you for your journey."

"My journey?" He sounded skeptical.

I put out my hand. He reached for it, and I pulled him up to a sitting position.

"Ouch ouch ouch," he said with a smile. His head flopped over on its side so he looked like he was listening for the sound of the ocean in his shoulder. I grabbed him by the hair and plopped his head down on his spine and twisted it a couple of small turns to wedge it into place. He screamed and laughed at the same time, if you can imagine such a thing. If I was prone to such reactions, I would have been unnerved.

"That'll help it heal," I said. "You need to be in tiptop shape when you eat your soup."

"I never much liked soup."

"You'll like this soup."

"What kind is it?"

"You have your choice."

"I just told you I don't like soup. I wouldn't *choose* any soup because I don't like any of them."

I closed my eyes and took a deep breath. Such a stubborn case. "You haven't even asked me where you will end up," I said.

"End up? What do you mean?"

"I mean what life you will have when you return."

"What life? What do you mean?"

"Never mind," I said. "Can you stand up?"

"I think so." He rose to his feet.

"Neck still hurting?"

"No," he said. The disappointment was an epic misery in his voice.

"Come along," I said, and hooked my arm out for him. He put his hand on my elbow and walked with me.

"I've enjoyed having you," I said. "I hope you've learned some things while you've been here."

"What should I have learned?" he said.

I sighed.

"No, *really*," he said. "What exactly was I supposed to learn? I'd like to know."

"Forget about it," I said. "Doesn't matter."

We got to the soup room, which was set up cafeteria style. You took your bowl from the stack, then went down the counter where there were all kinds of soups: bean, chicken, vegetable, split pea, minestrone, miso, noodle, tomato, and so on. We also offered condiments like salt, pepper, and hot sauce. Not to mention the crackers and bread for dipping. Rex let my arm go and got into line.

"I'll wait for you at a table," I said. I found an empty table in the corner. I sat and looked around. Thousands of people were eating their soup. The sound of so many people slurping is a grand sound, a symphony. I smiled at some of the musicians. They smiled back.

Rex came around the corner from the end of the counter carrying a tray bearing a steaming bowl. His head looked like it sat on his neck properly now, like the break had mostly healed. Rapid healing is one of the nice things about this place. I never tired of it. I put up my hand so he could see me. He caught my eye and headed in my direction. He put the tray down on the table.

"How come you didn't get any?" he said.

"I don't like soup," I said.

He looked at me with suspicion.

"It's a joke," I said.

"Ha ha."

"What did you get?"

"This one had noodles and beef in it. It looked mostly tolerable."

I saw he also had some crusty slabs of bread. He tore off a piece and dunked it in the broth and took a deep bite.

"You're going to have a very different life," I told him.

"This isn't different enough?" he said as he began eating his soup.

"Remember how you talked about the cactus stealing sunlight?"

"How'd you know about that?"

"I know everything."

He looked doubtful.

"I told you," I said, "I don't have any real power here. I can only observe."

"Yeah." He ate more soup. Evidently, it agreed with him.

"That's not quite true," I said. "I have one ability. I can decide what you are going to be when you go back."

He looked blankly at me. It was like he didn't know who I was. He looked down at the soup. Took another bite. Then looked up at me.

"Who are you?" he said.

"I've decided to make you a tree," I said. "You'll steal sunlight from the air all day long and take water out of the ground. All day and all night."

"What's a tree?" he said. "What's sunlight?"

"One other thing," I said. "The soup isn't just for sustenance. It's magic soup. It takes away your memory. You won't remember any of this or any of your previous life. It works out much much better that way."

He blinked at me. "Do I know you?" he said.

Chapter 12: Pride

Jake and Mort drove up the coast of California on Highway 1. The sun glinted off the blue Pacific to their left. They wound around cliff edges and reveled in the look of the beach sand when the road took them down to sea level. The sand was white and smooth and the wind shaped much of it into curved dunes.

"I've never seen the ocean before," said Jake.

"Me neither," said Mort, although he had the vague feeling that he was not exactly telling the truth. Not that he was lying, just that somewhere in the back of his mind he had some dim memory of salt water touching him, like he had waded into some waves. He supposed that was possible. Louisa had told him his father had come from the north, somewhere around Portland.

After Mort had stolen a car, they purposely waited until the sun rose to begin their drive north. They wanted to take full advantage of the coastal vistas.

Their car was a beater and Mort was not even sure it could take them all the way to Seattle, but he had told Jake that old cars were the best ones to steal. People often didn't even insure old cars, so they weren't always that interested in expending a lot of energy to find one. Also, since uninsured vehicles were illegal, they often weren't even reported to the police. Jake was skeptical of this, but let it go. He reasoned that Mort, obviously more experienced in the ways of thievery, was more likely to know what he was talking about.

"You steal a lot of cars?" asked Jake.

"No," said Mort. "I know how, but I avoid that. Much better to steal money."

"Yeah," said Jake. "More useful."

"Exactly."

"I wouldn't mind learning how to steal stuff. It might come in useful, you know?"

Mort sensed a hint of defiance in Jake's voice, like he was trying to sound tough and worldly, but he could not pull it off.

"You don't want to get into that," said Mort.

"Yes, I do."

"What happened to being an upright member of society? Working for your friend's landscape business and such."

"I'll do that," said Jake, "but until then we have a few days. Why not see what the other side of life is like?"

Mort thought about telling Jake what he did for a living, but decided neither of them was ready for that. They stopped at a small park and got out of the car and went down to the beach. They took off their shoes and waded into the water which was a lot colder than either of them had expected but not so cold that they had to get out.

A couple of families had stopped as well. One of them picnicked on a wooden table that had been put there for the purpose. Mort nodded at them, and they waved back to him.

"That's a good idea," said Mort.

"What?"

"We should stop and get some food."

They went back to the car, Jake driving this time, and resumed their route north. Mort noted that Jake was an unsure driver, his foot hovering over the brake at times, and slowing down long before getting to a slow patch in the traffic. They were both more serious, it seemed, all the reckless joy gone from them. Something about being in the water had sobered them, as if the cold froze out all their energy. Jake began to think it might have been a big mistake to hook up with Mort. He should have stayed on the train. Jake was a criminal now just as much as Mort. An accomplice to a crime. Car theft. That was serious.

Mort regretted bringing along an amateur on his jaunt north. Jake could only be trouble for him, completely ignorant of how to survive in a tough world. If you didn't steal, then you got stolen from. It was no more complicated than that, and Jake had not learned that lesson yet. Some people never learned it. Mort was pretty sure he had known it from the day he was born.

They rode in silence for half an hour, then saw a roadside diner up ahead: wooden siding rotting away, a roof streaked white from seagull shit, and an old neon sign at the edge of the property, still lit up in the morning light: THE GREASY SPOON.

"This looks like a good place," said Mort.

Jake pulled into the parking lot. They got out and took seats inside the diner. An older woman, who looked like she took no shit from anyone, deposited a couple of glasses of water on the table and threw down two menus, sticky from who knew what.

"Coffee?" she asked.

"Yeah," said Jake. "Black."

"Cream and sugar," said Mort.

She left to go behind the counter and pour the cups. Jake looked out the window. The ocean was just visible in the distance, white peaks of waves lapping up from the horizon, like blooms of flowers that died as soon as they were born. Mort looked around the diner. There were a few other tables but no other customers. Maybe they were the first of the lunch rush. Or maybe this place never got many customers.

The waitress returned with their coffees in thick white mugs and took their orders.

When she was gone again Mort asked Jake if he still wanted to ride with him.

"Why wouldn't I?" said Jake.

Mort shrugged. "It just feels like maybe you think you made the wrong decision."

"I never knew the ocean was so cold," said Jake.

"Yeah. So?"

"Just made me think how we could all die pretty easily."

"What?"

"Don't you ever think about that?"

"You mean dying?"

"Sure, dying. People die."

"Who the fuck cares about people," said Mort. "You're not dying. I'm not dying. So what the fuck are you talking about?"

"My dad told me people only get one or two chances to be successful in life."

"He read that in a book somewhere," said Mort, now disgusted by the turn of the conversation.

"Maybe," said Jake. "The point was that opportunity only comes once or twice. If you don't take it, you're dead. You ever think about things like that?"

"Listen," said Mort. "If you pay attention, opportunity comes knocking at least one or twice every five *minutes*. What's your father do?"

"Sells real estate."

Mort snorted.

"What?" said Jake.

"He's a criminal. He should know better."

Jake looked at him like he wanted to deck him. Mort did not break his gaze from Jake's eyes.

The waitress brought their orders and plunked down their plates with a clatter. "Enjoy," she said as she turned around and walked away.

"What are you talking about, criminal?" said Jake. "You're the one who steals cars and money and who knows what the fuck else."

"That's how I know," said Mort. "His job is to get the highest price he can for a property, right?"

"Yeah," said Jake.

"Why doesn't he just sell it for what it's worth?"

"He does. I mean, it's like whatever the buyer is willing to pay."

"Bingo," said Mort. "He's trying to get as much out of the buyer as he can. That's stealing, man. No one calls it that because it isn't illegal, but that's what it is. He's trying to get as much money out of them as he can and he'll do whatever it takes. That's the exact same description as my job."

"What you do isn't a job," said Jake.

"Sure it is. I keep regular hours and I report to my work sites on time ready to do my job."

Jake shook his head and looked down at his steak and eggs. He pulled the napkin out from under the knife and fork beside his plate and tucked it under his chin. He cut off a piece of steak and put it into his mouth.

Mort turned his attention to his bacon and eggs. They ate in silence for a while. Mort felt like he had made some good points. He must have been right, since Jake had no answer for him.

"But," said Jake suddenly, "the people want to give him their money. He doesn't take it against their will."

"That's a minor difference. He convinces them with sweet talk and by appealing to their vanity and need for status. I do it by being sneaky. It's exactly the same thing."

"There's something wrong with your logic. I can't figure out what it is, but it's wrong. Selling land is not stealing."

"You do anything with land that ends up with someone saying they own it, that's stealing," said Mort. "Pure and simple."

"People have to live somewhere."

"They don't have to own where they live."

Jake shook his head. "No no no. You've got it all wrong."

"Okay," said Mort. "Then tell me this. If you think real estate is so great, why don't you do it? Bet your dad would love to have you in the family business."

Jake looked pained. "That's a little complicated," he said.

"Why, because he beats you or something? You have an abusive father? Is that it?"

Jake looked away. The ocean appeared bluer than earlier in the morning. Something about the sun? He didn't know. The white caps still tossed up temporary flowers. He liked those a lot. Made him think of the white flowers on saguaros, when they bloomed in May. They only lasted a short time. Always made him sad to see them go.

"Maybe," Jake said, almost in a whisper.

"Maybe?" said Mort. "Did you say maybe?"

"He beats up my mother," said Jake. "I got sick of it. Hit him pretty hard, just to let him know what it felt like. Broke his nose." He shrugged. "There was a lot of blood and stuff. My mom told me to get out."

Mort felt his heart open up for Jake. He had wondered why a kid like Jake was running away from his home. But then, it was probably only temporary. His mother would call him to come back, and he would go back. He had planned to tell Jake that no matter how bad he had it, at least he had a father, but he decided that was not a good idea. He wouldn't want a father like that. He was better off with a father that deserted him. Jake would have been better off with a father who was thoughtful enough to leave his mother and him alone.

"So you did what your mom said."

Jake nodded.

"Even though he will probably hit her again."

"That's what they do. They'll be all sweet on each other now. For a while. Then he'll get pissed off about some stupid little thing. It's what they do. I don't have to stand around and watch it any more though."

"So you're going to Seattle with me," said Mort.

Jake shrugged.

"How does it feel to abandon your mother?"

"Fuck you," said Jake.

Mort sniffed. "I don't understand how you could just leave her like that. Why didn't you kick *him* out of the house?"

"I told you. It's complicated."

"You only get a couple of chances. Didn't you say that? That was one of them. You blew it, man. I should turn the car around and take you back there. Maybe you can still do the right thing."

Jake had lost whatever fight he had in him. Mort could see he was miserable, just thinking about the situation he had left behind. He didn't push him anymore. "Finish your damn lunch," said Mort.

"Breakfast," said Jake.

"Whatever."

Jake wasn't feeling hungry anymore, but he ate a few more bites of his eggs and finished off his toast. The butter had gotten cold and half congealed. He put some jam on the last piece and put it in his mouth with no enthusiasm at all. Jake put some bills on the table, along with a generous thirty percent tip, and the two of them headed for the door.

Outside they found four guys, a few years older than them, clustered around their car. Jake and Mort stopped. The guys smiled at them. They were all bigger than either Jake or Mort, and they looked like they worked out.

"This your car?" said the biggest of them, who put one foot on the bumper as he spoke.

Another one had pulled open the passenger door and was looking through the glove compartment. The other two leaned against the side of the car and stared at Jake and Mort with their hands folded in front of them. Mort was more than prepared to walk away. It wasn't his car. He could always get another car, though it might be tough here. No town for miles around. But they could hitchhike until they got somewhere. No big deal.

"Yeah," said Jake. "That's our car. What's it to you?"

The guy who had been in the glove compartment poked his head out from the other side of the car. "Funny," he said, holding the registration in his hand, "you don't look like Mary Phillips. Are you Mary Phillips? Do you have a fag name or something?"

Mort grabbed Jake's elbow. "Come on," he whispered. "Let's go."

"That's my mother," said Jake. "Leave her car alone."

Mort groaned. He didn't need this.

"Oh," said the big man on the bumper. "Your mother. She know you have her car?"

All four of them grinned.

"You know what," said one of the ones with his arms crossed in front of him. "I think we could probably roll this car over. What do you think, guys?"

"What?" said Mort. "Are you fucking kidding me?"

"Don't let them," said Jake to Mort. "Don't let them push you around."

"*Let* them?" said Mort. "They could push around an elephant if they wanted to."

"They're punks," said Jake. "We don't get pushed around by punks."

Mort shook his head at Jake. "What the fuck are you talking about?" he said in a whisper. Jake didn't answer; he just glared at the four guys.

Mort turned from Jake and put up his hands. "We don't want any trouble," he said. "You want to have fun with that car. Be our guests. We'll just be on our way."

The four of them got on one side of the car and bent down. They each grabbed a piece of the bottom edge, lifted it so the two side tires were off the ground and held it there for a moment. Mort could not believe they would actually do it. Jake's anger boiled in his belly. It wasn't his car, but that didn't matter. These guys were trying to make him look bad.

Then the four big guys heaved and grunted and the car kept going up. Mort and Jake saw the rusty underside, flashing like a glimpse of dark guts. Then the sound of metal scraping on sandy pavement, glass crackling, and the car rolling over onto its roof.

The guys all dusted off their hands by slapping their palms together, and then they turned to Jake and Mort, smiling as loud as they could.

"What the fuck?" said Jake.

"Just having a little fun," said the biggest one. "We can call your mother and tell her what happened if you want. Confession is good for the soul, you know."

"Confession," said Mort.

"Car theft," said the biggest guy. "It's a crime. Or didn't you know?"

Mort took a step back from the men. He tried to pull Jake back with him, but Jake was unmovable. He shrugged Mort off.

"You should pay attention to your friend," said one of the men. "He's got the right idea. Just walk away."

Jake took a deep breath of the sea air rolling over the hills from the shore. Something about it gave his thoughts a new clarity. He did not want to tangle with these guys. They were complete shitheads, and they were also big. On the other hand, he had hit his father. That hadn't felt good at all. His father was a shithead, too, but he was his father. It might feel good to hit someone he had no attachment to. Might cleanse his soul.

"Just one of you," said Jake.

"*Fuck*," said Mort.

"Pick one. I won't fight you all at once but one of you."

The biggest guy spit on the ground. He nodded to the one who had been rummaging in the glove compartment. He stepped away from the overturned car and took off his jacket.

"Don't do it," said Mort in a whisper.

Jake threw his own jacket to the ground. Mort picked it up, then immediately felt embarrassed. Why did he care about Jake's stupid jacket?

Jake and the other guy came closer, both with their fists raised. The other three guys circled around them, each one a few paces away. Mort groaned. Jake was going to get the shit kicked out of him. That much was clear. And maybe Mort, too, if he wasn't smart and *just walked away*. Now how hard was that?

Too hard, it seemed. He could not take a step back. Not one.

The big guy, Jake's opponent, dropped his hands and leaned his chin forward. "I'll give you a head start, kid," he said.

Jake did not hesitate. He moved like lightning and landed a quick jab on the bigger guy's eye. He stumbled back a step or two, laughing. "Not bad," he said. "Now try this on for size."

He took two long steps toward Jake and landed a quick blow to his belly. Jake doubled over and the man brought his knee up to Jakes forehead with a sharp smack. Jake went down and huddled on the ground. The man pulled his foot back as if to kick Jake but decided there was no point. Jake was coughing and had his arms wrapped around his stomach. Mort wanted to run to him, to see how he was, but he was afraid. Whatever courage he had or thought he had, was gone.

The four guys looked at Mort. "You want some of this?" asked the biggest one.

Mort shook his head. "No sir," he said. His voice quavered, like he was going to cry. He actually did want to cry. Jake groaned and spit. Coughed some more.

"Now tell me the truth," said the biggest guy. "You're a couple of filthy car thieves, aren't you?"

"Yes sir," said Mort.

"Say it."

"We're a couple of filthy car thieves."

"You're good for nothing, cocksucking, pieces of shit."

"Yes sir."

"Say it."

"We're good for nothing, cocksucking, pieces of shit."

That seemed to satisfy them. "We don't ever want to see you around here again," said the biggest guy. "Got that?"

"Yes sir," said Mort.

The four of them advanced toward him. He had already lost whatever dignity he thought he might have. He was prepared to lose his teeth now, if that's what had to happen. He wanted to run, but there was no chance he could outrun all of them. He gritted his teeth and waited, forcing himself to keep his eyes open.

They brushed by him, purposely knocking his shoulders as they went.

And that was all. They got into their own car and drove south on the highway.

Mort could hardly believe his luck. He was alive.

He heard Jake groaning from the ground and went to him and bent down. "You okay?" he said.

"I'm not a piece of shit or a cocksucker," he said, barely able to get the words out.

"I know," said Mort.

"And one more thing," he whispered.

"Yeah?" said Mort.

"I'm no kind of thief."

Chapter 13: Comfort

JUDY SOLD COPIES of *HomeTown*, a weekly newspaper that reported on the homeless and homeless issues. Her regular spot was on the sidewalk outside of the food co-op just a few blocks from Faith Village where she could catch the eye of guilt ridden health food nuts as they left the store with their granola and tofu. Each copy of *HomeTown* sold for a dollar. She got seventy cents out of that. The rest went to production costs and modest salaries for the staff and token payments to the contributors. On a good day, standing for six hours, which was about all she could stand, she sold twenty copies. Fourteen dollars. It wasn't much for a day's work, but it was enough for her to survive in Faith Village.

One morning, after selling her papers, she returned home to her tent for a snack and a nap before going back to her spot in the afternoon. A young woman, had to be no more than twenty, if that, stood near her tent with a notebook in her hand. She was obviously not from the village: her clothes were too new and her heels were too high. Not to mention the fact that she wore makeup. Judy couldn't remember the last time she put any kind of makeup on her face. It made her wonder what she had been thinking doing that sort of thing back in the day. All those products cost an arm and a leg.

Judy greeted the woman warily.

"Hello," she said. "Are you lost?"

"I'm Susie," said the young woman. "I'm doing a story for *HomeTown* on the village."

"*Home Town?*" said Judy. "I sell those."

"I know," said Susie. "That's how I found out about you. I want to interview you if that's okay."

Judy stepped past her to her tent. Other women stood outside their tents, looking at Judy and Susie. Susie looked a little nervous. She glanced over her shoulder several times. "Don't mind them," said Judy. "We look tough, but that's all for show."

"Oh, I know," said Susie. "You have to protect yourselves. That's what I wanted to talk to you about. One of the things."

Judy almost unzipped her tent and was going to invite Susie in, but she didn't want to talk to anyone about her life.

"I think *Home Town* already did a story on us, didn't they?"

Susie nodded. "Sure, but that was a while ago. Plus, no one ever talked to you. You started Faith Village."

"No I didn't," said Judy, maybe a little too forcefully. Susie was a nice kid. She wasn't trying to upset Judy. That was something she was doing to herself.

"That's not what everyone else says," said Susie.

"Everyone else is wrong. Faith Village was—it still is—a community effort. There is no leader or founder or anything. We've always worked together."

Susie still looked startled, like she had just arrived at an accident scene. Judy wondered how she ever got it in her head that she could be a reporter if an encounter with a powerless homeless woman knocked her off her stride. Judy watched, amused, as Susie struggled to regain her composure. Finally she flipped open her notebook and took a pencil from behind her ear. "Can I quote you on that?" she said.

"It's like this," said Judy. "I used to give interviews all the time, figuring that getting the word out about Faith Village would help the residents here. People would find out about us and either donate money so we could keep growing, or maybe just see that we were good people and leave us alone. But that never happened. The stories were never about *us*. They were about the writer and how marvelous he or she was for doing the story. You see what I mean?"

"Not exactly," said Susie.

"I got tired of working for them, of advancing their interests. We were just a stepping stone on their career. Once they came from all over the country to talk to us. Now, not so much."

"I know that," said Susie. "That's why I want to write about you now. It's been fifteen years. I'd like to do a summary piece."

"Evergreen piece?"

"Evergreen?"

"They used to do a story on us every year. In the spring. How we survived the winter and would we go on. The newspapers loved it. Every year the same story. An easy page in the paper to fill."

"This isn't that. I want to do some real reporting."

"How old were you fifteen years ago? Five?"

"Almost. Four."

Judy laughed. "You got pictures?"

"Beg your pardon?"

"Never mind. Come on in."

She bent down and pulled the zipper open so the two flaps of the door swung open. Susie bent down beside her.

"You'll have to excuse the mess," said Judy. "My cleaning lady hasn't been in yet this week."

"You have a cleaning lady?" said Susie.

Judy tried to keep from laughing but she couldn't quite manage it.

"Oh," said Susie. "You were joking."

"Something like that," said Judy. "You sure you're cut out for this job?"

"I'm interning. I'm hoping to learn how to tell when people are not telling the truth."

Judy stepped into the tent. A small cot filled one corner, a kerosene stove another, and a small table with a lamp—darkened—rested skewed on the uneven ground between them. "I had a generator for the light and for a heater," said Judy, "but it got stolen a while back. I'm saving up for another one."

"By selling the paper?" said Susie.

"Yup," said Judy.

"Is theft a big problem?"

"It's a problem because when you have things you feel like you're better than you were. But then if your things get stolen, you realize you weren't anything more than you've always been."

Susie blinked. "I'm not sure I know what you mean."

"Never mind. You have to be older to get it." And you have to have someone take the only thing you ever cared about in the world. Once that happens to you, you understand what possessions can do to you.

"How is it without light?"

"We get some filtering down from the city. It's never completely dark, but you learn to go with the rhythms of nature. You sleep when it's night. Wake up with the sun." She shrugged.

Susie wrote furiously in her notebook. "You need to learn shorthand," said Judy.

Susie blushed. "That's what people tell me. Where did you get the tent?"

"Oh, that was interesting. Soon after I staked out this ground, I started building a shelter. Out of wood and tin sheets I could find lying around. Some cardboard. That sort of thing. It was tough going. I couldn't find the tools I needed and it was just plain hard work. I was green, let me tell you. Knew nothing about scavenging or how to make do. I was still thinking I could recreate my life from before, even though that was long gone. So I went out into the suburbs. People put out all kinds of things, for free."

"Freecycling," said Susie.

"That's what they call it?"

"Yeah. My mom does it. She puts out stuff on the sidewalk in front of the house with a big free sign on it. Usually gets snapped up right away."

"By people like me, huh?" She smiled at Susie.

Susie smiled back. "Probably."

"Maybe I got this tent from your mom?"

"Doesn't look like anything we had."

"It had a big rip in it, but that wasn't any big deal. Some duct tape took care of that." She pointed to a length of gray tape across the roof of the tent.

Susie spun her head around and twisted her neck to look up. "Does it ever leak?" she asked.

"It has. But I re-tape it."

"I noticed other tents in the village. Did they get them the same way?"

"A sporting goods store was getting rid of some of their inventory and donated tents to us."

"How'd they find out you needed them?"

"Someone at the store read a story about us."

Susie looked up. "In a newspaper?"

Now it was Judy's turn to blush. "Yeah, you got me. In a newspaper."

"I wasn't trying to get you," said Susie. She looked around the tent. "Looks like you made it pretty comfortable. Do you ever think about getting back into society?"

Ten years ago that question would have made Judy angry. Today it just amused her. "This is part of society, honey," she said. "You write for a homeless paper. You should know that. Vagabonds, outcasts, down-on-their luck folks, beggars, we've always been part of society. It's just that a big part of society doesn't want to think about us. That just means they don't understand. It's nothing to do with us." She could have gone on. Wanted to, actually, but didn't see the point. Also, she didn't want to expend the energy. Susie didn't seem to get it.

"I didn't mean to offend," she said. "It just seems like you have a lot of skills in organizing and coping. Seems like you could easily get a job."

"If I wanted to."

"Right. If you wanted to. Does that mean you don't want to?"

"There's a community here. I appreciate it and everyone who lives here appreciates me. I never had that in my old life."

"I read that you had your baby stolen from you."

"I don't want to talk about that," said Judy.

Susie twirled her pencil in her fingers. She looked like she was going to write something in her notebook, then pulled her pencil back and left it poised over the paper. So this is why she came, thought Judy. To ask about Melville.

"I wondered if that was what got you to this place, losing your son."

"Look," said Judy. "You're a nice kid. I've invited you into my house. Please do me the courtesy of respecting my privacy."

"But—"

"No buts. You don't know what that kind of pain does to someone."

"That's why I'm asking," said Susie.

"Next question."

"But—"

"Next. Question."

Susie sighed. Judy could see her still trying to think up a way to approach the subject she wanted to pursue. It didn't matter what Judy wanted. It never did with reporters. That's why she tried to avoid them. She was beginning to wish she hadn't made an exception today.

But then Susie seemed to let it go.

"There are people," she said, "who accuse you of stealing."

"We have no thieves here," said Judy.

"The land that Faith Village stands on."

"It's citizen's land," said Judy.

"It's city land."

"Same thing."

"The city doesn't see it that way."

"But most people do," said Judy. "Let me ask you again, do you know the nature of the publication you're writing for?"

"We're homeless advocates."

"Exactly. And haven't you realized that homeless advocates don't exactly have a rosy opinion of the whole concept of land ownership?"

"I'm aware of it."

"So where is this question coming from?"

"It pertains to the legality of Faith Village. Surely you know people don't want you here."

"They used to not want us here. Now they'd rather have us in one place than all over the streets, sleeping in front of church doors, and such. Did you come here today to argue with me about the right of Faith Village to exist?"

"No. Where'd you get the cot?"

"Found it in a trash bin."

Susie tapped her pencil on her notepad. She was trying to think of another question.

"You might ask me about my friends."

"I'll go talk to them later. Any one in particular you want me to see?"

"Actually," said Judy, "what I want you to do is throw away your pencil and pad and live here. You think you could do that? Give up whatever life you have and become part of something here?"

"I don't know," said Susie.

BUT I DID. Judy was trying to get Susie to eat the soup, in a manner of speaking. To take the plunge and live a different life. But it wouldn't work. Susie didn't want to eat the soup. Rex didn't want to eat the soup either, but I convinced him. Could Judy convince Susie? No. I could have told her that if I had the power.

But, as I've mentioned at least a few times, I have no power. I can only observe. Do you believe me? Think before you answer.

After Rex ate his soup, I escorted him to the departing room. It was just a short distance from the soup line. He looked happy. I don't know if he was or if he wasn't, but he *looked* happy. I said goodbye. He didn't answer. Then I turned and left him.

I'm not exactly sure how he got back down. I'm not privy to that part of the scheme. Something about stripping away the outer body and transmitting the inner spirit. Or some such. Doesn't matter. Rex was part of the world again. He wore a tree suit. Tree flesh clothed him. Birds came to sit on his limbs. They tickled him and he invited them to return. They mostly did.

He was a big oak. They plunked him down in the middle of Portland. Close to Faith Village, if you want to know. Yes, I had something to do with that. I never drank the soup, you see. I didn't want to forget. That's why I'm still here. I'll stay here as long as I don't drink the soup. If I ever do. Then someone else will take my place, be the avatar of thieves. All you liars and thieves down there, you have an avatar. You don't know it, but I watch. I try to make things right by picking who you'll be. I can't let you keep memories, it doesn't work that way. If you don't eat the soup, you don't go back. It's just that simple.

I never wanted to go back because I didn't want to lose the memories.

Not that I had great memories, that's not what I'm saying. It's just that without memories you're nothing.

So I sympathized with Susie. She didn't want to lose what she had. I saw and understood. And Judy would have been happy to lose her memories. That's what being in the village was all about. If you don't live in the trappings of your former life, it's like you never had that life in the first place.

I watched them both.

Tension there in that little tent. Each of them hoping to get something out of the encounter but not knowing how to get it.

Rex arrived just about the time Judy was asking Susie if she could be homeless.

I was fascinated by the possibility of Judy noticing. A change in her energy field, you know. Would she feel it?

I thought I saw something pass over her face, but it could have been my imagination.

"I don't know," said Judy, imitating Susie's voice, and getting it just about perfect. "I don't know. I don't know." She was impatient with the young reporter. The *young* reporter. Too young. Too naïve.

"I just mean," said Susie, "that it's a big change. I'd have to prepare for it."

Judy felt a chill run up her spine. She shivered. It wasn't cold. Why was she feeling like this? Susie noticed the shudder.

"Are you okay?"

Judy shook her head and wrapped her arms around her shoulders. "Suddenly it feels like something—I don't know how to describe it." She saw panic in Susie's eyes.

"You look scared," said Susie. "Are you sick? Do you need some water or something?"

Judy looked up at the ceiling of the tent. Suddenly it felt claustrophobic in her house. Her house, this tiny stretch of fabric. How could she ever call it her house? It looked like the canopy that she had stretched over Melville's carriage the morning he disappeared. She sometimes wondered if that was the last thing he had seen, the inside of that canopy, and maybe that's why she wanted to live in this tent, to try to connect with him that way?

"I need to get outside," she said.

She pushed past Susie, who took a step back and ended up leaning against the canvas wall of the tent. Judy broke out into the open air and took in deep breaths. She leaned over with her hands on her knees and gulped air.

Susie followed and put her palm on Judy's shoulder.

I was startled by Judy's reaction. Just the presence of Rex in the vicinity caused Judy this much discomfort? I was not prepared for it. But it all made sense. The agent of her downfall was nearby.

Rex woke up in the tree.

Rex was the tree.

His leaves rustled. This amused Rex. He rustled them some more. The wind moved over his bark. Even if he had a concept of reincarnation, he probably wouldn't have thought it was possible to be reincarnated as a tree. But that's what happened to him.

Judy stood up and looked around, gazing over the tents of Faith Village. This was her place. Her home. Why did she feel like she was in enemy territory all of a sudden?

Other women came out of their tents. They stood in front of them, some with their hands up to their foreheads, looking around. A disturbance in the field.

Susie grew silent and looked around at the forest of women, all appearing as if they were cold, just like Judy, who had set her eyes on the oak tree at the edge of Faith Village. She stared at it, not knowing why.

But I knew why.

Go Judy, I said to myself.

Judy went to one of the women of the village, someone she knew had an ax.

"I want to cut down that tree," she said.

"Which tree?" said the woman.

"The one that's making me crazy," said Judy.

The woman gave Judy the ax.

Judy hefted it against her palm. It felt right. She turned and began walking to the tree where Rex now lived.

Chapter 14: Life

YOU MAY THINK I could have concocted a more direct way for Judy to exact her revenge on Rex. You're probably right. So why did I pick this method?

Trees take a long time to die. Even after they've been cut up and chopped to pieces, they're still alive, all those bits. Like the saguaro that Rex tried to steal. Even though it had been uprooted and essentially destroyed, it was still going to be alive for maybe ten years. That's how long it takes the flesh to truly understand that it has met its doom.

It isn't quite as long with oaks, but the principle applies. Even after wood has been butchered, you can feel it alive under your hand. It's a slow dying. That seemed just right for Rex. What do you think? Oh, I can feel you on the other side of the page, squirming.

Like, an avatar is supposed to be above sadistic feelings. I only wish it was true.

MORT TRIED PUSHING the car back over, but the roof had been dented in pretty good, keeping it stuck to the spot where it was.

"It's no good," said Mort to Jake. "It's not budging. And even if we could roll it back, I don't know that we could drive it."

Jake noted the fluid leaking from the front of the car and nodded. "We don't need this car," he said. "Let's get going."

He rose to his feet, still a little unsteady from the pummeling he had received. His forehead displayed a nasty bruise, wide, dark, and swollen.

"I wonder if they'd give us a steak to put on that wound," said Mort.

"Forget it," said Jake. "Let's just get out of here."

Mort looked over to the front of the diner. The waitress stood in the doorway and looked at them with unconcealed contempt. She pushed open the door. "You ain't leaving that car like that for us to deal with," she said.

"Wasn't our fault, ma'am," said Mort. He hurried over to Jake and urged him to get going.

"All the same," said the waitress, "I'm going to call the police."

"You do that," said Mort. "Your local vigilante committee would be pleased to hear from them, I'm sure."

The waitress, still holding the door open, glared at them. Jake and Mort began walking, Jake still in pain and leaning over a little.

"She going to come after us?" said Jake. "Am I going to have to deck an old lady?"

"Decking an old lady seems about your speed, from what I saw earlier," said Mort. He looked back over his shoulder. The waitress finally spat, in disgust, and stepped away from the front door. It slammed shut.

"Whew," said Mort. "Looks like we're safe."

They began walking on the gravel shoulder of the highway. "We'll just get going a ways, then start hitching for rides."

Jake nodded. "I think I'm going to be sick," he said. He walked off the shoulder into the grass next to the road. A gnarled old tree stood nearby. He went to it and put his hand on the trunk and leaned over and waited, breathing heavily. Mort noticed Jake's hand was bruised up pretty good. Must be the one he used to connect with the big guy's head. Fighting never helped anyone, especially a thief. Always much better to walk away, intact and ready for the next job.

Sweat popped out on Jake's head and the bruise there felt like a weight. It was giving him the biggest headache he had ever had.

Mort looked away, not needing to see vomit cascade out of his friend's mouth.

A few cars went by. He saw them in the distance as they approached. Some slowed down at the diner, obviously intrigued by the sight of an overturned car. Then they looked at Mort and just kept driving.

"Thank you very much," said Mort to their receding behinds. He heard Jake retching behind him, and lifted his gaze to the shore, not more than a quarter mile away, across the highway.

Jake finished what he had to do and came back and stood beside Mort. "You okay?" said Mort.

"I'm better," said Jake.

"There's five bucks for breakfast we're never going to see again."

"Yeah."

"You're going to need to get some water."

"Let's just start walking," said Jake.

"Was there any blood in it?" said Mort as they took up a leisurely pace on the gravel. The crunch under their shoes punctuated the silence with irritation. Mort walked with his hand outstretched and his thumb pointing at the sky.

"No blood," said Jake.

"You should probably be checked out by a doctor, but that'd be too risky."

"Who are you, my mother? I'm fine."

Mort didn't say anything. A few cars whizzed by. None of them slowed down. Some people might stop for one older teenager. Maybe. Not too many were going to stop for two, especially ones who looked like they had been in a fight. Mort started to worry about that. They couldn't walk all the way to Oregon.

"I guess your mom must have got beat up like that herself a few times," said Mort. "I mean by your father."

"Yeah," said Jake.

"Only, I bet your dad made sure he didn't bruise her where anyone could see."

"How do you know anything about it?" said Jake.

Mort shrugged. "Just makes sense."

"I tried hitting him a few times. When I was just a kid. He walloped me so hard my mother was scared for me. She told him to hit her instead."

"Did he?"

"I don't know," said Jake. "Probably. I ran from the house that night. Spent it in the woods."

"With the raccoons and the bobcats?" said Mort.

"Something like that. When I got back the next day, he just laughed at me."

"If we don't get a ride soon," said Mort, "we're going to have to figure something else out."

"What is there to figure?" said Jake. "We walk until we find a car we can steal."

"We?"

"You. Me. Us. Whatever."

They continued for another hour or so, both of them with their thumbs out. The sun had moved up higher in the sky and beat down on them. Neither of them had hats, so it made them feel groggy, filled up with a lethargic heat.

"Let's cool off," said Mort as they approached a picnic area off the side of the road. The picnic tables had shelters over them for shade. They sat at one of them. The air under the shelter still felt cool from the morning. Jake put his head down to the inside of his elbow and closed his eyes. Mort thought if he let him, Jake would fall asleep. Then maybe Mort could just walk away from him. He wasn't doing Mort any good. Mort had a good plan to go up to Oregon, then he met Jake and everything went to shit real quick after that.

"Where'd you learn to steal stuff?" said Jake in a soft voice from where his head met his elbow.

"School," said Mort. "I figured out pretty quick that lots of people were way more trusting than they should be."

"You stole from other kids?"

"No, dummy. From the teachers."

"Impressive."

Mort shrugged. "Like I said, it was pretty easy. I just had to pretend I was interested in what they were teaching and they'd forget that you have to watch kids every minute."

"But what made you think you could do that? Most kids don't think they can steal money from adults."

"There's no big mystery to it. It's what I was born to do."

Jake raised his head and looked at Mort. "That's crazy. No one's *born* to be a thief."

Mort shrugged. "Maybe no one is. But I was."

A van pulled into the picnic area, driven by an older man. Mort guessed he was close to seventy, maybe older. The man got out of the van and nodded to Jake and Mort, then walked past them to the restroom.

"You want to steal that van?" asked Jake.

Mort looked at the van, a beater, just like the car they had stolen earlier. It was tempting, that was for sure. But a good thief knows when *not* to steal. "It's too dangerous here," he said. "Not enough cover. We'd be obvious on the road."

Jake looked skeptical. "Weren't we obvious in that other car?"

"Not the same," said Mort. "We got that car in a crowded city. Here the guy saw us. He'd know who took his van."

Jake resigned himself to not stealing this vehicle. It was too late, anyway; if they wanted to take it they should have done it as soon as the door to the restroom slammed shut. Now too much time had passed.

"I don't want to keep walking," said Jake. "It sucks."

"I know," said Mort.

The man came out of the restroom. He looked warily at Jake and Mort. Mort put on his best benign expression and waved at the man. "Good morning," he said. "Nice day." He elbowed Jake, who slapped a smile on his face and raised his hand to the man.

The man stopped and looked at them. "You boys okay?" he said.

"Benn better," said Mort. "Some guys wrecked our car."

"That rolled over car?" said the man. "That was you?"

"Yes, sir," said Mort. "They also beat up my friend here."

Jake nodded at the man. "How do you do, sir?"

"You guys in some kind of trouble?"

"A little," said Mort.

"Anything that could hurt me?"

"We're just trying to get up north to some jobs," said Mort. "We don't want any trouble and we don't give any trouble. We just had the bad luck to run into some bad guys."

The man sniffed the air and Mort could see the calculations running behind the man's eyes. He wasn't sure he should do this. He probably had a wife whose voice was in his head right now telling him he absolutely should not even consider doing anything like what he was about to do. It didn't matter. People were hardwired to help others. It made them feel good. Mort understood that and thought it was the best thing about people. Absolutely the best. It helped him immensely with his work.

"I'm going as far as Santa Cruz," said the man. "I got a son there that needs some help with his business. You can ride with me if you want."

Mort grabbed Jake and pulled him up from his stupor. Jake rose, suddenly infused with energy, and both of them began walking toward the van. The man went around to the driver's side, got in and leaned over and unlocked the passenger door. Jake got in first and sat in the middle. Mort followed.

The man started the engine and put the van into gear and got on the highway. "Name's Gordon," he said. He didn't offer his hand.

"I'm Mort," said Mort. "This is my friend Jake."

"Where you boys from?"

"Tucson," said Jake.

"There aren't any jobs in Tucson?"

"We're the adventurous types," said Mort. "We thought it be fun to try a different part of the country."

Gordon nodded. "I went to Europe when I was a kid about your age. No reason. Just to see it."

"That's it," said Mort. "Just want to see another part of the world."

"You both look tired. We got another few hours to Santa Cruz. You can sleep if you want."

"I'd just as soon stay awake and keep you company," said Mort.

Jake glanced at him and rolled his eyes.

"I don't believe that," said the man. "I never wanted to sit and listen to old men when I was your age. Can't imagine it's changed much."

"You mentioned your son," said Mort.

"He's got a construction business, but he never hired a good accountant. His books are a mess."

"You an accountant?" said Jake.

"Used to be. Retired now."

"It's nice you helping out your kid."

Gordon shrugged. "No big thing. He's family."

They drove in silence for a few miles.

"You worked for a long time as an accountant?" said Mort.

"Yeah," said the man. "Forty years for a construction company down in Long Beach."

"You ever, I don't know, do anything you kind of shouldn't?"

Gordon laughed. "You asking if I ever cooked books?"

"Something like that," said Mort. He sometimes thought that's where the real money was. If he could get a job like this guy had, then he could have access to all kinds of easy money.

"Didn't have to, even if I wanted to, which I didn't. They paid me plenty. I did fine."

"I wasn't saying you were a thief or anything," said Mort. "I was just asking. You hear about people who steal money that way."

"Sure," said Gordon. "It happens. But most accountants know better. Unless you're very very good, you will get caught. There are safeguards set up all over the place. Believe it or not, you're not the first one to think of this."

Mort laughed. "No, I'm sure I'm not."

"What business you boys going into?"

"Landscaping," said Jake. "We got these friends in Seattle. They want us to work for them."

Mort had no intention of going as far as Seattle, and he wasn't about to work for any landscapers, but he didn't correct Jake.

"That's good honest work," said Gordon. "You don't get rich that way, though. Unless you own the business. You should work for them for a couple of years, learn how to do it, then strike out on your own."

Mort grunted.

"Oh, there I go," said Gordon, "being the wise old man, like I know everything."

"No," said Mort. "I—"

Gordon held up his hand. "Never mind. Tell me what you had in mind."

Jake shrugged. "I'm not planning anything real big," he said. "I just have these friends, you know."

"Yeah," said Gordon. "You said that."

"It's just a job is all," said Jake.

"Huh," said Gordon.

"Not everyone has a big plan for their life," said Mort. "The truth is, Jake comes from an abusive family."

Jake elbowed Mort hard.

"Oh," said Gordon. "You do anything to deserve it?"

"What?" said Jake. "That some kind of a crack?"

"I'm just saying sometimes I wanted to wallop my boy with the trouble he got into. Thought it might teach him something. I never did it. Just thought about it."

"I've wanted to hit people sometimes," said Mort.

"It's a natural thing," said Gordon. "You have to fight against your natural urges sometimes though."

"I didn't do nothing," said Jake. "He's just an asshole."

Gordon nodded. "There's lots of those around. I got some food in the back if you kids are hungry."

Mort twisted around and saw a cooler behind the driver's seat.

"Go ahead," said Gordon. "Open in. I always take my own food when I travel. Cheaper that way."

Mort opened the lid of the cooler and reached in and pulled out a couple of sandwiches wrapped in plastic. He gave one to Jake, who took it, but not with much enthusiasm. Mort unwrapped his own. "Looks like ham and cheese," he said.

"Yeah, my favorite. Eat up. You both look like you could use a meal."

Mort ate his sandwich and watched the road. "Can I get you one?" he said to Gordon.

"It's okay," said Gordon. "I'm not hungry yet. Just save me one for later."

"Sure," said Mort.

Jake finally unwrapped his sandwich and began eating it.

As they both chewed, they passed through a small town. Gordon slowed down the van to get under the reduced speed limit.

"Lots of speed traps in these little towns," he said.

Mort nodded. On the side of the road they saw a man with his thumb out. Gordon caught his eye. The man nodded at him. Mort noticed something passed between them, like they had an understanding. How could that be? They were complete strangers to each other.

Probably something about getting older, he decided. People get to make these little communities without ever even seeing each other. It was like they all knew each other after a while. A brotherhood of old people.

The man didn't seem upset that Gordon didn't stop for him. He waved as the van went by him.

"Lots of people out looking for rides today," said Gordon.

Mort liked Gordon. If he ever even wanted to steal his van, or take his money, he decided right then and there that there was no reason to. It wasn't right.

He also thought that this was dangerous thinking for him. Everyone was a potential source of income. Everyone. That was the way it had always been. Why was it changing?

He put his chin in his hand and leaned his elbow on the door. He thought about this new way of looking at the world. He wasn't sure he liked it at all.

Chapter 15: Power

ONCE, A LONG time ago, one of the avatars of lovers thought it would be a merciful thing to allow people the option of remembering one thing, and one thing only, from their previous life.

"And what one memory, if you had that ability, would you take with you?" I asked her.

"It would be a particular afternoon near the middle of my life," she said. "The last time I slept with my husband."

I could see that. It would be a good memory. "If I had to keep just one memory," I said, "it would probably be the time I took a candy bar from the store on the corner a block from my house when I was just six years old. I knew I shouldn't do it, but I did it anyway. It was such a thrill to feel like I got away with something, even something so insignificant, and nothing in my life ever quite matched it."

"Oh," she said. "That does sound like a nice one."

"I'll always have it," I said. "I won't have to pick it and drop all the others."

"No," she said.

"And you'll always have yours, too."

"That's because we're brighter than the soup eaters."

I laughed. We avatars are the smart and cunning ones. Have I not mentioned that? It's true. We figured out the soup and refused to take it. So we never go back to life. We stay here, in between lives, with all of our memories intact.

It does get crowded here in the way station. We do our best to keep the throngs going on their way, but the smart ones figure it out and some of them are fine with the complete memory wipe. They are eager to get a new start. Those are the ones who had a sad life or even a mostly happy life with one or a few truly awful memories thrown in.

Those kinds of people are more than eager to eat the soup. Any soup. Anything to remove the pain. Others are not. They cannot fathom life anew. They had truly happy lives and want to keep those memories. And some had the ordinary lives that most of us have and are not concerned with whether they are happy or sad or anything in-between. They just don't want to waste all that work. Some people spend all their lives acquiring skills and ways of seeing the world. It's like a culture. They don't want that culture destroyed.

I can understand such a point of view, but my job is to see that their view does not prevail. Now, admittedly, I have it pretty easy. Most thieves are not that excited about keeping their thieving days intact. I'm an exception that way, very pleased with all the stealing I have had. It feels right to steal. I was made for it. So I wasn't about to lose that panorama of my life.

But most thieves, my own case not withstanding, are sorry about their thievery. Do you believe it? Perhaps not, but it is so.

Most thieves, when they see that they may have an opportunity to be something else in the next life, something that doesn't involve stealing, they are eager to jump in and be that new person. They want redemption, even if it has to happen in another life. But such impulses are by no means universal.

I knew, for example, that Rex had no intention of choosing a new life with no old memories. He was too interested in what happened to his son. Or, at least, the boy he stole that he convinced himself was his son.

And that was why I gave him all those years. To satisfy that curiosity. And once that was done, he didn't have much else to keep him here. He was primed for the soup and I made sure he ate the whole bowl.

More thievery, I suppose. Stealing the memories of people is our stock in trade here.

I don't feel any remorse. Even if I had not been a thief in my time among the living, I would not have felt any remorse in my actions. Why should I? The universe unfolds in a certain way. We are all cogs in the vast wheel. Do you believe it? Should you believe it?

I can't tell you what to believe. I won't try.

Instead, I'll take you along as I watch Judy dispatch the oak.

Oh, before that, I'll tell you something else about the soup. We have a cook. A good one. She was the first to refuse the redeployment. Every day she makes pots and pots of soup. She tends a garden and she keeps animals. She harvests the herbs and vegetables, and slaughters the animals all to make the soup. I have been in her garden. It is the finest in creation, and I am not using that word symbolically. It truly is the finest garden ever created. And her chickens and livestock are the best quality. She works ceaselessly. She was a cook before she came up here. She wanted nothing more than to cook for the rest of her life. And that's what she does here.

The soup calls to me. Her soup.

I can't explain it, but when she makes her big pots, their aroma fills the air here and invades my nostrils and tells me that memory is a crutch. The pictures in my head that point back to long lost experiences an illusion.

I know all that. Life is illusion. No one has to tell me that. But the point is that the soup makes it more than knowledge; it makes it an imperative. I could see myself sitting down to a good bowl of the stuff. Maybe several bowls, sampling the different varieties. All the ones who eat the soup, almost to a person, report it as being the best soup ever. So it is a supreme effort of will to make myself *not* eat any of the soup.

I'm just letting you know so that you understand I am not a weak person. I do have willpower and I exercise it every day of my life.

So now, follow me to one of the viewing rooms. This way. Watch the door handle, it tends to stick sometimes. Nothing is perfect, not even here. Sure, take a seat over there. Are you comfortable?

Yeah, there it is. Faith Village. Charming name for a settlement, isn't it? Kind of a ghetto, I know, but I have a soft spot for Judy. Not so much because her child was taken from her, though that's part of it. Mostly for her previous career, where she had figured out how to embezzle. I love embezzlement. Even the word sends shivers up my spine. And to have done it for so many years, just amazing. She kept her greed under control. She could have tried for much more, but she knew that if she kept the sums low her activities would remain under the radar and not be detected ever. It never was, you know. Not once. What undid her was not her thievery, but someone else's. Rex's.

I believe I have stated earlier that I have no issues with basic garden variety thievery. The taking of things is a noble and venerable pursuit, crucial to the wellbeing of society, for if no one performed that task, all the wealth of the world would be concentrated with a few people and they would have so much power that the rest of the world would be miserable. So the taking of objects is the taking of power. Remember that.

Yes, there we are. The picture is coming in strong and clear. I like the bird's eye view, don't you?

What? You wonder why I made Rex be a tree?

I did not care for Rex's theft of the child Melville. That was beyond accepted norms of thievery, the kind of thievery I have been talking about, where the power and wealth of the world is made available to all.

Yes, I suppose it might not be so bad to be a tree, if you were so inclined. There is a nobility to it, I will grant you that, but the life is so restricted, don't you think?

Okay, yes, it would be restful. And trees do get a lot of respect. Okay, okay. So maybe my little punishment was not thought out quite far enough.

In any case, it will be good to watch this little murder. Oh, there's the avatar of killing. He often comes by to watch some of my little dramas.

Yes, he looks awfully scary, I will grant you that, but he's a softie. Weeps and weeps with every murder he remembers, and he remembers a lot of them. It's good he doesn't go back. No, seriously. I know the soup erases every memory, but some of his are so vivid and so bloody, I wonder if their sheer strength would survive the transition. I have not heard of such things, except as rumors, but it seems not altogether impossible. The universe holds many mysteries.

Oh, here it is. It's starting to happen.

Yes, okay, I'll be quiet now so we can watch.

Judy, holding the ax, walked toward the oak, with Susie tagging along beside her.

"You do this sort of thing often?" asked Susie.

"I've never done this sort of thing, but I've learned not to count on others. If I want something done, then I do it myself."

She walked with a determined pace. The ax felt good in her hands, like she had been born to this task, this felling of a living thing.

"That's the only real bit of greenery anywhere in Faith Village," said Susie. "You sure you want to get rid of it?"

Judy ignored her yammering. Why was she talking, anyway? Weren't reporters supposed to just listen? Wasn't that the most important item on their job description?

"Plus," said Susie, "the city owns that tree."

"No one owns a tree," said Judy.

"The city does. You may not agree with that societal arrangement, but that is the truth. You cut down that tree without a permit and you could be in trouble."

Judy laughed. "My whole life is a life without permits. Haven't you noticed?"

Susie slowed her pace, letting Judy get away from her. The tree moved in the wind. The leaves rustled and spoke to her. They said she was doing wrong. They said she shouldn't be hurting another living thing. They said a lot of things, but Judy didn't listen. She couldn't. A hand had seized her heart and squeezed it until it pushed tears out of her eyes. She ran her sleeve over them to try to dry them.

She didn't understand exactly what was going on, but she knew that tree had to go. Whatever it took.

She arrived at the base of the oak, where the ground swelled just a little where the roots pushed up. She stood on a knot of root that had looped out of the ground. She put out her hand and touched the bark. It was rough, of course, but it also had a softness to it, like it was made for dying. She thought she could put her hand through the bark and reach into the core of the trunk and pull the life energy out of the fiber. Then she would throw it to the ground and stomp on it until it was dead.

Such amazing thoughts. Such fervent impulses. She had never felt quite this power before, and a lot of it had to do with the instrument in her hands.

She had never before believed in any kind of divine hand of guidance, but this time, in this place, she could not explain what was happening to her in any other way.

The trunk was perhaps two feet across. She did not know how long it would take to fell it, but she was ready to begin the job.

She put the ax head down on the ground so the handle leaned against her leg. She spit in her hands, rubbed her palms together and took up the ax and raised it over her shoulder. She held it there for a split second, then brought it down on the skin of the tree.

A satisfying thwack sounded from the oak and the ax wedged itself in the wood. She wiggled it free and swung it into the bark again, higher and at the opposite angle so it created a wedge. Another thwack. She pulled out the ax and settled into a rhythm.

Residents of Faith Village emerged from their tents and wooden houses and came to watch.

Whispers: "What's she doing?"

No answers.

"Hey, Judy, you okay?"

"Never better," said Judy between swings. Her face was warm from sweat. Her body already ached, her arms were on fire, but she didn't stop.

"What's your beef with this tree?"

"It took my kid," said Judy, not understanding what she was saying, or even knowing she would say it until the words came out of her mouth.

"Are you crazy?"

"Maybe."

"Uh huh," came several murmurs of assent, though it was easy to see that no one believed it. Judy was the sanest of any of them and if she believed the tree took her child, then the tree must have taken her child. Whatever that meant.

Susie watched the proceedings with interest, writing in her notebook and keeping out of the way.

Soon some of the onlookers went back to their tents and returned with cutting instruments of their own. Saws and axes. They were ready to cut up the carcass of the tree when it fell. Some of them had wood heaters. That oak flesh would burn nicely, give a toasty warmth, and who wouldn't like that?

Judy kept working. She quickly grew tired, but did not stop. She was sustained as much by her sisters, gathered around her, as by the image of her baby. Her lost baby. Tucked under the canvas canopy of his stroller. Unprotected. The face of her baby hung in the air in front of her while her breath warmed the air around her.

REX DIDN'T HAVE a name anymore. At first, soon after slipping into the tree, he didn't know what he was. But soon he began to amass sensations. There was the feel of leaves on his extremities. He had a lot of extremities. There was the push of air over his limbs. He couldn't see, but he could hear. Vibrations in the ground rumbled up through him. His feet pushed down into the firmness of the earth. Warmth enveloped him there. He felt like he held the entire world. No, he felt like he *was* the entire world, and he had no need of anything. Everything that he required was here at hand.

It may be difficult for most of us to understand this state of being. Perhaps those who meditate often might have an inkling. It is something like a complete acceptance of the universe. It is something like a realization that you are the universe. But then it is beyond that. Realization drops away. Awareness drops away and you are left with only the is-ness of being.

It felt like eternity. But it was much shorter than that.

The first swing of Judy's ax severed Rex from any awareness of serenity. Flesh cleaved from his body. He felt pieces of himself tumble down, touching his skin as they went, falling on his roots. What was the agent of this assault? He had no eyes to see, no voice to ask. The power of an oak is illusory.

The world trembled and shook with each blow. Soon he felt himself begin to tilt. Or the earth to tip. It was so hard to tell from where he was. The sun grabbed for his leaves, but it could do nothing. Only kiss the leaves farewell.

Before long the earth began to speak to him. Not in a voice. It may be more accurate to say that Rex and the earth had an understanding born of contact.

The earth ground itself into his skin.

Feet climbed over him, on top of him.

More assault. His limbs dismembered. His consciousness torn to pieces.

Trees take a long time to die. Even after they are cut down, the tissue lives on. Survives.

Rex didn't know exactly how long, but he was resigned: His death was going to be a journey. He would not arrive for some time.

Chapter 16: Watch

Jake elbowed Mort in the arm. Mort woke up, roused from a deep sleep. "What?" he said.

"He's gone for another piss," said Jake. "I swear, that guy has to pee every half an hour."

"It's what happens to old guys," said Mort. He looked around. They were parked at a McDonald's just off the main highway. It looked like they were in a smallish town.

"We in Santa Cruz?" said Mort.

"No way," said Jake. "Still a couple of hours. We should take the van."

"No," said Mort. "I don't think so."

"Why not? He's probably got insurance on it. Look, he left the keys."

"We're not taking this old guy's van. He's done nothing but help us."

"But it'll help him. He won't be out anything. The insurance money will get him a newer and better van."

"You don't know what you're talking about," said Mort. "He'll only get blue book for this van. Maybe two thousand dollars. We're not taking the guy's ride. Period."

Jake sat with hands crossed in front of him. "Well, fuck," he said. "I thought you were this master criminal."

"I know who to take from and who not to."

Jake elbowed him again, several times. "Hey," said Mort.

"Get out. I want the window seat for while."

Mort opened the door and tumbled out onto the parking lot. Jake followed and held the door for him. Mort climbed back into the cab and took a spot in the middle of the seat. Jake got back in just as Gordon returned from the restaurant. He carried bags of food with him.

He climbed into the cab, tossed a bag to Mort and Jake, who tore it open and began eating the burgers and fries inside.

"A word of advice," said Gordon.

They turned to him.

"Don't ever get old," he said. "It's no fun."

"Why's that?" said Jake.

"Everything hurts and you have to take a piss all the time."

"Better old than dead," said Jake.

Gordon looked up for a few seconds. "I haven't decided about that yet," he said. He started the van and eased out onto the road. As they got going, Gordon let his gaze wander from the road to the waves.

"Thanks for the food," said Mort.

"Don't mention it. I suspect you generally steal your meals. Am I right?"

Mort stopped chewing with a wad of fries filling his mouth like cotton.

"Okay," said Gordon, "not exactly stealing meals but stealing the funds to get meals. That closer to it?"

"I don't know what you mean," said Mort.

"Look," said Gordon, "I'm not judging. I'm sure you have a history that makes such behavior understandable. Maybe even inevitable. I was just wondering why you haven't taken my vehicle yet. You've had lots of opportunities."

He talked about the theft of his car like he was talking about the weather. It seemed to have no importance to him at all.

"Why would you think we would take your van?" said Jake.

"Come off it, boys," he said with the same light tone. "When I saw you I knew you were trouble. I knew that turned over car was stolen."

"Why'd you give us a ride?" said Mort.

"Thought it'd be interesting. Learn a little about thievery. See, I think my son's been doing some stuff he shouldn't be. Needs me to hide his tracks. Using my accounting skills."

"You going to do it?" said Jake.

"Haven't quite decided yet."

"He's your kid," said Mort. "You've got to help him."

"Oh sure," said Gordon. "I'm going to help him, no doubt. The only question is, what is 'helping' in this case. Do I cover up his crime, or do I get him to face the music?"

There was no question in Mort's mind. His own father had abandoned him. That wasn't what family did to family. You didn't just run off.

"I think," said Jake before Mort could speak up, "that you hire someone else to do the dirty work. You don't need to get involved."

Gordon laughed. "Interesting take on it. Only thing is, that takes it out of the family. Harder to keep quiet."

Jake grunted his assent. "Guess you're right."

"Mort," said Gordon. "What about you? What do you think I should do?"

"None of my business," said Mort. "You know what you need to do. Or not do."

"I want your opinion," said Gordon. "What if it was you?"

"You mean what if I was an old guy with a kid who stole stuff for his construction business and wanted me to fix the books so it looked legit?"

"Yeah," said Gordon.

"I'm not an old guy who has to pee all the time."

"Just use your goddamn imagination," said Gordon. "Is that so hard?"

Mort bristled at Gordon's newfound irritation and suddenly wished they had taken the van from him. They could be driving down this road in peace, him and Jake.

"That depends on who you are," said Mort, speaking as mildly as Gordon had only a few minutes before.

"Who I am?" said Gordon, surprised by the question.

"You ever steal anything?"

Gordon looked like he was going to say something, then stopped. He wasn't sure how much to tell, Mort could see that. He had not admitted to anything, but he wanted to. This conversation was more of a confessional than a friendly chat. Mort could see that, too. The man had to get something off his chest.

"Twice," said Gordon.

"In your life?" said Jake.

Gordon nodded.

"You want to tell us about it?"

"First time was when I was a kid. About your age. I had a job at a hardware store. The owner liked me enough and trusted me enough that he let me close up. That was great. I had to lock the door and cash out the register and take the money to the bank. No big deal. But after a couple of months of this I figured out that no one expects the receipts to perfectly match the money in the till. It's impossible. So if I took a dollar or two every now and then out of the till, then made the deposit, no one would ever know."

"So that's what you did?" said Jake.

Gordon nodded.

"Just once?" said Mort.

Gordon shook his head. "A few times. Actually, more than a few. I worked for him for two years before heading off to college. I must have dipped into the till maybe a couple of dozen times."

"You said you only ever stole twice," said Mort.

"I'm counting the two years as one time."

"Okay," said Mort.

"Because I took from the same place over those two years. It was like one robbery stretched over a long period of time."

"I said okay," said Mort. "You don't have to keep justifying it."

"You ever tell the guy?" said Jake. "You ever give the money back?"

"Years later I mailed him how much I took from him, with a little extra for interest. I never told him though. Made sure it was anonymous. Typed the address on the envelope on a typewriter at the library so no one would ever know it was me."

"That make you feel better?" said Jake. "Giving back the money, I mean?"

"Not *really*. I should have told him. That would have been the right thing to do."

Mort shrugged. "He probably thought you were a great guy."

Gordon nodded. "I was, except for that one thing. When I quit he gave me a bonus, way more than he could afford, just to help me out going to school and all."

"Ouch," said Mort.

"Yeah," said Gordon. "He's dead now."

"Figured as much," said Jake.

"I'm beginning to get a picture of who you are," said Mort. "I steal from stores, but I don't think I would steal from an independent store like that. I go after chain places where the guys who own the chain make like millions of dollars a year."

"You think about that?" said Gordon.

"Damn right," said Mort.

"I think I underestimated you," said Gordon.

"Most people do," said Mort. "So what was the other time?"

"That one is harder to explain. I stole a watch."

"A watch?"

"I was on this cruise with my wife. Soon after I retired."

"So that would have been sixty years ago?" said Jake, then laughed at his own lame joke.

"Very funny," said Gordon. "I'm not *that* fucking old."

"Never mind," said Mort. "Tell me about the watch."

"Cruises are kind of boring, if you want to know the truth. You walk around the ship all day and then you eat and then you walk around some more and eat some more and sit around on the goddamn deck then listen to some asshole tell jokes on a stage." He stopped. "Ahhh, whatever. My wife likes them for some reason I can't figure out."

"The watch," said Mort.

"Yeah. It was the afternoon. We sat on deck chairs out in the sun. I have to admit, I did like the sun beating down on us. Warmed me up considerably. Just didn't see why we had to get on this stupid boat to get some sun."

"The watch the watch the watch," said Mort.

"Yeah. *Fuck.* The watch. Okay. Beside us was this younger couple, a man and woman, real young. I think they were newlyweds and this was their honeymoon. They nodded at us once, but mostly they paid no attention to us. Why would they? They had each other. The guy was in the lounge chair next to me, and there was a small table between us. He had taken off his watch and put it on the table. I noticed it right away. It was a pretty expensive watch, I could tell. It was self-winding. I figured the guy had to be rich to have a watch like that, or maybe it was a present from someone. In any case, I knew that watch was worth a couple of thousand dollars. Swiss made. Precision parts. I knew all that about the watch. I had seen other watches like it. I knew some guys who had watches like it.

"Anyway. The watch lay there beside me. I don't know why he took it off. They were holding hands and talking lovey-dovey to each other. It was like he completely forgot about his watch, which tells me it was new. Maybe she gave it to him for a wedding present. I don't know. But maybe he took it off because it was so new and he wasn't comfortable with it yet. Something. After a while they get up. Probably to go back to their room. Like I said, why not? That's what I would have done in their place.

"But here's the thing. He leaves the watch there on the table. My whole body feels alive at that point. Like suddenly something has been handed to me that I've wanted my entire life."

"The watch," said Mort.

"Fuck no," said Gordon. "It wasn't the goddamn watch."

"Then what?" said Jake.

"I wanted to call to the guy. Tell him he forgot his watch, but I couldn't make myself. My own wife was asleep beside me. Zonked right out and snoring like there was no tomorrow. I watched the guy turn the corner and disappear. I never went after him. People walked by in front of me. I nodded to them. They nodded back. I felt like I was bigger than a billboard, like my forehead had neon letters on it telling everyone I wanted that watch so much I was going to take it.

"And so I did. Just reached out my hand, grabbed the thing, and put it in my pocket." Gordon, with his left hand still on the wheel, rolled back his sleeve and turned his wrist so Jake and Mort could see the watch.

"That's sure a nice one," said Jake. "I can see why you couldn't resist it."

"But *I* didn't see why," said Gordon. "I still don't. I've seen stuff all my life that I wanted. I never just took it."

"Except for the money," said Mort.

"Except for that. And even then, it wasn't anything I *wanted.* It was more that I could do it, so I did it."

"What your wife say about the watch?"

"She doesn't know," said Gordon. "I keep it in the van, buried in the glove compartment. I like to wear it when I'm driving."

"That is pretty fucked up," said Mort, "if you don't mind me saying."

"I know," said Gordon.

"The guy ever come back for it?"

"Not that afternoon, at least not while I was there. I woke up my wife and said it was time for dinner, just so we could get out of there. I saw the guy a couple more times on the cruise. We nodded to each other, but he never asked me about his watch. So now it's mine." He looked down at it. Rolled his sleeve back over it. "I love this watch. I can't even say why, but I love having it and I love the way I got it."

Mort recognized the joy of having something that wasn't rightfully yours. He felt that euphoria all the time and knew that most people couldn't handle it. It was too strong. They got feelings of guilt from it. Which was crazy. They only had guilt because most people didn't have the guts to steal. Or they only stole in ways that society sanctioned: like making things cost way more than they had to. That was stealing. Or how about taxes. That was stealing, pure and simple. People worked hard for their money and then some fat cats in Washington DC picked your pocket for it? Those assholes didn't feel any guilt about taking your money. But relieving a convenience store of some of its profit? That was evil beyond evil if you listened to some folks. Mort didn't listen to them. They didn't know what they were talking about. Stealing was a basic survival instinct of human beings. He had thought that for some time, and now, listening to Gordon tell his stories about the thefts he had committed, he believed it even more strongly. Here was a stand up guy who wanted to help out his son and who probably had never done anything else wrong in his life, and something in him *made* him take that watch. It wasn't anything evil. It was just being human.

"Gordon," said Mort. "You're one of us. I say, help your son get away with his theft. He did it for his family, didn't he? Don't let him get in trouble for it."

"I thought you might say something like that," said Gordon.

"Is that what you wanted to hear, or what you didn't want to hear?"

Gordon gave a little noncommittal shrug. "Hard to say. Truth is, I never told anyone any of this. Ever."

"It was something you had to say," said Jake. "Stealing isn't the worst thing in the world someone could do. There's lots worse."

"I know. But doesn't mean it's right."

Mort was getting tired of the right/wrong debate.

"Forget that shit, Gordon," he said. "What you got to think of right now is survival. That's what it's all about."

"Damn right," said Jake. "The survival of your family."

THE PHILOSOPHICAL THIEVES. A whole van load of them.

I offered their remarks here at such length to give you a sense of the complexities of thievery. It isn't an easy thing to steal. It takes a lot of energy. It can be taxing to the emotional side of you. If you are of a certain bent, then stealing cuts to the core of your being and you aren't the same once you've stolen. You may think of yourself in a certain way, but theft is a stain. That's why the soup is so helpful to people. If you don't have any memories, then you can't feel bad. It's such a cleansing.

And why haven't I taken the soup, yet, you may ask?

None of your business.

The trio is approaching the outskirts of Santa Cruz. Let's see how their little trip ends.

YOUR GAS IS getting kind of low, Gordon," said Mort.

"We're almost there. We'll make it just fine."

Mort gestured down the road in front of them. "There's a gas station. Pull in and I'll pay for a fill up," he said.

"You don't have to do that. I've enjoyed the company."

"I feel like I should give you something. You may have saved our lives."

"Oh, I doubt that," said Gordon. "I just saved you a few steps. Someone else would have picked you up."

"Don't you have to pee?" said Jake.

"Damn. You're right."

"They have a bathroom," said Mort. "You go empty your bladder and I'll fill up your tank. It's like the balance of nature."

Gordon laughed. He slowed the van and turned into the gas station and stopped at one of the pumps. He got out of the van and went inside the food store. Jake pulled bills out of his pocket and fed a couple of twenties into the cash machine and put the hose in the van's gas tank, set it to stop automatically, and then pulled Jake out of the van and headed over to the road. They stuck out their thumbs and someone stopped within thirty seconds. They got into the back seat and Mort looked out the side window at the van. They went a long way down the road before Gordon came out of the store. He walked over to the van, then stopped and looked around, scratching his head.

"Where you boys headed to?" asked the driver, a hippie-looking guy with a bushy beard, smelly clothes, and a pony tail.

"Portland," said Jake.

"You're in luck," said the driver. "That's exactly where I'm going. You got money for gas?"

"Yup," said Mort.

"Excellent," said the driver. "This should be fun."

Chapter 17: Identity

I ARRIVED HERE so long ago I've forgotten how long, even though I haven't eaten any of the soup. My host was not present, so I wandered around on my own. It turns out he had more pressing matters, a lot of cases to deal with. I kind of slid under the radar. No matter. I've always been the independent sort. I saw the screening rooms, wondered why heaven would have movie theaters, and continued walking on. The whole affair looked exactly like a shopping mall. I had always felt comfortable in shopping malls, so I walked the corridors, passing storefronts with names and items I did not recognize or could not remember.

I arrived at the food court and realized I was hungry. People got hungry in heaven? It appeared so.

Of course, I was not in heaven. But on that first day, that was exactly where I thought I was. I had my own idea of heaven, many people do. I expected clouds and angels and harps, as many people do, but when I didn't see them I merely assumed my concept of heaven was mistaken and revised the picture in my head to conform with the reality as I was experiencing it then.

The food court was a little peculiar. There were no hamburger places, no Chinese food stalls, no cookie outlets, none of the food purveyors that I was used to in the malls I had been to. Instead, they all sold soup.

Who goes to a mall hoping to eat soup? I would guess next to no one.

But I was there. I was hungry.

I stepped up to one of the counters and looked at the menu. Oh, there was soup all right. Every kind you could think of. I saw gumbo, made with fresh okra pods; Spanish gazpacho, a puree of tomato and vegetables; cioppino, an Italian fish stew with tomatoes and shellfish; bird's nest soup from China, which, despite its name, I thought might be okay to try; tinola, a Philippine broth with chicken and green papayas; American corn chowder; a medieval beer soup, which the menu indicated should be poured over bread; a Korean rice soup with chicken, ginseng, and chestnuts called samgyetang; Chinese winter melon soup, which had been gently steamed for six hours; a cool cucumber soup; A Filipino soup of coconut milk, fruit, and tapioca called ginataan; your basic Japanese ramen; and more. The menu, in fact, looked to be infinite. It went down the wall, but the print grew smaller as it went, so by the time I got near the bottom I was looking at the tiniest print possible, and still the menu continued.

There were smells, too. Oh, the smells of the different soups. As I looked at each item on the menu, its smell seemed to permeate the air. How did they do that? I had no idea but assumed heaven had the technology to do just about anything it wanted to do.

Someone came out of the kitchen in the back. She wore a big wide apron streaked with stains. She had obviously been working hard.

"What can I get you?" she said.

Here a peculiar thing happened. I was ready to order some soup. I had settled on a nice chicken and rice because it reminded me of my childhood. I opened my mouth to tell her. Then closed it.

She looked at me.

Should I say an understanding passed between us? Behind me acres of tables with people at them slurping soup spread out like a kind of apocalyptic vision of conformity and acquiescence. It was unnerving and this woman in front of me, smiling like she knew something I wasn't supposed to know, didn't help.

"What happens if I eat the soup?" I said.

Her smile turned instantly stiff, like it had been painted on. "What happens? What do you think happens?"

"I don't know. Something you aren't telling me."

She stopped smiling. "Where's your avatar?" she asked.

"My avatar?"

"When you arrived, wasn't there someone to guide you here?"

"No. No one met me."

She put her hand to her mouth and chewed her knuckle for a second. "Wait here," she said, and turned and went back to her kitchen.

There was no possible way I was going to eat any of the soups they were offering me. Not after that little exchange.

I did not wait for her. I stepped away from the counter and hurried past the rows of soup slurpers. I noticed the same effect as with the menu: if I looked across the sea of diners, I saw that they extended further than it was possible to discern. They effectively receded to infinity. So many people. So much soup. Behind me others stood at counters, placed their orders and received their bowls, then walked over to tables where they sat and ate in silence. Complete silence. I'm no expert on social interaction, but the lack of conversation did seem peculiar. Isn't that why you ate with others, to partake of their friendship and camaraderie?

After they ate, they stood up, like zombies, if I may use the term, and walked out of the food court, a long line of them, in single file with heavy plodding steps. I felt a chill run through me. This wasn't heaven. How could it be? Where was the joy? Where was the happiness?

It did not occur to me that I might be in that other place, mostly because I never believed in that other place. I always liked the idea that even hell existed, but it would be empty. That made me think the universe was kind of okay, in the end, not malevolent or evil. That thought comforted me tremendously.

Now that I had passed on to whatever I had come to, suddenly it didn't seem so nice. Maybe hell wasn't empty and I was in it?

Oh, such are the thoughts of the newly dead.

You did know I died, right? I never explicitly said it, but I assumed by now that you got the idea.

Perhaps, in the interests of biographical completeness, I should tell you about that.

I was a shoplifter from way back. It may have started when I was just a kid. I'm not sure. What I do know is that from the time I could remember, I stole things from stores. The first thing was a licorice stick from a store in the neighborhood. I was there with my mother. I saw the red sweet ribbon of goodness, reached out for it, knew I was doing something wrong, and grabbed it and stuffed it into my pocket. I was maybe seven. All the rest of that day and maybe for the rest of the week, I thought something was going to swoop down and crush me. I truly thought I would die before long. Probably when my mother found out I had stolen the licorice. Back home, in my room, I couldn't even eat the thing. I thought eating it would compound the badness I had done. I tried tasting it, but it was vile. I couldn't make myself eat it. I tried, but no go. I was too young to understand what guilt was, but I was not too young to feel it. I was miserable beyond anything I had ever known before or since. I was sure the powers of the universe were going to crush me. The thought scared me so much that I began to compose my obituary. I didn't even know what an obituary was, but in my fevered condition I invented the form.

Neighborhood child, most evil person ever born, punished with death for her crime. All her family was so sad. They never knew just how horrible she was.

Then, after a few days, when I was not crushed by some cosmic hand of revenge, I realized I had gotten away with it.

At first that felt disconcerting. I had already heard crime doesn't pay. And if you do something wrong you will have to be punished.

But crime did pay. I stole something and thereby had an object I had not owned previously. That was amazing. And wonderful. Also, I wasn't punished. How great was *that?* I thought that if I had not been caught soon after the fact, then I was never going to be caught. I am amazed, now, at how sharp I had been. My early parsing of the situation was essentially correct: the more time that passes after the crime, the less likely you will be found out.

At seven, essentially powerless, such revelations are the stuff of which life-changing events are made. I had discovered a way to be powerful in the world. I never looked back. As the years progressed, as I grew up, I learned how to steal everything. When I was younger and still living at home, I was very careful to keep my thefts small and undetectable by my parents. I don't think they ever found out. That was a great source of pride to me. I was always the good and wholesome daughter to them. If they only knew.

As soon as I was old enough, I went out into the world on my own. I worked small jobs, part time, for the cash I needed for bills and such, but mostly I got the things I needed by stealing. I stole clothes, and learned to walk out of grocery stores with food. I never got caught, not once. I was so good, I looked so innocent, that mostly no one ever suspected I was capable of theft. That worked in my favor, obviously, but also I was very good at what I did and never committed any observable act that would contradict the benign impression people had of me.

And here's the thing that never stopped: the thrill of getting away with something. I constantly went back to theft because of that thrill.

I never thought it was wrong.

Let me rephrase that. I always *knew* it was wrong, but I never *felt* it was wrong. There's a big difference. I was aware of the cultural prohibition on stealing and was fully aware that most people in the culture considered theft, of whatever kind, to be bad. That was clear. However, I didn't share the belief. To me theft was not wrong. Why? Because everybody did it. They called it different things, but taking what wasn't yours was a basic human instinct, despite the platitudes against it. Or maybe there were platitudes against it because it *was* a basic human instinct, and a disruptive one at that, at least to those who already had wealth, power, and influence. It was certainly in their best interest to make everyone feel like theft was a horrible thing. A perfect way to keep the fruits of the earth to themselves.

Do I sound childish? Do my justifications make it seem like I have no adult sensibility at all? I will not argue with you on that point. Since my choice of career came out of a child's sense of entitlement and wonder, it is perhaps completely understandable that my justification of it would be the logic of a child.

But I grew old. I never married. Never had children. Didn't want them.

I stole and stole and stole and it was glorious beyond the telling. I never thought that any other kind of life could ever be as fulfilling or as rich with excitement and joy. I loved the world. Loved all of its abundance, because so much of that abundance was mine for the taking.

Here's how I died.

I was 53 years old. I needed some tissue so I stopped at a convenience store and walked the aisles nonchalantly, in the way I had learned to do. I found the shelf with the tissues and confirmed, in my peripheral vision, that the clerk at the register was not watching me. I picked up the small package of tissue and popped it into my jacket pocket in a quick motion, less than a half second that you would have had to have anticipated to even notice it had occurred. I was getting ready to walk out of the store when two guys came in who were obviously desperate. One of them caught my eye as he walked in. That was a mistake. Maybe the only real mistake of my entire life, but it was big.

He turned in my direction and stared at me. I looked away, but it was much too late. The other guy, his partner, went up to the register and demanded that the clerk give him money.

A peculiar feeling came over me. I wanted to pray. It didn't make any sense, but that was what I wanted to do. I didn't know any prayers. I remembered some hymns from when I had heard them on television when I was a child.

The guy who saw me looked at the door behind him, as if he was thinking about letting me go, then changed his mind. He pulled a gun from inside his jacket and pointed it at me and motioned for me to go in the direction of his partner. I thought to resist. These were amateurs, obviously. They had no sense of how to do a crime right. There was no way they weren't going to get caught. Maybe I should have run. He might have let me go. I don't know. It's hard to say, now.

I went toward the partner and clerk, who was busy stuffing money into a bag. There wasn't much. That was the thing. Stores don't have a lot of cash. These bozos didn't know that. Or didn't care. I don't know.

"Who's this?" said the first guy's partner.

"Just someone in the store."

"We can't have any witnesses," he said.

I caught the clerk's eye. He was so scared. I wanted to tell him there was no reason. Life was a blink in any case. No need to worry about it. That hymn, that famous hymn, "Amazing Grace," kept going through my head. Nuts.

I felt the tissue in my pocket. My last theft, and so small. A pity it wasn't something bigger to go out on.

The first guy swung his gun up straight at me.

I wanted to give the tissue to the clerk. A kind of atonement? Maybe. Or it could have been a boast. See, I took this and I'm proud of it. Even facing death, I feel happy that I took this from you.

I never had time.

I looked the guy with the gun right in the eye. "Please." I said.

He tightened his mouth and dropped his eyelids a fraction of an inch.

I closed my eyes.

I heard the beginning of a hard pop, but not the end.

AND THAT'S HOW I got to where I ended up.

The thing you need to know, about any place, is the rules. Not because you should necessarily follow them, although that's certainly allowed if you are so inclined, but because you need to know the consequences of your actions. If you violate certain rules you need to know what happens.

Those two guys, those inept thieves without sense enough to do things quietly and efficiently, ended up in a police shoot out, bleeding on the street. I never saw them again. Don't know where they went and don't care. Probably came up here, ate their soup like obedient little twits, and returned to life. Probably as slugs or something.

As for me, I kept walking through the mall. I left the food court behind, left the acres of tables and soup eaters.

The mall spread out before me. No one tried to stop me. I didn't see any signs warning me to stay away, or keep out.

I saw people in robes standing. They acknowledged me with quick little nods and a few murmured hellos. I answered back.

Did I have a big wound in my chest? Yes. Did it pour out blood as I walked. No. That would have been unseemly, yes? Besides the wound was temporary. It began healing pretty quickly.

And then something amazing happened. I found I was in robes as well. Just as I was walking, my clothes turned into robes. I sensed I had come to another zone in the mall.

Eventually I stopped walking. There were many other people in the vicinity. All wearing robes.

"You're an avatar?" said one of them.

My instincts for thievery had not died with that gunshot. "Of course," I said.

"You've refused the soup?"

"Of course. Who wouldn't?"

The robed one before me smiled. "Indeed." He clapped his hand on my back and pulled me into the circle of his friends.

I'm not saying this was the greatest thing that could have happened to me, but it was close. I never took the soup. That was the key. You take the soup and all your memories are gone. Every one of them: poof! Like they never existed.

I didn't want that. I loved my memories with the soup. I was going to keep them for as long as I could. Someone would have to steal them from me if I was going to lose them. That was the only way.

I learned what it meant to be an avatar. We helped people go back. Took away their memories. Assigned them a new spot. We could have fun with that, I could see. Some avatars remained for eons. Others got bored and took the soup and moved on. I wasn't sure where I was in that scheme. I would at least do the work for a little while.

It was fun to take memories from people. Give them clean slates. I took to it with gusto. I watched and marveled.

People had so many resources.

They could learn to steal anything.

Chapter 18: Words

Susie watched Judy and her friends bring down the oak and did not interfere. When the tree was completely destroyed, Susie approached Judy where she stood amid chips of fresh oak flesh littering the ground.

"You came for a story," said Judy. She took in great gulps of air. Her face was wet from sweat, cheeks bright red. "Did you get one?"

"I think so," said Susie.

"Yeah," said Judy. "I think so, too."

Some of the residents, who had come out to help Judy by cutting up the limbs into smaller pieces, clapped Judy on the back and told her how amazing she was. Judy acknowledged them with a slight nod of her head, like this was nothing.

And, in truth, it was nothing. She had cut down a tree. Happens every day. But to Susie it had the air of something bigger and more important.

"I'll try not to identify you in the story," said Susie. "Since you could get in trouble over the tree."

"They won't bother me now," said Judy. "Maybe years ago, when I was first starting Faith Village, they might have. But now they are resigned to my existence."

"I wouldn't be too sure about that," said Susie. "That sort of thing can change pretty quickly. What were you feeling as you cut the tree down?"

"Feeling?"

"Wait. Back up. What made you cut the tree down in the first place?"

Susie had put her notebook away.

"It was—" said Judy. "I don't know. I'm not sure I can explain it. A fog came over me and all I could think about was that tree."

"You'd noticed it before?"

Judy looked up at the sky, overcast and gray. It lent a melancholy mood to the day. "Sure," she said. "That tree's been here all along. I loved that tree."

"I'm sure others loved it, too."

Judy nodded.

"So if you loved it?"

"It made me think of my lost son."

"Your lost son? I thought you didn't want to talk about him."

Judy shook her head and put her face in her hands. She held it for several seconds, then looked up into Susie's eyes. "I don't expect you to understand. I don't expect anyone to understand. It was just that at that moment I felt this pressure on me. Like if I didn't do this thing I would suffocate. It sounds crazy—"

"Not necessarily," said Susie.

"Sounds crazy to me."

Susie nodded. "What intrigued me was how your friends jumped in without even thinking. They are very loyal to you."

"Sure," said Judy. "We support each other. That's what Faith Village is all about."

The oak tree was mostly gone, all the pieces of it cut up and carted off to the various tents and shacks, to be used later in the wood stoves and makeshift fireplaces.

"You didn't want any of the pieces?" said Susie.

Judy extended her foot and pressed on some of the chips, pushing them into the soft ground. Ax chops and saw scars marked the stump. The raw yellow wound exuded a deep and satisfying odor, more inviting than freshly baked bread. Susie liked the smell. It made her think of spring.

"I don't think I could take any of the pieces," said Judy. "They'd just make me sick."

Susie nodded. "The aroma of them?"

"That," said Judy. "And something else. Some spirit in them."

"Spirit?" said Susie.

Judy shrugged. "I don't know how else to say it. Are we done? Let's be done, please. I need to get back home and rest up a little."

"Of course," said Susie. "Thank you for your time."

Judy turned from her and began walking back to her tent. Susie watched her open the front flap, walk inside, and zip the tent closed from the inside. Susie went and stood next to the stump of the oak and bent down to the ground and picked up one of the chips that Judy's ax had liberated from the body of the tree. It felt smooth on one side, rough on the other. Ridges, closely spaced like fingerprints, bumped against her own fingerprints where the grain curved over the surface. The edges of the chip were cut smooth and it felt heavy with tree sap, like a bandage weighed down with blood.

Susie felt like a murder, of a sort, had taken place here, but she didn't want to dwell on the thought. After all, it was a tree, nothing more. People cut down trees all the time and no one ever thought of it as murder, except maybe crazy eco freaks. Not that there weren't plenty of those around. But Susie would never consider herself one of those. Still, there was a void in the world now. Susie felt it as a void in her heart. She wanted to sit on the stump, but the shape of it, the way Judy had cut it on the round, didn't lend itself to that. She put the chip into her pocket. Maybe it would help her when she was writing the story. It could give her sense memories of this place.

She stood next to the stump for several minutes, long enough to begin questioning her own sanity, then stepped out of Faith Village. She walked a block or two, past warehouses and railroad tracks near the village. Workers stood on loading docks, smoking cigarettes and drinking from plastic cups. They nodded at her and she nodded back. She got to a main street, one with four lanes of traffic, and turned the corner and walked until she came to a bus stop where she stopped and waited for the bus to arrive. A couple of other people stood with her. No one looked at anyone else.

The bus came and heaved to a stop. Susie and the other people shuffled close to the door and rearranged themselves into single file, all of them polite to each other, as though this boarding of the bus was the most intricate thing you could imagine.

Susie took a seat in the back and pulled out her notes and looked them over. There was so much good stuff here. *HomeTown* should be happy to get it.

No one sat beside her, which was fine with Susie. She didn't need any company right now. She had work to do. She was a journalist on a story.

The bus stopped a block from *HomeTown*'s offices. Susie had not told Judy that she had no contact with the editors of *HomeTown*. This story was completely speculative. If *HomeTown* didn't take it, she didn't know what she would do with it.

She walked into the building and down the hall to a small office way in the back, barely bigger than a closet. Two older guys sat at desks behind computers. Piles of paper and old editions of *HomeTown* littered every free surface.

"Yeah?" said one of the men.

"I've got a story for you," said Susie.

"That right?" said the man. He wore glasses, which he now slid down his nose to look over them at her.

"It's about the woman who started Faith Village."

"Judy Bryant. We've done stories on her."

"Not like this one," said Susie.

"You know Judy?"

"I just met her."

The other man, who had been tapping on his computer up to now, ignoring Susie, looked up. "Just met her?" he said with a smirk.

"She cut down a tree."

"Huh," said the first man.

The second one returned to his screen.

"With an ax. She got possessed and attacked this tree."

"I don't think that's news," said the first man. "Even for us."

"Don't you get it?" said Susie. "She's not the same person she was. She's changed. The Judy from a few years ago would never have cut down a tree."

The man smiled. "How do you know, if you just met her."

"I read all your stories about her."

The man studied her carefully. "You write the story yet?"

"I'm going to."

"Come back when you got something to show me."

Susie was elated. "Then you'll print it?"

"I didn't say that. I'll *look* at it. That's all I can promise."

"Okay," said Susie. "When do you close?"

"We're here all night. Deadline."

"I'll be back," said Susie. "Today."

The two men looked at each other and smiled. "We can't wait," said one of them.

Susie nodded and left the building. Okay, they didn't say yes, but they did say maybe. That was something. The main library was just a few blocks from here. She walked to it, quickly, as though her life depended on her getting there in the shortest time possible, and she went up to the third floor and found herself a quiet table in a corner, one with a computer. She logged onto the internet and began searching for an article that began with a description of a homeless encampment. She spent a good ten minutes diligently researching until she found a pretty good essay on a pretty obscure site of a very small circulation magazine. The hit counter was in the low double figures. Perfect, she thought. An easy steal. Hardly anyone's seen this.

She copied the first page or so of the article and pasted it into a word processor document. She read it again, with her byline at the top of the page. It looked real good. Perfect for her needs. The editors at *HomeTown* would be completely unable to resist this once she brought it in to them.

She typed out her notes in the same document.

As she worked, she considered the complete turn around her life had taken. Up until yesterday she had never thought about writing for a newspaper. Indeed, she had never thought much about writing anything at all.

Then she had that dream. An odd thing it was, unlike any dream she had ever had before. Whereas most of her dreams, when she remembered them, were incoherent, surrealistic, and kind of silly, this one was more like a set of instructions. In it she looked into a mirror, one of those distorting mirrors that made your waist fat and your head small, and the image, the warped image of herself, talked to her from inside the mirror. It told her she needed to leave her job, the one where she went to a shoe store every day and sold shoes to people. That part of her life was over. She was to go to Faith Village, the place where all the homeless people lived, and talk to Judy Bryant. She was then to write an article about her for the homeless paper, *HomeTown*.

The dream was so clear, so precise, and so adamant about what she should do that Susie had no decision to make. She called her boss and told her she quit.

Then Susie put on her jacket and took the bus to Faith Village and found Judy. All the while she had no idea why a dream would tell her to do these things.

And now, seated at the library computer and tapping out what she hoped would be a real story, she began to doubt the reality of the dream. Which was absurd. Because a dream wasn't real in the first place.

Doesn't matter, doesn't matter.

Bigger things going on here. She was not in charge of her own fate, at least not at the moment. Wasn't it amazing that she had this dream and was told where to go, at precisely the same time that something momentous happened to Faith Village and Judy Bryant?

At least, she thought it was momentous. Wasn't it? Cutting down a tree like that? She supposed it was her job to make it momentous.

She read over the opening paragraphs again and then began telling her account of what happened to Judy Bryant. And the tree. She put the wood chip down on the table next to the computer. It was startling in its brilliant purity. A pale yellow, but pale never looked so bright, so otherworldly. Somehow the presence of this chip of oak tree spurred her on. She wrote the article, the first one she had ever done, in a flash of inspiration, not stopping for a moment during the next half hour until she was done. When she thought about the process later, it felt to her like the article wrote itself, that she was not involved with the process at all.

When she came to the end, she didn't even read it over. She simply pressed the print button and went down the aisle to the printer to retrieve the pages. Then she walked out of the library and back to the editors at *HomeTown*. The editors both looked up as she walked in.

"Oh," said one. "You're back. Need more instruction?"

"I finished," said Susie.

He looked doubtful. He laughed. Susie didn't mind. She would probably have laughed in his place. He held out his hand. Susie dropped the five pages on his palm. He looked at the top sheet.

"You didn't double space," he said.

"I didn't know I had to," she said. The truth was, she didn't even know what double space meant.

"You've done this before, haven't you?"

Susie shook her head. "Never."

"Hmmm," he said and began reading.

Susie stood in front of him as he read. She felt her head turn warm. She was so uncomfortable having him read her pages while she stood in front of him. It felt like he knew way too much about her now. Like he had seen her naked.

"I like the opening," he said. "Very tight." He got to the end of page one and passed it page to the other guy who grabbed it and read it quickly.

"Not bad," he said. "Does she keep it going?"

"Gets even better," said the first editor. He read through to the end while Susie felt her head expand. They liked her story? That was the best news. Her dream was going to be fulfilled, less than twelve hours after she dreamed it.

The second guy read the last couple of pages while the first guy put his hands behind his head and looked at Susie. "Where have you written before?"

"I told you," said Susie, "this is the first thing I've ever done."

"That's hard to believe. This is first rate stuff."

Susie shrugged.

"Did you suddenly wake up this morning and get religion about the homeless?"

"Something like that."

"You have no clips?"

"Clips?"

"Material from your previous publications."

"No," said Susie. "I'm telling you the truth. There are no previous publications."

"If you say so. Look for it in the next edition. It'll hit the street in a couple of days."

"Great," said Susie. "Thanks."

"If you have anything else, bring it in."

"Oh," said Susie. "I won't. That's it. What I did there is all I'm ever going to do."

She left the office and returned to the street. She fingered the wood chip in her pocket. It was still a little damp. And warm from her pocket. She had a feeling that she would keep this chunk of oak for the rest of her life. She felt a little bewildered by her day. How could someone go to bed as one person and wake up as a completely different person?

And what did she do now? Go back to her job at the shoe store? After she had seen a part of life she did not even know existed before? After she had seen a homeless woman wreck a tree just because something in her soul told her to do it?

No, it was impossible now.

The only thing was, she didn't know what was possible, now, here, in her new life.

Chapter 19: Shelter

"TELL ME AGAIN," said Jake, "how it was wrong to take the old man's van, but it was right to take the hippie's car."

Mort was driving. They were north of Redding, California, on Interstate Five, heading into the mountains that would take them over the pass and into Oregon.

"Gordon was an okay guy," said Mort. "He was like our friend. He gave us a ride, a long one, and he gave us food, and he told us about his life."

"The hippie guy gave us a ride."

"But no food or stories."

"Stories?"

"About what he stole."

"The watch, you mean?" said Jake.

"Yeah, the watch. And the money. It was obviously a big deal to him, hard to tell it, but he told us."

"That's the difference?" said Jake, obviously doubting it could be the difference.

"Louisa always told me you don't piss where you swim."

"Who the fuck's Louisa?" said Jake.

"She raised me after my father ditched me."

"She told you not to pee in the pool? Everyone knows that."

"Jesus, were you born stupid, or did you have to study? It means you don't mess up the place you're living in. You don't screw with your friends. Get it?"

Jake shook his head. "I think you make all this stuff up as you go along and it doesn't make any sense. You liked the old guy, so you left him alone. You didn't like this last guy because he made us pay for gas, so you took his car. Simple as that."

Mort looked ahead to where the freeway started going up. It looked like a pretty steep incline and the tops of the mountains were lost in dark clouds. Did that mean a storm was coming? He used to see clouds like that in Tucson just before the monsoons unleashed torrents of rain. But they didn't get monsoons in Northern California, did they? Weren't they only a desert thing? Mort thought so, but he wasn't sure.

"You okay to drive for a while?" asked Jake. "I'm going to sleep."

"Whatever," said Mort, glad to have him quiet for a while. Jake sure asked a lot questions.

He endured Jake wrestling around on the seat, thrashing this way and that, trying to find a comfortable place for his head. Nothing seemed to work. Finally he took his jacket from the back seat and bunched it up into a makeshift pillow, jammed it up against the window, and put his head on it. He was snoring in a few minutes.

By that time they were in the hills. Some light rain fell. Mort turned on the wiper blades, and they chattered across the windshield. Jake had made a few points, Mort had to concede. It wasn't easy to be consistently ethical about stealing. The hippie wasn't so bad. Except he kept going on and on about his wife—his old lady—he called her. How she had decided he wasn't worth being around anymore and she found some other guy and ran off with him. It was obviously the most important thing in the guy's life, ever, but it was beyond boring to Mort, so when they stopped for a late lunch and the guy went to the bathroom, Mort slid into the driver's seat and drove away. Without even thinking. And why not? Stealing cars was the most natural thing in the world for Mort. He wasn't sure why that was, but he didn't fight it. He had free and quiet transportation for a while. At least until he had to ditch the car. You didn't keep a stolen car for long. You had to drive it hard to get away from the scene and you had to keep it for only a short time, before all the cops everywhere got on the lookout for it. And you had to obey all the rules because if you were ever stopped they'd know it was stolen in half a second.

Right after he took the car, Jake said he shouldn't have. The hippie guy was nice. And he had a sad life. He thought he'd be happy with his wife for the rest of his life and then she ditches him. Jake told Mort he should understand, since he was ditched himself. Not by a woman or anything, but his father.

Mort's head began hurting, listening to Jake. He was getting to be worse than the hippie. The worst thing was that Jake didn't even try to understand Mort's way of thinking about stealing. He was never going to get ahead in the world if he didn't start thinking about how and why to steal.

Mort had asked the hippie if he ever stole. The guy clammed up. He was suspicious of them. Like if he told them about what he stole (and Mort knew there was something because everyone stole, everyone who was ever alive stole something in their lives) then they'd have power over him and be able to blackmail him. That was the craziest thing ever, but that's exactly what he thought. Mort could tell. That made Mort dislike him right there. Who was he to think Mort was some kind of agent for the police? It was insulting, is what it was. If he had told about how he shoplifted something when he was a kid, or took something from his Mom's purse, or even sneaked into a movie without paying, Mort would have left him alone with his vehicle and his heartache. But since he didn't want to do any of that, screw him. His car was Mort's now. On a short term loan. Mort laughed at the thought: He wasn't stealing a car, he was renting one with a very good rate.

The rain started falling hard. The wipers stopped their chattering and swept sheets of water away from the windshield. Traffic around them slowed down considerably. Mort didn't see why. The freeway had widened to three lanes, with the big eighteen-wheelers taking the right most lane as they creeped up the hill. Mort took the car around them and got into the left lane and revved the engine to climb the hill quicker. He began passing cars that had slowed down, mostly because the trucks had slowed down, he thought. Not because they had to.

He turned on his lights. The sun must have been setting, except he couldn't see it with all the clouds.

He got to the crest of the hill and the road leveled out. He had passed all those cars going up the hill, so now he had clear road in front of him. He was tempted to speed through this part of it, but he remembered he had to keep his speed under the limit.

The road straightened out, too. No curves. It looked like he was up in the mountains. He saw the bottoms of white covered peaks off in the distance. Jake, beside him, had his mouth hanging open, with his head rocking against the window, lightly going thump thump thump.

Mort looked ahead. The road seemed to go on for some time. He thought it might be nice to be in Jake's position. He'd been driving for a while and a break would be just the thing. Some sleep. Not long, just enough to get his energy back.

He woke up with the car's headlights illuminating a flash of bushes going across his field of vision from left to right so fast that he only registered a flickering array of shadows. He was aware of Jake screaming (the idiot screamed!) and he put his foot on the brake but it didn't do any good since the car was spinning. Somehow they had drifted into the median. The car's wheels slid over grass. They were going sideways and the back end hit a barrier that the California Department of Transportation had put up in the middle of the median to keep cars from going into a small creek that crossed under the freeway. Metal squealed against concrete. Mort and Jake were both thrown to one side, and then everything was completely still.

Except for the wipers. They still went back and forth. Mort turned them off and also turned off the lights. The engine had stopped. Mort turned the ignition key to try to start it up again, but nothing happened. The engine or the battery must have been damaged. He didn't think he could fix it, not in the dark like this.

"What the fuck?" said Jake.

"Come on," said Mort. "We've got to get out of here."

He opened the door and stepped onto the wet grass. It was cold and raining outside. They were in for a miserable night.

Jake was still looking around. Mort went around the other side and opened the passenger door. "Get out. We can't be here when the cops find this car."

He grabbed Jake's arm and pulled him out. Jake tumbled onto the grass and got up on his knees.

"What'd you do?" he said. "Are you crazy?"

"Fell asleep," said Mort. "I guess. It happens."

"It happens?" said Jake with an edge in his voice. "It *happens?*"

Mort didn't see any cars stopping for them. That was good. Someone calling 911 on their cell phone was the worst thing that could happen to them right now.

"Let's start walking," said Mort. He looked across the highway to what appeared to be barbed wire hung between a series of wooden posts. Probably someone's land and they didn't want people on it. That was one thing that was hard to steal, thought Mort: Land. You couldn't just take it, you had to be clever about it, use paperwork. Mort admired people who could steal land.

Jake stood. "Why no," he said. "I don't think I'm hurt. Thanks for asking."

"Don't you get it?" said Mort. "If we get caught with the car then we go to jail. You want to go to jail?"

Jake glared at him.

"I'm going across the highway," said Mort. "Check out that ranch, if that's what it is. You can come with or stay here. I don't give a rat's ass."

He went to the edge of the northbound lanes and stood on the shoulder. It was too dark and deserted to hitchhike here. No one would see them until they were too far past to slow down. And who would even want to slow down for two guys out alone in a deserted area on a night like this? Had to figure they were two guys up to no good. That's what Mort would have thought.

Jake came up beside him. He had put on his jacket and lifted the back over his head for shelter from the rain.

"How could you have fallen asleep?" he said.

"Let it go," said Mort. He saw headlights way down the highway. Plenty of time to cross. He sprinted across the lanes of traffic. The vehicles came up quicker than he expected. He heard their rumble behind him, then turned and saw Jake was still on the other side.

"Come on," said Mort, shouting across the lanes.

"This is a good way to get killed," Jake shouted back at him.

"Yeah," said Mort. "And what do you have to live for?"

Jake didn't answer. He waited half a minute for a gap in the traffic and ran across the lanes and began walking with Mort down the slope to the fence, strung with red "No Trespassing" signs every twenty feet.

"Someone doesn't want us in here," said Jake.

"You ever hear of an easement?" asked Mort.

"Easement?"

"It's this thing where if a path has been used for a long time, then even if someone comes along and buys the land that the path is on, they can't keep people from going on it because it's like a tradition and you can't break a tradition."

"There's no path here," said Jake.

Mort stopped at the fence, which was three strands of barbed wire between wooden posts. He stepped on the bottom strand so it sunk down to the ground,and pushed the middle strand up so it touched the top strand.

Jake, with his jacket still deployed over his head, looked like he was considering the advisability of staying with Mort. Mort waited. Jake had no other option.

Jake bent down and stepped between the space Mort had created. Then he clamped his foot on the bottom strand and pushed the middle strand up so Jake could follow. When they were both on the other side of the fence, Mort spread his hands. "Two people following the same route. Probably on a trail that other people used. I'd say that qualifies as a path."

"So we made an easement?"

"Yup," said Mort. "Let's go this way." He pointed to a blurry building in the distance that looked like a barn. He thought they could spend the night there. Or at least be somewhere dry until the rain stopped.

They started walking. The ground was soggy and soft. They passed piles of cow shit. Mort kept on the lookout for cattle. If there was a bull, they could be in trouble. But no livestock approached them.

"What would get us into more trouble?" said Jake. "Getting caught stealing a car, or getting caught trespassing?"

"Hard to say," said Mort. "Except people will shoot you quicker if you're on their land than if you just take their car."

Jake didn't have anything to say to that.

It felt like it was getting colder and colder all the time. Mort started shivering. The blurred spot of color he had seen earlier was not resolving into a barn, as he had hoped. In fact, it looked more like a billboard now.

"Crap," he said.

"Yeah," said Jake. "Crap."

Mort thought they had been walking away from the freeway, but the road had taken a curve and come back on them. Whoever owned this land had put up a sign. As they got close to it, the sound of traffic became stronger. They dipped down into a depression in the land, then rose up. The headlights of traffic glared at them. The sign directed people to the next exit to stop for a home cooked meal at a restaurant.

"Let's go there," said Jake.

"It's ten miles away," said Mort. "Can't you read?"

"Fuck," said Jake. Then he perked up. "Hey," he said. "That's not a sign. It's a truck trailer."

Mort, who had turned his attention to the road, trying to figure out a way to get another ride, turned back to the sign and stepped toward it. "Hey," he said. "You're right."

They had passed several old truck trailers earlier in the day. They were obviously too old for service, but people had parked them close to the road and turned them into makeshift billboards. This was one of those.

"Let's see if the doors open," said Jake.

They ran to the end of the trailer. The doors were closed and a padlocked chain was wrapped around the latch.

"Dammit," said Jake.

"Don't give up yet," said Mort. He went around to the side of the trailer. The tires were old and the supports that held up the end without the tires were bent and rusty. The trailer itself had a pretty serious accordion fold in it, which was probably why it was taken out of service in the first place. It was a beat up old trailer, but if they could get into it, they could at least dry out and get a little comfortable.

Mort bent down and looked underneath. That's where truckers often kept tools they needed to maintain their rigs on the road. Probably whoever had this trailer had taken away the tools, but you never knew. The little bay where the tool box was sometimes kept was gone.

Mort looked down in the grass under the trailer. Jake came around the other side and ducked his head. "Having fun under there?"

"I'm looking for a crowbar or something."

"Let's get out of here. We aren't getting into this thing."

"Don't give up. Even if we can't get in, we can sit under the trailer."

"The ground's all wet here," said Jake.

"Not as wet as out there," said Mort.

"You have an answer for everything."

"That's the only way to survive," said Mort. He ran his hand under the cab and waddled down to the back of the trailer, to where the wheels were. It was dark and he was a little concerned that he might run into snakes or rats but nothing like that happened. He put his hand on one of the back tires and touched something.

Bingo.

He grabbed it. His hands were numb with cold, but he recognized the object easily. It was a key.

"Got it," he said as he came out from under the trailer, directly into the rain. It spattered against his face.

"What did you get?" said Jake from the other side.

Mort didn't answer. He went to the padlock and inserted the key and turned it. Seized up with rust, it didn't budge at first, and he felt a strong disappointment deflate him, but he wiggled the key around and kept trying until it scraped something inside the padlock and snapped it open. Jake clapped his hands. "Oh man," he said. "Let's get inside."

Mort swung the big door open. The smell of turpentine assaulted him. It was dark inside, but he thought he could make out piles of paint cans to one side.

"They must keep this stuff here for when they need to redo the sign. Or touch it up and stuff."

"I don't care," said Jake. "It's dry, that's all I need."

He put his hands on the edge of the platform and lifted himself up and onto the cab bed, then rolled over and put out his hand for Mort. Mort grabbed his wrist and Jake pulled him in.

The turpentine smell didn't last too long. Either it escaped into the outside air when they opened the back, or they got used to it. Either way, they were happy to be there. They pushed the brushes and cans to one side. Mort heard a leak, drip dripping at the other end of the trailer, but there was a slight slope in that direction, so water did not come to where they were. The cab bed was dry. Metallic pings sounded through the trailer: raindrops hitting the top. It wasn't warm, but at least they weren't getting rained on anymore.

"How long you think this rain will last?" said Jake.

"I'm not a fucking weatherman," said Mort.

"I hate rain."

"You hate rain but you're going north to where it rains all the time," said Mort. "You're kind of a low watt bulb, aren't you?"

"I didn't fall asleep when I was supposed to be driving," said Jake.

Mort's eyes were starting to get used to the inside of the trailer. It wasn't completely dark. A gap where the accordion fold was let in a tiny sliver of air, and with it a thin dribble of star light, enough to make him think he wasn't in pitch darkness.

"I feel like we're hobos on a train," said Jake.

"Except we're not moving," said Mort.

"Yeah. Plus hobos usually have cans of beans or something, don't they? I'm hungry. Aren't you hungry?"

"Go to sleep," said Mort. "We'll find something to eat in the morning."

Chapter 20: Soup

You know the story of Prometheus. He stole fire from the gods and paid for it the rest of his life. Here's my question: why didn't the gods steal it back? Did they have power or didn't they? Looks to me like they didn't. Not real power anyway.

That's the position I was in. I had sent Rex to that tree. Nothing wrong with that, it's part of my power. Even part of my privilege if you want to call it that. After he took down that saguaro, it only seemed fitting to lock him into a plant. So now there he was: dismembered and strewn about Faith Village. And it wasn't like he was just *in* the tree. The way it works is that Rex *was* the tree, just as earlier he *was* the guy who took Melville Bryant from his natural mother.

So, just to give you an idea of what goes on for one of these people, let's listen in on Rex for a while.

DON'T KNOW WHERE I am. Nothing to see. Feel motion. So many parts. I was whole, now scattered. A body. I have a body, but it won't stay together. Sap running. I'm bleeding. Cuts everywhere. The air scrapes across my cuts. I've become pain and reach for something to ease it. What am I? How can I be in so many places? Darkness everywhere, but the warmth of something enveloping me. I take some of it in, through my leaves. Leaves? What are leaves? I don't know but I have them. I used to grab the ground, firm. Now my feet are lopped off. I float. My leaves are still there, somewhere. I feel them as phantoms, floating about in the void. Come back come back. The cutting is done. But now parts of me are burning. Oxygen laces into my flesh, so hot, my cells are collapsing, blackening. I reach for something, but I have no motion. Can no longer move, but am moved. All the parts of me. I am so aware, but what good is awareness now? What does it do for me? There must be something else. Existence cannot be simply pain. I take a moment to compose myself. An inventory of what I have lost. I am many where once I was one. But the many are not connected. We are floating islands drifting in nothing. I want to remember. Need to find something before the hacking. There is something about being here I cannot understand. How did I get here? Who rendered me separate from my selves? Why do I have separate selves? I should be one. Make me one again. I'm losing track of all the pieces. How many? That one and that one and that one and so many more. Reaching for one another. But we don't find each other. We are broken. We are sad creatures, chunks of creatures. We hope for unity but live as parts of things. Sad, so sad. The ground is still there, for some of us. Touching not at the roots (where are the *roots?*) but at the bark. Ground against bark. So wrong. I wish I was in my roots. They are there, the roots. They grab soil, take it for themselves. They steal water from the ground and flush it through the system. My system. Or they used to. Now they writhe. Nothing for them to do. A stump above them. Seeping tears.

AND SO ON. You see the futility of a tree's thoughts, especially a cut down tree?

Now let's drop in on Judy's thoughts.

SUSIE, WHAT KIND of a name is that for a reporter? I shouldn't have talked to her. Shouldn't have shown her my crazy side. Not that I'm crazy. Except for cutting down that tree. What was I thinking? Why did I need to see that tree destroyed? Nuts. Nuts. I am cuckoo. Living in the streets does that to people. I need a job. No. I have a job. My job is living. Staying alive even with Melville gone. Oh but, Susie. She saw me chop down a tree. It's probably historic. A historic tree. The citizenry will be after me. I'll be the crazy homeless woman, batty, with an ax. Today the tree, tomorrow she'll be in your house chopping you up. Would that be so bad? Some people need chopping up. The one who put me here. Who is it? Who took my son? I'd chop him up in a minute. Or her. Probably a her. Some woman who couldn't get a baby of her own. She took mine. Maybe it's okay. Maybe he's still alive. Yes, he's alive. Has to be. No one takes babies just to kill them. Oh, I can't say kill. I don't want him killed. Please please please make him be alive. Don't make him be like the tree I just killed. Susie. What will I do about Susie? Nothing. I can't do anything. She will write her story. She will do what she wants to do. Wish I believed in something. God. It's hard when God does something like this to you. He was a small child. Why did he have to be taken from me? Please let him be alive. Maybe there is a God. God God God. The word makes me sick. Stop it stop it stop it. There's nothing to do about it now. Please, God, make him be alive. Even if he wasn't alive up to now, just wave your hand and stroke your beard and bring him back to life. Bring him back to me. Me me me. That tree. I did that. I killed the tree. I have power, God, but it's a reverse power now. I took life, but once I gave life. Remember that? Me. I did it. Oh that tree. I wanted that tree so dead. Susie saw me. Why was I so interested in killing? Did you take my son because I stole from my company? Couldn't you have just taken my house? Wouldn't that have been fair? Not my son. Why my son? If I had a job I'd just have money. That's all. I don't need a job. I just want my son. My baby. I would have given the money back. People do that. They change. What is so bad about stealing, anyway? Everyone steals. Oh, God, why did I kill that tree? Someone tell me. The tree had something in it. It called to me. Oh God. My hands are on my head. I'm pacing. Stop it. Stand still. I can't. The city will come and shut us down. We'll be forced to leave. I can't move to another city. How would I do that? I can't just walk somewhere. This city has to leave us alone. I know. I'll confess. I'll go to city hall and tell them it was me. I cut down the tree, but I'll plant more. I'll plant so many tress no one will care about one old oak tree. It would have come down in a storm anyway. All trees do. It's not like they live forever. Oh, Susie. Why did you have to come here today? Why did I have to read the thoughts of a stupid old oak? What was in that oak? What made it so evil? I'm not evil. I stole some money, that's all. There is much worse evil in the world. Much worse. I'm so hungry. I need food. I should go out and fly my sign. I'm still pacing. I'm hungry. Wish I could eat an oak tree. Wish that oak tree never lived. Wish so much. Wish I never left Melville alone. Wish wish wish. No use to wish. Just do.

You see the contrast, I'm sure. I thought my little experiment in placement would give her more satisfaction. This was the best way to allow her to kill the person who stole her child without killing an actual real live person, since that would do nothing more than get her into prison. Now, granted, she might not have cared. She might have gotten supreme satisfaction from offing the soul that got her into her current situation and made the last two decades of her life something like a slow torture, thinking about her son. But it didn't seem right to tempt her with that particular opportunity. I didn't want to see her behind bars. Who would?

However, my alternate plan failed, didn't it? She appeared not to derive any satisfaction from the act of dispatching Rex in his current incarnation.

Is this my fault? Yes, in a way. I should have simply deployed Rex randomly, as I do with all my cases. Or most of them. It's just that sometimes, when the mood strikes me, I like to try different things. What is the point of having minor godlike powers if you don't get to have fun with them sometimes?

But, like Prometheus, I can't undo what I did. Judy killed the tree, but did not have satisfaction. I cannot now unkill the tree and thereby allow Judy to be more content. I do wish I had that ability.

What I wish I could do is arrange matters so that Melville, aka Mort, could be reunited with his mother. Sounds so simple, doesn't it? But Mort is his own free agent. I cannot interfere. Not while he is still alive. Now, if he were to die, then I could send him down to close proximity with his mother, so they could be reunited in some way. Perhaps he could be a young down-on-his-luck person who wanders into Faith Village one day and Judy undertakes to help him survive. Or, conversely, he could be a rich benefactor who is moved by the plight of the homeless and helps his mother into a life off the streets and becomes her friend. Or some other such scenario in which they mutually help each other and come to know each other as kindred spirits. Such a turn of events would be possible to engineer. But it requires the death of Melville.

Don't blame me. I didn't make the rules.

Ah, but, you say, Melville is slowly making his way up towards Portland. Surely they will be reunited then.

Perhaps. I cannot say. I do not predict the future.

When I first got here, I thought such things were possible. I hung out with the other white-robed avatars and asked them about life in heaven. I thought it was heaven.

"This is not heaven," said one of them, a young kid, maybe eight years old. She looked funny in the white robes. Like a trick-or-treater getting ready to go out on Halloween.

"Then what is it?" I said.

"A way station. They come up here to rejuvenate themselves, then we send them back."

"We."

"The avatars," said the kid. The other avatars drifted away from us. They seemed like an anti-social lot.

"How did the avatars get to be avatars?" I said.

"The way you just did. We don't eat the soup. We don't want to forget our lives."

I wondered what an eight-year-old could possibly want to remember for the rest of existence.

"Why don't I have a name?" I asked. "I think I remember being named, but I can't remember what it is."

"None of us have names," said the kid. "Names make us specific beings, but we aren't specific. We're more of a concept than an individual being."

I couldn't quite wrap my mind around that thought. Maybe later.

"We're not in hell, though, right?"

She looked at me with an amused expression. "Is that what you think?"

I shrugged. "It's possible. I mean, it's a fair guess, given what I've seen."

"You should rest easy. This isn't hell. Or heaven. It's—"

"Just a way station," I said, irritation in my voice. I wasn't getting any of the answers I wanted. I wasn't getting any good answers at all.

"Exactly," said the kid. She started moving away. Not quickly, but definitely drifting. Was I so obnoxious that no one wanted to be anywhere near me?

"Why us?" I said.

"Not sure," said the kid. "Don't worry about it. Could be we're the rebels. You ever do bad things?"

Was this a test? I wasn't sure if I should answer. "Hasn't everyone?" I said.

"Sure, but some of us like the things we did, the bad things, so much that we don't want to forget them. They feel too good."

"What did you do?" I said.

"You first."

I sighed. Was the afterlife just a bunch of games that people played? Was that all we came down to?

"I spent my life stealing things."

"Oooooh," said the kid. "So awful." She laughed.

"I didn't say it was awful," I said, thinking how dumb it was to be justifying myself to this child, this avatar, this nothing. "What did you do?" I said. "Take candy from a school mate?"

"I helped kill the father of my best friend, who was doing things to her he shouldn't have been doing. We did it together. We used his gun. We knew where it was, in the closet. First she shot him then I was supposed to shoot him. We were going to take turns. We thought then they wouldn't be able to tell who did the killing, so they wouldn't be able to blame it on either one of us. It was our way of protecting each other, we thought. We were best friends. We were going to be in this together. Plus, we kind of knew that we were too young to be responsible for what we were doing. If you're going to kill someone, it's way better to do it before you're too old. We were saving my friend's life. His father was a bad man."

I blinked. "Oh," I said.

"Only thing is, my friend didn't exactly know what she was doing because in the confusion of her father bleeding all over the place she started shaking with fear and ended up shooting me too."

"That's how you got here?" I said.

"Yes."

"That's quite a story," I said.

She shrugged. "Just before I died, when all the blood had drained out of me, and my friend was screaming, I hoped she was going to be okay. I wanted her to be okay. I hoped she wasn't going to go to jail or get into big trouble or anything."

"And did she?"

"She was too young to go to jail, but she's having a hard time. Lots of counseling and stuff. Her mother kind of abandoned her to the system."

"So you're staying on here to watch over her?" I asked.

"Something like that," said the kid. She was still drifting. I let her go.

"See you later," I said.

"Probably," said the kid, "but don't count on it. Just do your task and everything will be fine."

Advice from an eight-year-old. I never thought someone so young could have anything useful to say to me, but it turned out to be exactly the right thing. I never saw her again; the avatars don't mix too much. But I still remember her.

When I finally decide to go back, if I ever do, I'll miss the memory of meeting her. She was so flush with life, even in this place, even after what had happened to her and her best friend.

But if that ever happened, if I ever went back, I would have to swallow my disgust at the thought of eating the soup. The soup that erases your memories.

After meeting the killer eight-year-old, I wondered how anyone could live with that kind of memory. I decided no one should have to. I returned to the cafeteria and got into line and asked for a bowl of soup.

The guy on the other side of the counter studied me carefully. "You don't want soup," he said.

I felt myself turning red. How can an avatar turn red? "Of course I do," I said.

"No," he said. "You're not ready. Move along."

"I want a bowl of soup," I said.

He raised his chin and said very slowly and deliberately: "Don't make me mad. Move along and come back when you're ready."

I didn't move.

The guy lost it. It was amazing to behold. His face filled up with rage. It was like he wanted to strangle me. I half expected him to leap across the counter and take my neck in his hands and snap my spine. "Get the fuck out of my fucking line you fucking shithead," he said. Real loud. All the soup slurpers stopped and looked up. At me. I stepped back from the counter.

The guy smiled at me. He had gone back to being calm and quiet. Just like that. In an instant. "Got it?" he said.

"Got it," I mumbled.

The slurpers went back to their slurping. People after me in line pushed past me. I didn't know where to go, but I didn't want to be standing there doing nothing, so I walked through the dining area. Some of the slurpers looked at me. Most were intent on the bowls in front of them.

One thing about being an avatar is that you have these robes, which can be very useful. I passed empty tables, where empty bowls of soup with spoons in them lay like weird headstones. I snapped up one of these bowls, one that had a couple of spoonfuls left in the bottom, and hid it in my robes. Simple. The sort of thing I used to do all the time when I was a free agent back on earth.

I had stolen soup. One of my best lifts ever. I took the bowl and went back to where the eight-year-old avatar had been. She needed this soup. She had to forget what happened to her and her friend. That kind of memory was too much for anyone. And it was even worse that she seemed to *want* the memory. I was determined to help her. My first good deed in the afterlife.

But I never found her.

Never found out what happened to her.

I kept the bowl and searched for days.

In the end, the soup at the bottom of the bowl dried out and turned to powder. After I had decided I would never find the eight-year-old, I scraped off the dried soup with my fingernail and let it fall, like ground pepper, to the ground.

Chapter 21: Fire

A SERIES OF thumps and bangs on the wall of the trailer roused Mort and Jake from a fitful sleep.

"What's that?" said Mort.

Jake rose up on his elbows. "Someone's out there," he said. They heard a muffled voice.

"Get out, whoever's in there. Get out of my trailer."

They both looked at the doors. A tall slit of light marked the spot where the two doors almost met. The slit widened and the door creaked. Sharp morning light spilled into the cab, stinging Jake's and Mort's eyes. They put up there hands for shade and squinted. Mort saw a guy in profile, holding a rifle or a shotgun, he couldn't tell which.

Mort raised his hands over his head.

"We just needed to get out of the rain," said Jake. "We didn't damage anything."

Mort elbowed Jake, who was then quick to raise his own hands.

"It isn't raining now," said the man.

"We'll go," said Mort.

The man leveled his gun at the two of them. "I don't think so," he said. "I've called the police. They'll be here shortly. I believe the two of you are in some bigger trouble than trespassing in a trailer."

Mort could now see that the man was older, maybe in his seventies. And he had no intention of shooting them. All Mort had to do was convince the man that he was harmless.

"I don't know what you mean by bigger trouble, sir. Our car broke down last night and we needed to find shelter."

"Why didn't you just stay with the car?"

"It was leaking," said Mort.

"Leaking?"

"Yes sir."

"How'd you get in here?"

"We found the key," said Mort. "Thought it was okay to just spend the night and get dry. We were going to leave a twenty dollar bill to pay for the night's accommodation."

Mort stood up. Jake stood with him.

"Get back," said the man.

"All we want to do is leave your property and be on our way." Mort took his wad of cash from his pocket and peeled off three twenty dollar bills and dropped them to the floor of the trailer. The man looked at the bills, then at the bigger stash going back into Mort's pocket.

"Where'd a couple of kids like you get that much money?" said the man.

"We work for a living," said Mort. "We're on our way north to find our dad. He deserted us a long time ago."

The man was only half listening. He pointed the gun at Mort's pocket. "How much money you figure you have?"

"Just enough to get us to Portland."

"Bullshit," said the man. "You've got hundreds of dollars there. Hand it over."

"What?" said Mort. "Are you serious?"

"This just turned into a robbery. Hand over that money."

"Jesus," said Jake.

"I thought the cops were coming," said Mort.

"By the time they get here you'll be gone and I'll tell them I couldn't hold you here."

Mort shook his head. If he ever needed proof that everybody was a thief, this was it. He reached into his pocket and flicked off most of the cash from his roll, leaving a few bills to help him and Jake out later. He didn't think the old man would notice the motion, but he did. He raised the end of the gun so it pointed directly at Mort's head. "All of it," he said.

Mort sighed, put the roll in his other hand and fished the remaining bills out of his pocket.

"Just a twenty," said Mort. "Leave us something." Mort could always get money if he needed to, but he still didn't want to give this guy everything. It was humiliating. Just because he had a gun. Which was wrong. A gun shouldn't mean you won. He used a fake gun in his robberies sometimes, but it was fake. That was important. No one was every going to get hurt. Here, he was a split second from getting his head shot off. All that had to happen was for the old man's finger to start shaking.

"Just drop it all on the floor," said the man.

Mort let the bills flutter down. He estimated there was close to a thousand dollars there.

The man swung the gun over until it was pointing at Jake's head. "How about you? You have an money?"

Jake shook his head. He pulled his pockets inside out to show they were empty.

The man studied the both of them for a couple of seconds, then stepped back from the end of the trailer. "Now get out of here," he said.

Mort and Jake slowly walked toward the open doors. When they got to the lip, the man was several paces in front of them, with his gun still raised. Mort had a pretty good idea that the gun probably wasn't loaded, but he didn't want to take the chance. Let the geezer have his money. It would be a good story to tell his geezer buddies. Maybe this was his first robbery. A crime of convenience, and more power to him.

Mort looked down on the ground. The blades of grass were all edged with whiteness that gleamed in morning sun. A hard frost last night. No wonder they had been cold.

They jumped down from the trailer and the man motioned with his gun toward the highway. "I'm giving you a head start with the cops," he said. "Get going and we'll call it even. You don't have to thank me."

"Thank you?" said Jake.

Mort grabbed him by the elbow and dragged him away from the man. "You've been more than kind, sir," he said to the man as Jake stumble-walked with Mort. Mort didn't look back. He hurried his pace. Jake held back at first, then matched his speed. They trotted over frosty ground, with their footsteps crunching under them.

They were both tired, hungry, and thirsty. They got to the barbed wire fence and helped each other through, as they had done the night before to get onto the property. Mort looked back at the trailer with the sign painted on its side. The doors were closed. He thought he saw the lock back on them. He couldn't see the man with the gun, then looked further away, toward the mountain rising far in the distance, and saw the man walking over a rise in the grass and then dipping down into a depression. Off to the side, just away from the mountain, Mort saw a house, white, with trees all around it. Probably the guy's house. He wanted to ditch Jake and turn around and rob the house. He could have done it. Nothing to it. Get his money back and maybe a little more. But he didn't want to. He got a kind of strange pleasure from the old man doing a robbery and getting away with it. He shook his head as he watched Jake bend down to get through the space between the strands of barbed wire. Crazy for him to be happy about getting his money taken.

"We should get on the other side," said Mort.

"Why?"

"Our car spun out on this side. They'll be looking for us going north."

"No one's going to be looking for us," said Jake.

"They will when they find out that car's been stolen." Mort looked back to where they left the highway last night. He couldn't see the car; they had gone too far. But it was there and it was probably being investigated by the cops. They waited for a break in the traffic, then sprinted across the two north bound lanes. The median was wide at this spot in the freeway. It dipped way down and was covered with weeds. Mort and Jake waded through the vegetation, which was now melting off it's frost so their feet got wet and even colder. They trudged up the other side of the median. Mort legs felt sore. They walked across the southbound lanes and across the paved shoulder to the gravel on the other side.

"We can't hitchhike from here," said Jake.

"We aren't going to hitchhike," said Mort. "We need to get off the road."

They kept walking to the field on the other side. They encountered no fence. The grassy hills, like a sea of yellow and green, looked like waves thrown up around them. "We'll get lost in here," said Jake.

"That's the idea," said Mort. "We stay away from the road and just keep walking. After a few miles we can go back and hitch a ride."

Jake looked like he wanted to argue, but quickly acquiesced. They walked in silence for a mile or two.

"Why'd you tell that guy you had money?" said Jake.

"Doesn't matter," said Mort.

"It does matter. We're broke now."

"It's just money. There's always more money around."

"Maybe for you," said Jake.

"For you, too, if you want it."

The sun began to warm them. Mort felt it in his bones. His clothes, still a little damp from the night before, began to heat up and dry out. It felt good.

"I don't know how to steal."

"Everyone knows how to steal," said Mort.

"I mean steal important stuff and get away with it."

"You think money is important?" said Mort.

"Without it you can't do anything. Not in this world."

"You're wrong," said Mort. "Money is a convenience, but life goes on without it. Always has. Cave men didn't have money."

The sound of the interstate retreated to a dull hiss and rumble off to their side. They were far enough away from it that they couldn't see it or any of the traffic on it. That was the way Mort wanted it. They could follow it without being seen. They crossed fences. Some made of piled stone. Other's barbed wire. And some made of wood. People here sure liked to fence in land. They also walked next to herds of cows, the creatures chewing and staring at them like cows always did. They also passed quite a few no trespassing signs, but neither of them paid any attention to those. They just stepped over all the fences and kept walking.

"We aren't cave men," said Jake.

"Yeah we are," said Mort. "We wear fancy clothes but we're just animals."

Jake kept quiet again. He was in no mood for arguing with Mort. What he wanted was some food. When were they going to get some food?

The sun got higher in the sky and started to warm the air. Mort and Jake began to sweat.

"We're going to get sun burnt," said Jake.

"It won't kill you," said Mort.

"We need water," said Jake. "We can't keep walking like this without water."

He stopped. Mort stood with him. "Just a couple more miles," he said, "then we can get back to the road and hitch a ride."

Jake looked around. Nothing but hills and cows as far as he could see. He put his hand up to his forehead and slowly spun in a circle.

"What you looking for?" said Mort.

"Nothing. I'm just tired of this." He stopped and stared.

"What?" said Mort.

Jake pointed to the horizon. Mort followed his finger and saw a glint, like a piece of metal. He squinted against the glint and thought he saw a flash of color, red and green. "What's that?" said Jake.

"Who cares?" said Mort.

"I do. Let's go see what it is."

"That's near the highway," said Mort. "We need to stay out of sight."

But Jake didn't listen. He hurried toward the reflection. Mort scratched the back of his head, considering his options. He could follow Jake and they could see what the stupid spark of light was. Or he could let Jake go and continue on his own. That might be okay for him, because maybe they would catch Jake and not even think about looking for him. Except Mort couldn't be sure Jake wouldn't rat him out. Best to keep close to Jake and try to get him to see reason. He saw Jake running fast toward the highway. He sighed and began running after Jake.

The reflection soon disappeared, but the color remained: bright red, like fluorescent paint. As they got closer, he saw metal parts. At first it looked like the wreck of a car, but as he caught up to Jake and they began running, he saw it was something else: not randomly strewn pieces of metal, but deliberately constructed pieces of metal. It was a sculpture made of old parts from cars, tractors, maybe some appliances like fridges and stoves. It curved up and down. It had a tail. And a head. And some curled metal, painted orange and red, sprouted out of the thing's mouth. They dipped down into a small hollow so that the thing disappeared, then rose up and saw it in its entirety.

A dragon, exhaling fire next to the freeway.

They both stopped to take in the magnificence. Whoever put it together had some kind of genius for matching part to function. The scales, now that Mort was closer to it, appeared to be made of old CDs. The tail was crafted from the chassis of a car. A series of spikes from a threshing machine formed the spine. An old car bumper formed the jaw.

Mort and Jake, both mesmerized by the thing, walked up to it and ran their hands over the body of it, feeling the smooth belly, made from fridge doors.

"Who would put a dragon here by the freeway?" said Mort.

"Yeah," said Jake. "Stupid."

"Probably stole all the parts for it."

"Or had it donated by people. Or scrounged around for it."

"Still stole it. No matter how you get things, you steal it from someone."

Jake didn't want to argue with him. He walked around the dragon several times, admiring its artistry. "Wish I had a camera," he said.

Mort stepped back. The dragon did look impressive. Cars whizzed by on the highway and Mort could tell they were looking at the dragon. Who wouldn't? It was something, standing out here. He looked at the fire. It was hard to tell what it was made of. It was some kind of curly metal. He stepped up to the flame. The paint was bright. Probably what they saw glinting on the horizon.

He reached up to the flame, just above his head, and ran his hand along the edge, sharp, but not enough to cut him. The metal gave, just a little. Probably aluminum.

"This is the most fantastic thing I've ever seen," said Jake.

Mort nodded. "It is that," he said.

He touched the end of one of the flame tips. The eye of the dragon seemed to look through him to the ground behind his head. How could this pile of old junk make him feel so sad? "What do you steal?" asked Mort. "Air to make fire?"

"What?" said Jake.

"Nothing," said Mort. He took a hold of the tip of one of the flames and bent it back, creasing the metal an inch or so from the end. He bent it back the other way so the crease deepened. He wiggled the piece back and forth until it was creased good and strong. Then he grasped the metal on both sides of the crease and tore off the tip.

"What are you doing?" said Jake. He was genuinely shocked that Mort would damage the sculpture on purpose. "Someone worked hard on this. You can't just fuck with it like that."

"We don't have a camera," said Mort. "I wanted a souvenir." He put the tip of the dragon flame into his pocket.

"Fuck," said Jake. "You have no respect for anything."

"Don't get all weird," said Mort. "It's just the tip. No one's going to notice it's gone. Come on."

Jake looked at the flames coming out of the dragon's mouth. "It's all wrong now," he said.

"Come on," said Mort. "Let's get walking."

"The balance is off."

"There's no balance," said Mort. "The people on the highway won't see the missing tip." He felt the jagged edges of the tip in his pocket, pressing into his thigh. He didn't know why he took the flame. Why did he need something like that? It was just a piece of metal that was probably going to cut him eventually. He looked at the hills beyond the dragon, where they had come from. Then he looked at the highway, just twenty yards from the dragon. People had already seen them.

"Come on," he said. "Let's go hitch a ride."

He trotted toward the shoulder.

"What about keeping out of sight?" said Jake.

"Never mind that. You want to ride or you want to walk?"

Jake, still upset by the theft of fire, stood next to the dragon. Mort thought he looked kind of puny beside the sculpture. Whoever made it knew about scale. The dragon had to be big. Had to.

Jake finally left the dragon and crossed the highway with Mort. They stood on the other side and put out their thumbs.

"It didn't have a no trespassing sign," said Mort.

"What didn't?"

"The dragon."

An eighteen wheeler thundered by them. Mort thought he might be slowing down, but he didn't. Several more cars went by, slapping wind into their faces.

"It doesn't have to say that," said Jake. "It's obvious."

"Not to me," said Mort. "It's there for the taking. Everything is there for taking if you look at it the right way."

Chapter 22: Bread

SUSIE WENT BACK to Faith Village a few days later. She found Judy in her tent, with a wood stove that had not been there previously. She leaned back in a chair and was   smoking a cigar.

"Come on in," she said.

Susie entered the tent and sat on the edge of Judy's cot.

"You want a cigar?" said Judy. She flipped open a cigar box next to her and extended a cellophane wrapped cigar in Susie's direction.

"I'll pass," said Susie.

"Got them from some guy passing by on the corner where I fly a sign. Said he was quitting. Just decided to quit right then and there. I took them, why not? I haven't smoked in years, but thought I'd try these. They're nice. You smoke?"

Susie shook her head.

"Too bad. I'm celebrating. Not exactly sure what, you know? Just feels like time for a celebration. Hand me some of those twigs." She pointed to a corner of the tent where a small stack of wood lay against the canvas wall.

Susie picked up some of the sticks and handed them to Judy, who opened the door of the stove and stuffed the wood inside.

"Oh man," she said. "That feels good."

"Did you see the article?" said Susie.

"No. I don't read that paper."

"It's all about you."

Judy waved her hand. "Never mind," she said. "I'm sure your article is great. I just don't want to read about myself. What's your next story about?"

"There is no next story," said Susie. "I'm not a real reporter. That was the first and probably the last story I'll ever write."

Judy opened the door of the stove and stoked the wood inside, sending up a shower of sparks and putting even more heat into the tent, which was quite warm already.

"So you lied to me," said Judy.

Susie nodded. "I wasn't trying to do anything bad. I just wanted to talk to you. I had this need to tell your story. Don't ask me why. I don't know."

"It's like that tree, I guess. I don't know why I wanted it cut down, but it was the most important thing in my life. I had to do it. Now that I have, I just want to celebrate."

"Uh huh," said Susie.

"I'll tell you something else," said Judy. "I can't stand this place anymore. I just want to get out."

Once, oh I don't know how long ago, a scientist came up to the way station. He was well regarded in his previous life. He won awards, got acclaim for his theories and papers. A physicist. He came to me because he had stolen some ideas from his colleagues and published them as his own. He was so highly thought of that when the wronged scientists claimed he had done what he in fact did, which was to steal their work, no one believed them. The thief got all the credit. He wasn't a bad guy. He just thought that his way of doing science was the right way. I suppose you could blame him for being dishonest and for sullying the profession. I wanted to. I did. I wanted to send him back as a proton, or something. They live for bazillions of years before they decay. He'd have all that time, lonely time, to stew about what he had done. I know: protons don't stew, I get that, but the symbolism of it appealed to me. He stole credit and glory from members of his own tribe. That deserved some kind of punishment in the next life, didn't it? Sure. Except that I ended up liking him. He was a cool guy, a lot of fun to be around. We played games, chess and go, mostly, and we talked. He loved to talk about physics. I didn't know anything about physics, but I listened. It was fascinating. He loved talking about the balance of the universe. Everything was made just so. The amount of energy in the universe was just so. The strength of all the forces was just so. The size of the atoms was just so. How they fit together was just so. If any part of the structure deviates from what it is, even by so much as a millionth of a billionth of one percent, then the whole house of cards just collapses and you don't have stars, you don't have planets, and you don't get life. All fascinating stuff. "I'm an atheist," he told me. "It's common in my line of work to not believe in the divine. But when you see how it all links together, it's hard not to believe in something. You have to have a lot of faith to think there is no god."

You see what I'm saying? He knew how to make you think and he made sure that you liked him. Which I did. I liked him a lot. He thought of not eating the soup, but he said it would get too boring up here. After a week or so he asked for the soup. I didn't send him back as a proton. I couldn't. I liked him too much. Instead, I made him a chef. He was happy.

I'm telling you all this to make a point. I can be swayed in my opinion of people. And stealing something, anything, doesn't necessarily mean you're evil and will be punished in the next life. That may be unfair, but I don't have to answer to anyone. For example, when Judy comes up here, she's not going get punished by me. Sure, she stole, but she already paid for it in the same life. She doesn't deserve even more suffering in the next.

The physicist guy made me look at the balance of things. And how, since I'm one of the orchestrators of the universe, it's up to me to make that balance work for everyone, as much as I can.

So let me explain Susie.

You remember Stella, I'm sure. Rex's wife? When she killed herself, which seems like eons ago now, she came up here and found me. Turns out she was involved in a lot of petty crime over the years. That was before she got depressed, which usually takes all the energy from a person and makes them neglect their work, which is what happened to her. She did a lot of scams on people. Street scams where she told someone she had lost some money and then talked the person into giving her money to replace the lost money, only she did it by giving them a check for more than the lost money, as a reward, only the check was, of course, bad. It's a classic scam, so old it's amazing anyone still falls for it, but she was good. She worked it several times a day and made a good living. Then she met Rex and they wanted children together, but they couldn't have any. Neither of them had legitimate jobs or a nice place to live, so adopting was going to be impossible for them. So they resigned themselves to no children. Until Stella got so depressed that Rex decided to help her out with a little kidnapping. But you already know that part.

When Stella came up here she didn't want to linger. Not for an instant. She didn't want to look at her life or Rex's life or Melville's life, the baby that would have been hers. She wanted to eat the soup and move on.

I admired that determination. She was depressed, but she saw the way station as a perfect opportunity to get beyond the depression and she wanted to seize it. I barely had time to find a new slot for her. I looked for someone with an upbeat name. Stella seemed so formal. Susie was perfect. Who wouldn't be happy with a name like Susie? By the time I got that far, she was all the way to the bottom of her bowl. She looked up at me, blankly, and I escorted her to the staging area and off she went.

Now, usually, I like to put people in some other place than where they came from. Makes it easier. Even though the memories are gone, there's still some residual awareness of the previous life. If you've ever had a déjà vu experience, you know what I'm talking about. That feeling that you've lived the experience before means that you very probably did, in another life, but don't remember it now. And how about seeing someone and thinking: I know that person. Even though you don't. Most people have that too. Well, that's someone you knew previously. It can get inconvenient and confusing. So if someone comes to me from Oregon, say, I usually try to put them in a place like India, or Australia. Far away. Unless, like with Rex, I want the collisions with previous lives.

But with Susie, she kind of caught me off guard. She was so ready to go that I didn't have time to do the proper deployment investigation and she ended up right back in Portland, Oregon. Right next to where she had lived before. Right smack dab up against Faith Village where Judy lived. The woman whose baby Rex stole.

You'd think it wouldn't matter. But it did.

Susie had an obsession with Judy. It was like she knew there was a connection between them, but she didn't know what that connection was.

And now, sitting next to her, feeding pieces of Rex into the wood stove, she still didn't know.

"You're leaving Faith Village?" said Susie.

"It's time to move on," said Judy. "I won't be needing this tent anymore. You want it?"

Susie blinked and laughed. "You mean move in here?"

"Sure. Why not? It's an experience, let me tell you."

"I don't think it's an experience I want," said Susie.

"Then what are you doing here?" Judy took a puff from the cigar and blew smoke into the air.

"I don't know, exactly. This is going to sound strange, but I mourned for that tree."

"Not so strange. I hated that tree. If I can *hate* a stupid tree, then I guess you can *mourn* it."

"I never noticed trees before. Ever. They were just there. And then this one. I feel like I came here the other day just so I could be near the tree."

"I never hated a tree before. So we're even, I guess. We both got things from that tree we didn't expect."

Susie looked around the tent, as if she was trying to find a way out. Judy watched her, amused. "You look like you want to climb the walls," she said to Susie.

"I want the walls to come down."

"I don't know that you mean by that, but never mind. You know I used to be an accountant?"

"Yes," said Susie.

"I'm going to go back and do that. I'm going to get a job. I have some money. I've been saving it. Should get me a room somewhere. A small one, but that's all I need. I've gotten used to living in a small place. You can't get a job without a place to live, you know. It's almost impossible. I mean a real place. One they consider real."

"When are you leaving?" said Susie.

"Soon. When all this wood is burned up."

Susie picked up a chunk of the oak tree. "This is why I came back," she said.

Judy reached over and swung the door of the stove open. Susie put the chunk of wood on the bottom edge of the opening and held it there, balanced for a few seconds. "I feel like if I can help burn up this oak, I'll help something move along."

"Me?" said Judy.

"Um. I don't think so. Someone else."

"Who?"

"That's just it, I don't know."

Judy motioned with her head. Susie shrugged, laughed, and pushed the wood into the stove. The flame inside caught the bark and crackled. Judy swung the door shut and Susie put her open palms up to the stove. The heat felt good. Waves of it touched her face and wrapped her in comfort. She glanced up at Judy, who smiled at her and blew cigar smoke into the tent.

OKAY, SO YOU maybe think I shouldn't have punished Rex. He was just trying to help out his wife. A noble gesture, I will agree, but he didn't have to do what he did. Stealing a baby, that's simply going too far. He had to pay for that in some way. The only thing is, he came back pretty quick.

That was my fault. I should have realized that once Judy burned him to a crisp, he was going to return. He did so piecemeal. A bit of him came back when the first chunk of the oak burned up. It was odd, let me tell you, to see a piece of Rex. He was tiny, just a little smidgen of a soul. I went to see him, but he had no faculties. He had little of anything. He was a bare bones soul. Not even any bones.

I noted his appearance and resolved to return to see him again when he was a little more complete. That didn't take long. As each chunk of the tree went up in smoke, Rex got a little more complete. Within a few days he was able to converse, a little. It was kind of like he was coming out of a coma. Awareness came first. He realized he was in a different place. He thought it was heaven, as most people do, but after a while he realized it was something else. A few days later he was able to speak. Not converse, exactly, but speak. He said a word or two, pushed it out like he was still learning what they meant. Maybe he was. I told him everything was going to be okay. I don't know if he understood me or cared. Then, when Judy and the other residents had completely destroyed all traces of the oak, including the bark and all the twigs and little branches, Rex came into his fullness as Rex.

"How are you?" I said.

"I spent my short life as a tree, then I got incinerated," said Rex. "How do you think I am?"

"You should feel proud," I said. "You didn't kill anyone or steal from anyone or cause anyone harm. Not once during your life on earth."

He studied me like I was a text he needed to decipher. "Have I been here before?" he said.

"Yes. Everyone who's here has been here before."

"What happens to me now?"

"Depends on what I decide," I said.

"You decide?"

"Yes."

"So there must be a test or something."

"Not exactly," I said. "I just need to decide if you would benefit from a, for lack of a better term, higher placement."

He thought about that. I could tell he liked the idea of a more exalted existence. But he also seemed to like being a tree. There was serenity in that, had to be. A certain freedom in not having to go places all the time. You knew what you were and you knew what you would be, everyday.

"I liked having leaves," he said.

I nodded.

"I liked *being* leaves, if you want to know the truth. The chopping down and burning up wasn't the best thing going, but before that, it was fantastic. You think you could put me back into a situation like that again?"

I have to admit I didn't expect that.

"I was thinking more of an animal," I said.

"What kind of animal?"

"A predator. Maybe a hawk. Or a mountain lion."

"Why would you make me a killer?"

I was at a loss. "Just seemed right," I said. "You earned the freedom. You would make a good predator."

His eyes lit up. I could tell he thought that was true. Then his face dimmed. "I tell you what," he said. "I know about these cactus. Saguaros. You've heard of them?"

"Sure," I said.

"They're like people. Ever notice that?"

"People?"

"They have their wood on the inside, like we have our bones. And then their flesh is hung on the wood, just like our flesh hangs on our bones."

"I see," I said.

"Plus, they have arms. Like us."

"Okay."

"I wouldn't mind being one of those for a couple hundred years. It would be peaceful. I could get into that, soaking up the sun."

"They have thorns, too," I said.

"To keep away predators?"

"Something like that."

"And birds tunnel into you. They make nests."

He laughed. "I heard about that too. They steal space inside me."

"Some people like to think of it as donating space to the birds."

He waved his hand. "Whatever," he said. "Can you do that for me? Can you put me in one of those cactuses?"

He got the plural of cactus wrong. He got the whole reincarnation mechanism wrong: you didn't inhabit one of the creatures or plants, you *became* a person, place, or thing. But it didn't matter. If I asked him, I figured he wouldn't have any real idea of what a soul was. So what? He still had a big heart. I had seen to it that he lost his emptiness. Why not let him revel in his joy for a century or two?

"Sure," I said. "How tall would you like to be? And how many arms?"

REX THANKED ME, like I had saved his life. Which I did, but I did that all the time. No need for thanks. He ate the soup like it was the best meal he would ever have. The best meal he *could* ever have. Just before he went back, he passed one of the avatars who was experimenting with baking. We get hobbies, sometimes. This avatar took flour from the soup cook and used it to make bread.

Rex saw the bread, loaves of it cooling on racks. As he went by the rack, he took one of the loaves. Just grabbed it up. Without thinking and without guilt.

His last theft? Maybe, although he didn't think of it as theft. It was a gift from the universe in his mind.

I began to think of it in exactly the same way.

Chapter 23: Dreams

SOMETIMES PEOPLE APPEAR here in the way station, and they know exactly what's going on without anyone telling them. The procedure and the set up exactly fits with their view of the afterlife. Not that they had a premonition or anything, I'm not saying that. It's more a matter of blind luck. Chance. People are very inventive about their various conceptions of what goes on after they die. Some of them are bound to get at least part of it right at least some of the time. So that's what happens. The people whose traditions or belief systems include reincarnation, they slot right into the routine here. They know I'm their guide, they realize that they will be going back, and they accept the little quirks of the system, like how we have these ridiculous robes, and how they can view the earth on a screen, and how they have to have the soup if they want to go back.

Then you get the ones who are completely incredulous about the whole thing. They think there's a joke being played on them and they wait for their buddies to appear from out of the shadows and yell "gotcha!" Or they think they've been kidnapped by UFOs and I'm an alien. Or they want to talk to God. It doesn't matter what I tell some of these people. They will not ever believe that the system is the way it is. So I tell them that I will let them see God, or go to the place where all their family is, or even talk to their dog again, if that's what they want, but I convince them that they need to eat. They look so worn and hungry. They must have had a terrible trip since their death. Not to mention that death itself takes a lot out of you, so they start to feel like they could use a meal and I show them to the cafeteria with all the soups. Just about everyone likes soup. They get a bowl to their liking and eat it and voila, my work is done. They lose their memory and are compliant as can be. Makes my job so easy and avatars are nothing if not lovers of ease.

Then there are people like me. We know what's going on, and we don't want to lose our memories. Simple as that.

But you know, everything loses its luster after a while. When I saw Rex, so happy to be returning as a saguaro, I started thinking maybe he had a point. Maybe it was time for me to give up this avatar life. After all, I wasn't getting anywhere here. This wasn't truly a life that mattered. And it was the same thing day after day.

Also, my memories from my previous life were not giving me the pleasure they should have anymore. Yes, it had been a thrill to steal all those things and it was a thrill to remember stealing all those things, but such memories were nothing to hang an existence on.

I had had some of those thoughts previously, but I just chalked them up to the general ups and downs of life that we all go through. Even avatars. But this time was different. It didn't feel like it was going to go away. I wanted something to look forward to, just like Rex. I wanted to be a saguaro cactus, or a rabbit, or even a stupid rock. Yes, I would be a rock and be happy about the choice.

Only thing is, an avatar has no say in where he or she goes. We are at the mercy of another avatar, just like anyone else.

What I didn't want was to be put in the body of someone unsavory. Murderers used to be someone else once. Yes they did. They have souls, just like everyone else. I didn't want to be one of those souls. It could happen. You never know. Every entity is a blank slate when they go down. The randomness of the universe could result in anything. Avatars, most of us, try to avoid such an occurrence, but we make mistakes, and we can't see everything.

In some ways, the risk seemed too great, so I stayed at my tasks, receiving newcomers, showing them the way, and sending them back.

Only thing was, that kind of no-risk life was no way to live. Even for a dead person. Even for an avatar.

But I remembered that little girl, the one who had been through the awful death before. She was an avatar with a difference. She would help me get back. I resolved to find her.

SUSIE DIDN'T KNOW what she should have expected from her visit with Judy, but she had hoped that they would bond in a greater way than simply subject and interviewer. That didn't happen, which disappointed her tremendously. Judy seemed to treat her as part of the furniture. She was not the least bit impressed that Susie had written about her. And why should she be? It did nothing for her life. If anything, it gave Susie some bragging rights, but even there, it didn't do much of that.

Susie did, however, feel like she had come close to some kind of divine force by coming to Judy's tent. The wood they put in the stove, just touching it and feeling its texture, gave her a delight she could not describe. It was as though she *knew* the wood, if that made any sense. The grain and the feel of it, the rough bark, the heft of it, there was so much *right* about that wood. There was a way in which it seemed to fall into her and hold her, like it had a spirit inside it that wanted to take *her* spirit, but not in a bad way, more like a melding. And she would have accepted the melding, if she knew how.

Judy ran her fingers over the floor of the tent where the last few scraps of wood bark and leaf debris remained. She scooped them up in her hand, and tossed the pieces into the stove then slammed the stove shut.

"Done," she said.

"What?" said Susie.

"That's the last of it. Nothing left of that tree now. Once it burns up those last scraps, it's gone."

"Except for the stump," said Susie.

"Sure, except for the stump, but the stump is dead. The tree is dead."

"That makes me feel sad," said Susie.

"Not me," said Judy. "It's gone. I feel like a burden has been taken from me. A weight, isn't that what people say? I never exactly knew what that meant, but I do now."

Susie smiled. "That's great," she said.

"What you going to do now?" said Judy.

"Go home, I guess."

"No, I mean, what are you going to do with your life?"

"Are you the interviewer now?" said Susie.

"I suddenly want to know what everyone in the world is planning to do with their lives. Isn't that crazy? I think I'll spend the rest of the day asking people. Won't that be fun?"

Susie nodded. It did sound like fun. You'd probably get a lot of people thinking you were crazy, but then you'd probably also get a lot of people telling you some fascinating things.

"So?" said Judy. "You'll be the first. What are you going to with your life?"

Susie had not given that sort of thing much thought, but she thought about it now. "You know," she said. "I think it would be kind of fun to go down to Arizona and see the big cactus there. I've never seen them and they've always seemed like amazing things. I could live there with them in my backyard."

Judy nodded and smiled. "See," she said. "That's just the sort of thing I was talking about."

A GROUP OF avatars, kind of dimwitted ones if you ask me, had decided they knew the real scoop about the way station. They held meetings where they convinced each other that this was all a dream. A very elaborate shared dream. An elaborate, shared, vivid, lucid, incredible dream. That's what the way station was and they were going to prove it.

I don't know how they could possibly prove such a thing, but that didn't stop them from trying.

The girl sat next to the group, listening to their blather. I stopped and waited until she saw me, then I waved to her. She waved back. I went over to her.

"I didn't know you were interested in the fringe theories," I said.

"I'm not exactly interested in the theories," she said. "More in the need for *them*—" she indicated the group of avatars with her thumb "—to invent crazy theories. It's fascinating."

"There's another group that thinks we're a computer program, running endlessly, and what we think is our soul is just a ghost in the software."

She laughed. "I guess for some the truth is just too much to take. I kind of wish this was all a dream. I wish my life was a dream."

"It can be nothing," I said. "If you go back, it can all be erased."

"Maybe," she said.

"You don't believe it?"

"I think something residual remains. If I go back I won't have the memories, but I will have the vague feeling of dread, like something dark and awful is there at my core. I wouldn't want that."

I could see her point, but even if there was a residual dread, couldn't one just ignore that and live a life? "As unpleasant as that would be," I said, "Wouldn't it be better than having the full blown memories? They have to be the most awful thing imaginable."

There is no correlation between wisdom and age with us. A two-year-old can be more worldly and savvy that a seventy-year-old. By a long shot. That's because the souls that travel around the cosmos are often old and full of experience. Just because they happen to inhabit a young person doesn't take away from that wisdom. I was not being condescending to this eight-year-old girl in any way. She knew exactly what she wanted and needed. I was simply asking her opinion to understand her position better.

"Having the memories puts the dread in context. Without the memories, there is no context. I can't blame it on anything. It would just be this mysterious and terrifying feeling that I would always have with me."

"So you think you'll be an avatar for the rest of your life?"

She shrugged. "It's not so bad up here. We get to help people."

I liked the sound of that, but needed more information. "Help people?" I said.

"When we send them back. We can give them benign places to live."

"Is that what you do?"

"I try to. But you can't always predict, can you?"

"No," I said.

"Why are you asking me all these things?"

"I'm ready to return."

"Haven't you been here a long time?"

"That's why I'm ready to return."

"And you want me to make your assignment, is that it?"

I nodded.

"Why me?"

"You seem like a forgiving soul."

"Do you have a lot to forgive?"

"I used to steal a lot. All the time."

She considered this. "That's not so bad. There's lots worse things people have done."

I nodded. One of the dream group saw us and asked if we would like to join them. "It's an informal group," she said. "We debate philosophical issues."

"We'll pass," I said.

"Suit yourself," she said, but did not turn back to the group right away. It seemed like she wanted something from us.

"Sorry," I said. "Are we bothering you?"

"It's just that if you aren't going to participate, I wish you wouldn't eavesdrop. It's kind of rude."

The little girl, the wise avatar who I was hoping would keep from a horrible fate, gave the other woman the finger. "Screw you," she said. "This is a free realm." She laughed.

The woman looked even more annoyed.

I raised my eyebrows at the girl.

"What?" she said.

"I didn't know you had that kind of fight in you."

"I don't like it," she said, "but sometimes it comes out in me." She went over to the group. The woman who had been talking to us had turned her back to us. The girl touched the woman's leg. "I'm sorry," she said. "I didn't mean to be an ass."

The woman, robes fluttering dramatically, looked like she wanted to slap the girl, but that had to be wrong. Why would she want to do that? She inhaled in a slow deliberate manner and looked down at the girl and then her expression softened.

"It's okay, kid," she said.

I expected the girl to be insulted by such a condescending remark, but she wasn't. Instead she beamed at the woman and everything was forgiven. The woman drew her into the group and everyone greeted her and wished her the best. The girl touched all of them, mostly on the knee or calf, some on the hand where they reached down for her to see their palms. She curled her hand around fingers. She looked very much at home in the midst of the delusional dream believers. How could she not? She was an avatar among avatars. Why would she go back to where she had been part of brutality? Why wouldn't she stay here?

After a while, once she had received gobs and gobs of attention and love, she extricated herself from the group and came back to me. The group continued its discussion. They had devolved into esoteric minutiae of technical philosophical points. No, not exactly how many angels can dance on the head of a pin, but close.

"Let's go," she said.

I walked with her. We passed over oceans of blankness, a blinding white. Why had I never noticed that all the white here was hard on the eyes?

"That was interesting," I said.

"I like to be swallowed up by some of them sometimes."

"Them?"

"The weirdos. The ones who won't accept what this is."

"There are some I've seen, they cluster together all the time and they're convinced they live in a department store changing room. Pretty soon a store employee is going to unlock the door and let them out."

"That's one of the nuttier ones," she said.

"You should have a name," I told her.

"I don't remember my name," she said.

"Make one up."

"You make one up for me."

Usually no one forgot their name. This was unusual, but not unknown. Even so, I had never named anyone up here. Now that I thought about it, why did we even need names. Why did anyone?

"You're small," I said. "How about Pixie?"

"Yuck," she said.

"What's wrong with that?"

"It's a stupid name. I'm not a pixie. I'm small because I'm a kid. Try again."

I sighed. I wasn't going to be any good at this. How do you name someone? It was ludicrous to ask me. "I need a book of baby names."

"We don't have one. Use your imagination."

"Um," I said. "You're an avatar. How about that?"

"What? Avatar? You want my name to be Avatar?"

"Sure."

"Wrong. Try again. One more time."

She said it like I *really* did have only one more try at it. Impatience on her part, I thought. Wasn't there a flower called impatiens? Would she like that as a name? Probably not. Sounded like a criticism. What about another flower?

"Rose," I said.

"That's not bad."

"Oh, you like Rose?"

"Sure. Rose. Rose Rose Rose. It fits me. I rose from the dead."

Okay. But we all rose from the dead. "I was thinking more the flower," I said.

"Whatever," she said. "Either one. I'm a flower who rose from the dead."

She seemed happy so I was happy.

"I got something from those people," she said. "When I was hugging them all, I reached into them and pulled out their dreams."

"You can do that?"

"Sure. Can't you?"

"No. I don't think anyone can."

She looked ahead, not wanting to catch my eye, I suppose. Or just walking and paying attention to what was there in front of her.

"I can," she said.

"You stole them?"

"Borrowed them."

"You're going to give them back?"

"It doesn't exactly work that way."

"Then you stole them. I know about stealing, remember? I know how it works."

"Fine."

I wasn't judging her, just setting the record straight.

"What are you going to do with them?" I asked.

"I don't know if I even want them."

"Why did you take them?"

"They needed someone to prove to them that they didn't know what they were talking about. So what if this is all a dream? I don't think it is, but what if it was? It doesn't change anything. We still have a job to do. They should buckle down and do it."

I was beginning to think I might have made a mistake coming to Rose. I wasn't sure she was as generous as I had hoped and thought she was.

"What are some of the dreams like?"

"I'm saving them for later."

For later?

"When I feel bad, I'll use some of their dreams to make myself feel better."

"Makes sense," I said.

"Now, about your assignment," she said. "I've been giving it some thought. You want to go to the cafeteria now?"

"Sure," I said, with a little more life in my voice than I felt in my heart. "Let's go."

Chapter 24: Bandage

"WHAT DID YOU have to take that piece of the dragon for?" said Jake.

"What do you care?" said Mort.

They had hitched a ride with a truck driver all the way to the outskirts of Portland where he had dropped them off at a truck stop. He was going to be there for a few hours, getting some rest and eating, before continuing north to Canada. He told Jake and Mort they could ride with him then if they wanted to wait. Neither did. They thanked him for his help and went out on the road and put out their thumbs.

"It just seemed like a stupid thing to do," said Jake. "That was a piece of art."

Mort fingered the metal tip of flame, still stowed in his pocket. It had been about eight hours since he had taken it from the side of the road in California. During that time he had come back to it often, and had liked the feel of its sharp edges against his finger.

"So?"

"So, someone worked on that. It wasn't just nothing. It wasn't just a car that someone bought. You can steal a car, that makes sense, that's okay, but to steal someone's art. Even a small piece of it, that's like stealing someone's soul."

Mort scratched his head, not sure what to make of Jake's words. He seemed too interested in this silly chunk of dragon's breath.

"What do you know about souls?" said Mort.

"Everyone knows about souls."

"I don't." He said it flatly, hoping to shut Jake up about it. He hated that kind of talk. It made him think about how little he knew. Usually that didn't bother him: he knew enough to survive, which is all that any living thing should know. But sometimes it made him feel stupid not to know what other people were talking about.

"You do," said Jake. "Everyone does."

"You said that already."

"Okay," said Jake. "It's like this: you steal stuff from people."

"Yeah."

"That's your soul. You're a thief."

"Bullshit. That's just what I do. It's nothing to do with my soul."

"All I'm saying is whatever you do, whatever you think is important to do in life, that's what your soul is. The guy who made that dragon, that's what was important to him, so that's what his soul is. You stole his soul."

"So what? You say I'm a thief, that's my soul. I stole the flame. I was doing what my soul wanted me to do. What's wrong with that?"

"You could have stole anything. You didn't have to steal that. Why did you?"

Mort had unconsciously stolen things in the past. He didn't always know why he did that, but he wasn't inclined to examine the motives behind the acts. He saw things, and he wanted them. Not for long, usually. Money, for example, didn't ever last. You spent it and it was gone. Food, too. You steal food and it's not a long term thing. It's gone in a day or two. Other things: he sometimes took things from stores. Just for fun. But when he had the things, whatever they were, he usually wasn't interested in them. He'd toss them in the bottom of his closet or throw them away. It didn't matter. None of the things mattered because they were all temporary. He had not thought of it in that way, but listening to Jake made him realize that's what it was. Life was completely temporary, why keep things? Like this piece of orange metal. Jake made a big deal about it, but it was just a chunk of metal. Who cares why he wanted it? He saw it and liked it and took it. He supposed it could be a good luck charm for the trip. Keep him and Jake safe. Maybe he was thinking that, even though he didn't think about things in that way. Jake looked at him, as if he was expecting an answer to his questions. Only sometimes there wasn't a real answer to a question. He put his hand in his pocket, took out the tip of flame, and handed it to Jake.

"You think it's so important," he said, "you go back there and put it back on."

Jake, startled by Mort's movement, put out his hand and Mort dropped the triangle on his palm. He didn't exactly want the flame. What he wanted was to understand Mort. Still, he wrapped his hand around the metal, puncturing his skin and drawing blood.

"Ouch," he said.

"You need to be careful with it, dummy," said Mort. "It's sharp."

"No shit," said Jake. He opened his hand and retrieved the piece of metal with his other hand and tired to give it back to Mort, who put up his hands and stepped back. Jake thought about just dropping it to the ground, but something about it made him want to take care of it. That's how he thought about it, like it was an orphan that needed a parent. He slipped it into his shirt pocket. Then he put his thumb against the cut. It wasn't a deep cut, but it hurt. It was also annoying, leaking blood. He tried to wipe the blood away, but more oozed up.

"We should get you a bandage for that."

"I'll be fine," said Jake.

"Come on. We'll go back to the truck stop. The store there will have some bandages."

"I said I'm okay."

Mort ignored him and walked across the wide parking lot with rows of eighteen wheelers rumbling the ground and the air. Jake watched him walk away. A car pulled up beside him. The driver leaned across the front seat. "You need a ride?" he asked.

Now how was it that he could stand in a place for half an hour or more with Mort before they got a ride, but he could stand here without Mort for about thirty seconds and a ride shows up? He wanted to get in the car, but he couldn't.

"Waiting for my buddy," he said.

"Suit yourself," said the driver. "I can't wait for him."

"Thanks for stopping," said Jake. The driver pulled away from him and sped up to the freeway. A perfect chance to dump Mort, and he passed. What was wrong with him?

Mort entered the store and kept his head down, to keep from being seen and, perhaps, later identified. Stupid cameras everywhere these days. There was a long line at the check out counter and lots of people milling around the store. He would have liked to rob this place, but he didn't have a quick way to get out of the vicinity. Besides, there were too many people around. Instead, he went to the shelf with first aid supplies and picked a package of bandages from next to the alcohol and antiseptic creams, and slipped it into his pocket. Then he went to the other side, grabbed a bottle of pop and a bag of chips and got in line at the counter. When he got to the counter, the clerk rung up his snacks and Mort patted his pocket.

"Oh, crap," he said. "I forgot my money in the car. Be right back."

"No problem," said the clerk, who pushed the pop and chips to the side and looked past Mort to the next person in line.

She's never going to remember me, he thought and walked out of the store, past the trucks, to where Mort was waiting. He took the package of bandages out of his pocket and opened it and pulled out one of the strip? "Hold out your hand," he said to Jake.

Jake spread his hand, palm up. The bleeding had mostly stopped, but there was a real cut visible there. Mort took the bandage out of its wrapper and put it over the cut.

"You get any money for us?" said Jake.

"No," said Mort. "Too crowded in there."

"I thought you could steal anything from anyone."

"I never said that." He pressed the bandage so it adhered tightly to Jake's palm.

"Maybe not," said Jake, flexing his hand and feeling the comforting alien sensation of the bandage on his skin. "But you want me to think it. You want everyone to think it."

"I don't want anyone thinking about me," said Mort. "People know me, that kills my chances of success, right there."

"You know what I mean," said Jake.

"I figured you'd be gone by now," said Mort.

"I wanted to," said Jake. "Wanted to run."

"So why didn't you?"

"Guess we must be soul mates."

Mort didn't say anything. He motioned that they should get walking.

"You know what soul mates are?" said Jake.

"No," said Mort.

"We knew each other before we were alive."

Mort rolled his eyes. "Not more of this bullshit."

"My mom explained it me. She believes in all that."

"She believe in astrology, too?"

"Never asked her."

"Bet she did. She had a terrible life. People with terrible lives always start believing in bullshit. It makes them feel better."

They fell into a slow walk, each of them holding out their hands and feeling the whoosh of air as cars passed by them.

Jake couldn't argue with Mort's assessment of his mother. She did have a terrible life and maybe that's why she was drawn to stuff that he thought was mostly nonsense. But so what? Didn't mean it wasn't true.

"What's wrong with feeling better?" said Jake.

"Nothing, except it isn't real."

"Feeling better isn't real? Then what's real? Feeling like shit all the time? Getting beaten up?"

"I'm just saying things are not all okay just because you believe in something. It doesn't work that way."

The sun perched low on the horizon. They had been walking for half an hour and still no ride. No one wanted to stop for two young men. It felt dangerous. Jake was not looking forward to spending the night somewhere cold, without any shelter, and no food. Mort was thinking they should have waited for that trucker. It wasn't too late. They could go back.

He heard the sound of a car slow down behind them. He turned around and saw a smiling face what looked like a happy guy behind the wheel of an SUV. It rolled to a stop a couple of hundred feet in front of them. Mort and Jake started running to the vehicle as the backup lights came on and the SUV began approaching them. They reached the passenger door in a few seconds and tumbled into the front seat.

"Thanks mister," said Jake.

"Yeah," said Mort, "we were getting worried no one was going to stop."

"It's getting dark," said the man. "Dangerous on the highway after sunset."

"Yeah," said Mort.

"Where you guys headed?"

"Faith Village," said Mort.

"Never heard of that," said the man.

"It's this encampment. Under the bridge downtown."

The man looked puzzled. "There's lots of bridges downtown. You know people there?"

"No," said Mort. "We just heard it was place to get started. You know, they take you in and get you back up on your feet."

The man looked doubtful, but he didn't let it trouble him too much. "How about I drop you off downtown and you figure out how to get to your village?"

"Sounds good," said Jake. "How far is that?"

"Oh, about half an hour or so. You boys running away from home or something?"

"Something," said Jake.

He nodded. "I remember when I was your age. Couldn't wait to get away from home. Stayed away for a while, then I came back. It was good to roam the world, you know. I saw Europe and went to Africa. Spent a few months in China. Teaching people how to read and talk English." He shrugged. "But my heart wasn't in it. I wanted to come back here. Missed the rain." He grinned. "Where's home to you?"

"Arizona," said Jake.

"Oh man, you're in for a change then. It doesn't get too hot and dry here."

"I know," said Mort.

The man looked like he wanted to keep talking, but Jake and Mort were holding back, unwilling to engage in real conversation.

I hope it all works out for you," said the man.

Mort wanted to rob the man, but he was such a dweeb, he couldn't make himself do it. Besides, maybe it was time to quit stealing from people for a while. He was coming to a new town. It would be a good time to try something new.

They rode in silence for a few minutes. Mort watched the sky dim and the road in front of them light up as opposing traffic turned on their headlights. A stream of red lights snaked into the city.

"Lot of traffic tonight," said the man.

Jake was leaning against the seat with his mouth open, taking in sleep breaths.

"Yeah," said Mort.

"Your friend here," said the man. "He's an old soul."

"What?"

"He's been here before. Lots of times. You're lucky to have him as a friend."

This was another crackpot? He couldn't get away from them, it seemed.

"You're welcome to him," said Mort.

"I met people like him, on my travels. You can always tell when someone has been through the process a few times. They have this seasoned quality to them, like they could be anything. Like they have been everything."

Mort wondered how some people could get things so wrong about other people. Jake was the farthest thing from a wise old soul he had ever seen.

"I hate to kill your illusions," he said to the man, "but Jake is just some mixed up kid who's running from a father who is a violent motherfucker who beats up his own wife."

"Okay," said the man, completely nonplussed by Mort's remark. "What about you? What you running from?"

Mort felt his face get warm. Did the man have nothing better to do than grill him about his stupid boring life?

"I got things," said Mort.

"Everyone has things. Your friend here, he's more than your friend. I could tell as soon as you got in the car. He's got a deep connection to you. You were something important to each other in another life."

LET'S LEAVE MORT for the moment, squirming away in the SUV, trying to find a way out of talking to this man with all the peculiar notions, while I tell you a little bit about Jake. He wasn't my case, but I knew about him. He came up here soon after Melville got kidnapped, which should have been a big deal to him, since he was Melville's father. But it wasn't because he didn't know about that. He didn't even know about Melville. Judy's pregnancy was the result of one encounter with Jake. He wasn't known as Jake then, of course, he was a business man in Portland. I saw him on the screens.

Unlike most of the people in this story, he wasn't a thief. He was mostly a good guy. A little too trusting, sometimes, and married. One day he was robbed by Rex. No big deal, it happened all the time. Rex had seen him from a distance, deduced that he had some cash in his back pocket (Rex was good at figuring out that sort of thing from the subtlest of clues) and arranged to bump into him, oh so slightly, at which point the money was taken from his back pocket. Just business as usual. Nothing personal on Rex's part, he was just surviving and saw an opportunity. You don't give a lion a hard time for taking down an antelope, do you?

Anyhow, a few minutes later he noticed the emptiness in his back pocket. He frantically searched for his money, but it was gone. He was so upset he couldn't see straight. He realized he'd been taken advantage of. No one likes that, I guess. It's hard on the ego to be duped so completely. He stopped, right there in the sidewalk and screamed. People have singular ways of dealing with things. He liked to scream. Judy, who happened to be walking past at that time, saw him and felt some kind of compassion for him. He seemed so upset. She was sure it had to do with something important. She went to him and asked him what was the matter. He told her. She laughed. "Is that all?" she said.

"Is that all? It was a couple hundred dollars."

"He probably needed it."

The man wanted to tell her she was full of it, but he didn't. She seemed like a kind person, in a strange way. She was trying to get him to lighten up about the money.

"So what if he needed it?" he said. "I need it. And it's mine."

"Not anymore," said Judy. "It's his. When you lose something real important, like your child or your best friend, then you can scream at the universe."

He was taken by her, no doubt. He remembered something a friend had told him once, that whenever something bad happens to you, something good will come along soon. Often right after or even at the same time.

"You want to have some coffee?" he said to Judy.

Judy accepted immediately. She wanted to get to know a man who would bellow at the sky. They spent the rest of the afternoon together.

Some would see fate at work here, but you have followed my tale long enough to know that fate is not a force in the world. It is a chance occurrence. You might even say that the two of them got together so that Melville could be born. I won't necessarily argue with you. Though I am an avatar, I don't have all the answers to everything. Who could? There are so many mysteries. Judy and the man had an afternoon together of the type that neither of them had ever had before. Neither of them were prone to such encounters, and in the normal course of events they would have felt shame for their behavior, then forgotten about it. This did not happen. They saw the day for what it was: a gift, temporary and sweet.

Then they parted.

They never met again.

But that afternoon, Melville, aka Morris, aka Mort, was conceived.

Judy never considered aborting him or giving him up for adoption. She loved him as soon as she knew of his conception, and she was determined to raise him by herself.

Most of the rest, you know. Melville was born and stolen by Rex.

Though up until now you didn't know this:

When Melville was Morris, about the time he had turned five, his father, (not Rex, but his real father, the one that gave him half his DNA) was struck and killed by a light rail train in downtown Portland when he stepped out from the sidewalk at precisely the wrong moment. The train ran whisper quiet, and the man, at that moment, was reminiscing about his brief encounter years earlier with Judy and fleetingly wondering what might have become of her, not knowing that she had taken up residence in a tent not half a mile from where he stood, and he looked up just a split second before the front of the train met his flesh.

Up here, in the way station, he was assigned to the avatar of stupid errors, who, in a singular act, motivated by job fatigue and disgust for all the stupid people in the world, put him into Jake's body, the tormented Jake, unable to help his mother.

Jake, who met up with his natural born son in the form of Mort.

Chapter 25: Youth

WHEN I LIVED back on the earth, before I became an avatar, I attended funerals. Not because I particularly enjoyed them. For one thing there was never anything to steal at a funeral. People usually did not bring money to a funeral. Funeral homes did not normally display a lot of items that I would want to take. For another thing, they are dismal affairs. Everyone so morose. Also, the deceased is never seen in a true light. Death exalts everyone. Everyone. You never hear the bad stuff about the dead person at a funeral.

But there are obligations in life. You need to take care of yourself by eating properly and getting enough sleep. You need to raise your children. You need to respect your parents.

And you need to go to funerals. So I went.

If only I knew then that death was no particularly momentous occasion. Everyone dies and everyone comes to the way station. It's just a natural transition and hardly worthy of marking, let alone exalting.

So when I came up here, I didn't much bother with funerals, except when I wanted a laugh, which wasn't often.

But here's the funny thing. Just about everyone that came up here was recently the subject of a funeral, or a memorial, or some kind of remembrance. Not everyone, because some people die without anyone knowing, (like Rex) and others without anyone caring, and some because that's what they wanted: no service. That's fine for them. Nothing says you *have* to, and probably some of them know the truth about the universe and have the intuition that memorials don't matter, but those that did, the vast majority, they want to see what was said at their memorials.

It makes sense, I suppose. It's kind of interesting to think about what people think about you. And even more interesting to see and hear people talking about you after you're gone.

All of which is a long winded way of saying that Rose wanted to see her funeral.

"You sure about that?" I said.

"Of course."

"Why haven't you seen it before?"

"Never wanted to before."

"Why now?"

She was annoyed by my questions. "What does it matter?" she said. "I want to see my funeral. Didn't you see your funeral?"

"Yes," I said, "when I first arrived." It was a thoroughly depressing affair, and I left in the middle of it.

"So why are you so weird about me wanting to do the same thing?" said Rose.

The main reason was that she had been here for a long time already. What would make her want to look at her funeral now?

"I'm concerned that you might be having an unhealthy interest in your death."

"What's it to you?"

"I'm worried about you."

"This is nuts. I'm going to go look at the loop of my funeral. You coming?"

I wanted to say no. But I decided I would go with her.

We found a viewing cave and settled into a chair. She called up the old loop. It popped up on the screen.

The loops are like old video tapes. They're stored in a vast library somewhere. I'm not familiar with the details of how that works. Think of an infinite library with an infinite catalog for accessing it. I don't know if that's what it is, but that's what it seems like, and since it works, that's how I think of it.

The view from high up, a church, lots of people gathered, wearing dark clothes. I didn't know people still wore dark clothes at funerals. Rose up front. Her coffin small. It didn't look real. How can a coffin be so tiny? Much weeping. Her parents holding each other.

And what else could one expect? The funeral of a child has to be one of the saddest thing on the planet. I glanced at Rose. She was mesmerized by the scene. She didn't seem upset.

The spool played out.

I started getting fidgety. Once you see the beginning, there's no reason to see more. A still picture would have given about as much information as the full spool.

Several people got up to say things about Rose. I learned her real name. Not that it matters. May. Her name was May. One syllable. Odd. Like the one we came up with for her.

People who spoke said how delightful a child she was. I don't want to belittle the scene or the event, but what more can one say about someone so young?

An aunt said May was so kind and polite. She shared her toys and always made people feel welcome.

Huh. An eight-year-old making people feel welcome. That sounded a little off. I didn't say anything, though. If I did, if I said anything at all, it wouldn't have been nice. I would have made fun of the whole proceedings. Probably cracked completely tasteless jokes.

Eventually the holy guy in charge said a few more words and the whole thing was over.

When it was finished, we just sat there for a few seconds. I didn't want to say anything until she did.

Finally: "I think I like Rose better than May."

"Me too," I said.

"My parents looked so sad."

"Well, sure. Their child died."

"I want to go back," she said. "I'm tired of being an avatar. They all seem so alive down there."

That shocked me. Alive? They were so morose and drained of energy. How could anyone consider that being alive?

"You know," she said, "how they feel things so strongly. We don't do that up here, us avatars. We're too caught up with all the details of what we have to do for people. Get them to eat the soup, then figure out where to put them. It takes away what makes us human."

I wanted to tell her that souls aren't human or non-human. All souls are just blanks until you put an entity around them, but I think I knew what she meant. Humans seem to use souls to the fullest. In so many other animals, (and plants) the souls just kind of sit there. Only humans seem to take full advantage of the power of a soul.

Not that all people are good. I'm not saying that. Just that the souls mean more to them.

"Are you sure?" I said. "You won't remember anything."

"I know."

"What about the dread?"

"I don't like the idea of dread, but maybe I can learn to live with it."

"It cripples a lot of people."

"I know. But I want to try. Will you assign me?"

"Of course. I would consider it an honor."

We walked back to the cafeteria, mostly in silence. I never noticed how our feet made tiny squishy noises as we walked, but I noticed it then, like it was the loudest thing in the universe. As if my awareness was heightened for some reason.

"You hear that?" I said.

"What?" said Rose.

"Our footsteps."

She listened. "That's funny," she said. "I never heard that before."

"Me neither."

We got to the cafeteria. All the chairs were filled. There was a long line snaking out of the dining area and into the hall. It seemed to go on for a long time.

"What's this?" she said.

"An upsurge in a war," I think. "I could tell because most of the people in line were young men. There were also women and children. I knew from previous visits to a line at the cafeteria that this was what war meant: young men as soldiers, dead, and women and children as civilian casualties.

"I don't want to get in this line. I might change my mind."

"You want to go now?" I said.

She went to the front of the line and asked someone if she could step in front of them. But even in the afterlife, even here in the way station of the universe, the primacy of the line was paramount. You simply did not cut in front of anyone. She asked others. All rebuffed her. She returned to stand beside me.

Now she looked anguished.

"I can't wait," she said.

I had the soup powder tucked away in a fold in my robes. I pulled it out and arranged it in a pile on my palm and put my hand out to Rose.

"Spit," I said, conscious that her mother might have had her do such a thing when she wanted to wipe some dirt off her face.

Rose leaned forward and spit out a small bit of saliva.

"More," I said.

She did more. I stirred it around with my finger.

"Soup," I told her.

She looked doubtful, but ate it.

"You'll put me somewhere beautiful?" she said. "Keep me out of war zones and give me a life I can believe in?"

I nodded.

"And make me human. I want a full life this time around."

I nodded again. "Of course," I said.

As the soup coursed through her, I saw her eyes go from pained to relaxed. It was working, she was losing her memory. I guided her toward the departure area.

"Where are we?" she said.

"You're safe," I told her.

I considered what she had asked for. To have a full life as a human. But that funeral had been so sad. I did not want to subject her, I did not want to subject anyone, to that kind of memory when she came back here. And that dread that Rose had talked about before. I felt I needed to keep her from that as well. Who needed dread like that? If I put her back to live a life from the beginning, then when she reached the age of her previous death she would access all of that old dread.

And the thing is, I can't put her in a baby's body that will have a good life. I can't know that. I can't predict the future.

So I did something she didn't want me to do. I put her in someone older. Quite a bit older. I put her in a healthy and happy woman of 72 years, a woman with lots of good memories. Rose was going to spend a good decade or two with her childhood safely behind her, and, as far as I could tell, only good memories of a life full of love and happiness.

Yeah, I stole her youth. For her own good.

So sue me.

I LET HER go and suddenly I didn't want to go back anymore. Her words about life as an avatar made me think how I couldn't be doing this for the rest of my life. Could I?

Whatever the rest of my life means.

I wanted her to assign me to whatever new life I might have back on earth. But she was gone now.

Thanks to me.

I don't feel like I did the wrong thing. I was trying to help her. If I couldn't do that every once in while, then what was the use of being an avatar?

Another avatar approached me as I walked along, absorbed by my own musings.

"I couldn't help noticing that you seem preoccupied," he said.

I looked up, startled. She approached me, I guess, because she was concerned for me.

"I just assigned someone contrary to their wishes."

"Why would you do that?" he said.

"I wanted to help her. She had a bad time in her last life."

He nodded. He appeared to be an experienced avatar, which meant she knew the kinds of considerations I had in mind as I weighed my options.

"I'm sure you did the right thing."

"I'm hoping so."

"Have you ever considered what this place is?"

"I don't indulge in speculation of that kind."

"How can you not?"

"I just don't."

"I'm part of a group that debates the existence of mirrors."

"Mirrors?"

"Yes. We all fell into mirrors. That's how we came to be here."

I tried to walk around him. "Excuse me," I said.

He stepped in front of me. Gently, but she was still there. Why would I care what this man and his friends think about the nature of reality? We all have ideas in that direction. Doesn't mean they carry any weight.

"Even if you never agree with what we believe," said the man, "you should spend some time with us. It will make you see other ways. It'll open up your life."

"I don't need that," I said, trying to step around him again.

He made to step in front of me one more time, but I looked at him sharply and he stepped back, giving me room.

I walked by him.

"We're here regularly," he said. "Come by soon. You'll like it."

I didn't answer him or make any gesture in his direction.

And now it's time to let you know what happened to the other players in our little drama.

We'll just drop into the proceedings.

Mort elbowed Jake in the shoulder. He woke with a start.

"We're here," said the driver. They were stopped in a parking place on the street, next to a tall bank building. "Downtown Portland. Hope you both find what you're looking for."

Mort opened the door and stepped onto the sidewalk. Jake followed him. They waved at the driver and he waved back and then drove away.

"Nice guy," said Jake.

"How would you know?" said Mort. "You've been asleep the whole time."

"I could tell," said Jake.

"Where's the bridge?"

"What bridge?"

"The one where Faith Village is."

"What do you want to go there for? It's a slum, isn't it? Some giant squat where people who can't get jobs or money go?"

Mort ignored him.

"I came here for one reason," he said. "To see Faith Village."

"That's crazy. Why don't you go rob someone or a store, and we can take the money and get a couple of rooms in nice hotel. Maybe some good food, too. I'm hungry. Aren't you hungry?"

"*You* rob someone."

"That's not my area of skill," said Jake.

"What *is* your area of skill? Annoying the shit out of people?"

Jake didn't answer. He kicked at some piece of paper garbage at his feet. It skittered across the sidewalk and into the street.

"Jesus," said Mort. "Are you going to pout now?"

"So where is this village at?"

"I told you, under the bridge?"

"*Which* bridge, moron?"

Mort felt himself fill with anger, then realized it wasn't his anger. It was something he wanted to feel because Jake was so incredibly annoying and needy.

"Dad," said Mort, "you need to let me go."

As soon as he said it, he didn't understand what he said or why he said it. It felt wrong and right at the same time.

"Dad?" said Jake. "You called me Dad."

"Figure of speech," said Mort. "Let's try this way." He pointed across the street and walked down to the corner, just half a block away. Jake followed.

"What did you mean by calling me Dad?"

"It's just a word. You ever heard the word Daddio?"

"No. What's Daddio?"

"It's—I don't know. It's something I've heard people say. It's like—it doesn't mean anything. It's just a word. Like cool. Coolsville. Something."

"Coolsville?"

"Stop asking me questions," said Mort. "Just stop it."

They crossed against the light, Mort leading the way with a brisk pace, Jake hurrying to keep up with him. Drivers in cars blew their horns as they went by. Someone stuck his middle finger into the air out of his window. "Jerks," he called.

Mort waved at him. On the other side of the street he kept walking, hurrying his pace, in fact, while Jake kept badgering him. They passed between two buildings and Mort saw the span of a bridge, rising in an arc, higher than he would have expected. Two flags fluttered at the top, way up there, tiny ruffles of cloth, barely even identifiable as flags. Was that the bridge? It looked to be a couple of miles away.

"Coolsville," said Jake. "I kind of like it. I'll use it from now on. Whenever you call me Dad again."

Mort put his hands over his ears. Maybe he could outrun Jake.

He came to another corner and ducked around a building and kept going toward the bridge. He didn't have to get the actual bridge. The village was under the bridge.

Jake stopped talking to him, but he still kept up with him, trotting behind.

After a few minutes of both of them running, he called to Mort. "Slow down," he said.

Mort didn't answer and he didn't slow down. He picked up his pace. It felt good to be running like this, after so many days of sitting in cars driving.

The buildings began to get smaller. He was leaving downtown.

They passed Susie, who had just left Faith Village. She caught their eye as they ran by her. Mort felt a twinge of panic, seeing this stranger. She seemed to know something about him. Jake felt a connection as well. All three of them did. Their lives paused for a moment, as they all searched their memories for traces of the other.

None came to any of the three.

Jake and Mort kept running, although, out of shape as they were, their pace had slowed down considerably.

Susie looked back at them, feeling something familiar in their presence, but then decided it was nothing and kept walking.

Jake and Mort stopped at a railing, high above the base of one of the pillars of the Fremont bridge.

Mort pointed to the collection of tents and makeshift wooden structures surrounding the pillar. Warehouses surrounded the little village.

"That's it," said Mort. "That's what I've been looking for."

"Just a bunch of roofs," said Jake. "Why do you want to go there?"

"I just want to."

"That woman we passed. You know her?"

"No," said Mort.

"Looked like she thought she knew us."

Mort shrugged. He hopped over the rail. A steep grassy slope extended down to the level of the village. He began gingerly walking down, conscious of the possibility of falling.

When he set out on his journey, he did not even know this is where he wanted to end up.

Now here he was. He felt like he was coming home.

Chapter 26: Nothing

With Rose gone, I was surprised at how much I missed her. I had barely even known her, and now it felt like she took away my reason for even being here in the way station. I saw that she got to her new home safely. Her new name was Clara. She lived with her son and his wife in a house in Florida. All of them retired and enjoying the good life. Clara had this odd feeling that something had changed, but she couldn't tell what. She didn't let it bother her. Life was never better for her than now, with her family around her and her days full.

Then I realized this was why I was here. I wanted to put people in good situations. I wanted to see Rex end up where he ended up, where he wanted to be. I liked seeing Rose get a good life for a change. Who wouldn't want to do something like that with their lives? Not changing the world, exactly, but doing something for the world and the people who live in it. Not stealing from them, but letting the world come to them.

Not for nothing have I come to this conclusion. Can you imagine what it is for me? But no need for that. I do not have to tell you of my travails. I have outlined some of my activities, my daily deeds, as it were, in the pages previous to this. We have arrived at some kind of formality. The need to tie things up and tidy the events. A narrative calls for such things, does it not? Perhaps. It may be that narrative is a false kind of knowledge. Even a deplorable activity, but we should all engage in such at some time or other. I made a career of deplorable activities. I have met many here who did the same. We are, all of us, to a person, fulfilled individuals.

You may ask how this can be. I do not wish to convince you of my point of view, especially if you truly believe otherwise. Why should I? It would do me no good and only irritate you. Simply put aside your judgment for the moment, and observe the events taking place on our stage below.

MORT AND JAKE almost fell down the slope. It was so steep that neither of them could keep up with it. Their shoes skipped across the grass. They had their arms up like birds ready to fly, and they stared down at their dancing feet, with the grass a blur flowing past.

They got to the flat expanse of the village and stood surveying the area.

"We can stay here for nothing," said Mort.

"Nothing is about all it's worth," said Jake. "Let's look around, sure, but we don't have to live here. There's no reason for us to live here."

Mort ignored him and walked toward the cluster of tents. A couple of women, one older, one probably still in her twenties, came out to meet them.

"Hello," said the older one.

"Hi," said Mort. "We were hoping we could move in."

The woman looked at him with suspicion. "Move in?"

"Yeah, we heard places like this are where people can get their lives in order."

"There are places like that," said the woman, "but you would have to find another. This is for females only."

Jake slapped Mort on the shoulder. "See?" he said. "Let's get out of here."

"Women only?" said Mort. "You sure?"

The younger woman laughed, then spit on the ground. "Yeah," she said, "we're sure."

Mort could hardly believe this turn of events. Why didn't he know this? "I thought you took anyone."

"I don't know where you got that idea? You two new in town?"

Mort nodded. "We came from Arizona?"

"Arizona? Why'd you come here? You got tired of the nice weather?"

"We both needed to get away."

The two women looked tough. Protecting their turf. What else did they have but this little patch of property under the bridge? Mort could understand why they didn't want males around. Males were trouble. Or they could be.

"You're lucky," said the older woman. "It isn't too cold right now. You'll do fine on the street. You could fly a sign for a while, that'll get you some food. Try the employment office. Should be able to get you something. You have any money at all?"

"Oh yeah," said Mort. "We're fine with money. We're good that way."

She didn't believe him, but Mort was not going to take money from her. That would have felt awful, to take money from someone who lived in a tent city.

"Not that I care," said the woman. "I wasn't going to give you any, that's for sure." She smiled and her eyes shined a little.

"No," said Mort. "That would be crazy."

Jake was behind Mort, urging him to get out of here. "Let's goooooooo," he said in a whine that Mort found annoying.

"In a minute," he said.

The women had crossed their arms in front of them. "Anything else we can do for you?" said the younger one.

There was something in the village. That's all Mort knew. Something for him. He didn't know what it was, but it was strong. Something drove him from Arizona to this bridge in the middle of a city he had never been to.

"Can I just look around?" he asked.

Jake groaned.

"What do you want to look around for?" said the younger woman. "It's a bunch of tents and shacks. Our neighborhood. It's where people live. What's to see?"

"I don't know," said Mort. "You can both walk with me if you want. I'll only be a few minutes and then I'll be gone."

The women whispered between themselves. Mort waited patiently. No need to push these ladies. They were being more than polite and generous to him. He stepped back while they spoke. Jake pleaded with Mort. "Come on," he said. "Let's go steal some money. Let's get out of here."

"No," said Mort. "I'm not stealing again."

"What?"

"I'm done with that. You don't need to steal to live."

"We don't have *any*thing," said Jake. "Or haven't you noticed that?"

"I noticed."

"We can't get anything here. They don't *have* anything."

"I know that," said Mort. "That's not why I'm here."

"Then why *are* we here?"

"Still trying to figure that out," said Mort.

The two women walked up to them.

"Okay," said the older one. "We talked it over. You can come in. We'll escort you the whole way, and you leave when we tell you. In any case, no more than ten minutes."

"Great," said Mort.

They turned and headed toward the entrance to the village. Mort followed. Jake hung back, but in the end he sighed, shook his head, and followed Mort.

They passed the oak stump. Chips still littered the area around its base, and the cut surface, where the trunk of the tree had once risen, bore the imprint of ax and saw.

"You cut down this tree?" said Mort. He stopped to look at the stump.

"It was in our way," said the older woman, unconvincingly.

"In your way?" said Jake, equally puzzled.

"The village is over here," said the younger woman.

But Mort did not move from the stump. He was completely captivated by it. The other three people could see he was being transformed, in some strange way, by the sight of it.

"You see something there?" said the older woman.

"When did this get cut down?" he said.

"Not too long ago. A few weeks."

"There's someone used to be in it," said Mort.

"What?" said Jake.

"I'm glad you cut it down," said Mort. "Because if you didn't, I would have."

"I didn't cut it down," said the older woman.

"Neither did I," said the younger.

"Then who?"

I NEVER EXPECTED Mort to give up thievery. But I was pleased by it. Which also didn't make sense. I was a thief, after all. It defined me for a long time. Years. But thieves grow up, I suppose. Even old ones like me find something else to do.

I contacted another avatar. Someone who understood me. She was a liar. A long time liar. Almost everything she said when she was on earth was a lie. She got all the liars. I asked her if she would assign me to a new life.

She nodded. She didn't *say* anything, she just nodded. That was how she functioned here. If she didn't have to speak, then she didn't lie.

Strange, sure, but you didn't think things were normal here did you?

Did you?

JUDY SENSED, BEFORE she heard, the conversation around the oak stump. She had just about packed up all her belongings, at least the ones she still wanted to keep, which weren't much. They included a worn and creased photo of her child, Melville, and besides that only a few items of necessity like her clothes and some papers.

She left the tent as clean as she could. The wood was all burned up. The next person who came to live here would have an easy time of it.

As she was getting ready to leave, she thought about the tree again. She was still puzzled by why she had wanted to cut it down, but she felt no remorse or shame in it. It was the right thing to do, for whatever reason.

She walked through Faith Village, the place that had been her home for so long, the place that she never thought she would ever leave, and approached the tree stump. She saw Mort and Jake and Olivia and Linda. At first she thought something might be going on, like they were in trouble. But then she saw it was a completely innocent meeting. Who were the two boys?

One of them turned to her.

She felt a sensation like lightning go up her spine. Her skin felt like it was on fire and her vision darkened, for just a second.

Then the other boy turned.

She knew this one, too. She knew them both.

Mort nodded at her.

Jake just stared. He saw something in her. Knew her from somewhere. He thought briefly, of the mystery of knowing someone. Did it ever happen that you thought you knew someone and you didn't?

He watched Mort walk toward the woman.

They stared at each other.

Were they in love?

It couldn't be.

"Hello," said Mort.

"Hello," said Judy. "Are you visiting our little settlement?"

"I came all the way from Arizona. I heard about your experiment."

"It's not an experiment. It's our life."

He pointed to her small suitcase, almost an oversized purse. "Are you leaving?" he said.

She nodded.

"You ever think you know someone when you meet them?"

She nodded again. "Some people say it's a dim memory, like you both knew each other before, in another life."

"I don't believe in that stuff. Do you?"

She thought about it. "I don't know. How could you ever prove it or disprove it?"

Mort nodded.

"Ever since my son was stolen from me, I don't believe in a lot. Just myself."

Mort nodded again. "Would you like to have some coffee with me?"

"Coffee?"

"Yeah. I think we may have some things in common. It feels like we might be family."

She laughed. "You know, that sounds about right. We were probably related in another life."

She stepped forward. He stepped aside and put our his arm. She took it and they walked past Jake, whose mouth had fallen open.

"I don't have any money," said Mort.

"Don't worry about it," said Judy. "I have some saved up."

I ASKED THE liar avatar for her advice. She wouldn't give me any. Then I told her whatever she thought I should do, that's what I would do.

She told me to eat the soup.

I hesitated, but not for long.

I ate the soup.

You just have read **Thieves** by Emen. Copyright © 2019 by Emen.

ISBN: 978-1-949644-53-1

This book by Emen. No fair for you to be copying this book, so don't do it, okay.

Picture of baby carriage: ID 120875230 © Marianna Lishchenko | Dreamstime.com

Emen no dedicate books so don't ask him for to dedicate book to you, okay.

Another book by Emen:
The Institute

About the author:
Emen is big name writer now. Just look at cover. See how big is his name? Almost half of cover. That is big name. Case is resting. I am dropping mic. Emen has fans now. They want to know about Emen's life. Like what kind soap he uses to wash hands. Can you believe? Emen don't tell such things. Is private. Even if not embarrassing, still private. You want know world of Emen? Read books, yeah. That is all. Still no picture of Emen on book. You don't need picture of Emen. Believe me.